TO BURY OUR FATHERS

A novel of Nicaragua
by Sergio Ramírez

translated by Nick Caistor

readers international

The title of this book in Spanish is *¿Te dió miedo la sangre?* published originally by Editorial Monte Avila in Caracas and most recently by Editorial Argos Vergara in Barcelona.

First published 1984 in English by Readers International, Inc., London and New York, whose editorial branch is at 8 Strathray Gardens, London NW3 4NY, England. US inquiries to 9 East 46th St., New York, NY 10017 USA. US Subscription and Order Department: P.O. Drawer E, Columbia, Louisiana 71418 USA.

Vignettes by Dieter Masuhr
Typesetting by Red Lion Setters, London WC1N 2LA
Printed and bound in Great Britain by Richard Clay (The Chaucer Press), Bungay, Suffolk

ISBN 0-930523-02-4 hardcover
ISBN 0-930523-03-2 softcover

Library of Congress Catalog Card Number 84-061849

To Peter, to Inke

THE MAIN LINES OF THE STORY

Taleno, Jilguero, and Larios, known as Indio, kidnap National Guard Colonel Catalino Lopez in Guatemala City and take him off to Lasinventura's brothel in Mixco, where he pays for his crimes.

Santiago Taleno, known as Turco, after a wandering childhood with his father and brother, enters the military academy and eventually becomes an aide to *el hombre*; later though he is caught and kept prisoner in a cage.

Pastorita and Chepito the barman talk of their lives, their songs and their sorrows, in *El Copacabana* on Lake Managua, and they remember Lazaro, Jilguero, and the trio *Los Caballeros*.

Pursued in the hills by the National Guard, Mauricio Rosales, otherwise known as Jilguero, remembers his grandfather, who had won the presidency but was robbed of it by fraud, and his sister, who was set to win the Miss Nicaragua competition but was also robbed of victory, as well as many other events.

National Guard Colonel Catalino Lopez, one of the first to be sent out to fight Sandino, talks of his faked wound and his cowardice, and of Pedron Altamirano's head brought on a stake to Managua.

Larios, one of the earliest rebels against *el hombre*, dies in exile in Guatemala, and we read of his son's journey back with the body to Leon for burial.

PART ONE

The skylark was born before all beings and before the earth itself. Its father died of illness when the earth did not yet exist. He remained unburied for five days, until the skylark, ingenious of necessity, buried its father in its own head.

Aristophanes, *The Birds*

—¿ Mató chancho tu mama?
¿ Te dió miedo la sangre?

Has your mother killed the pig?
Were you scared of the blood?
Nicaraguan nursery rhyme

CHAPTER 1

Blood red navy blue bottle green Jilguero reeled off to himself as he waited, picking out the leaded glass panes on the screen that led from the back of the shoeshine parlour into the depths of the billiard room, coffee brown golden yellow and again blood red. Turco, back from inspecting the sentry position on the far side of the gully, stops by the dying campfire and says to Jilguero, remember: from the other side of the street at noon, *El Jardin de Italia* had the look of a cavern, through the entrance of the crumbling doorway on Sixth Avenue. The walls, daubed with gloss paint, reflected the light from the fluorescent tubes with a scaly sheen, and the bootblacks floated in the radiance as they knelt on the worn tiled floor in front of the wooden thrones; only the customers' trouser legs and their shoes on the metal plates were visible from the lookout post when leaning back against the window of *La Samaritana* where a dusty dummy showed off a knitted sweater. Walking on a few steps and standing in the porch of *El Cairo*, at last one had a clear view inside *El Jardin de Italia*.

Jilguero shares out his pack of Esfinge among the men around the campfire, then lights the last for himself with a stick, and with the ember glowing and lighting his features: yes, he can still see the coloured screen at the entrance to the billiard room, the table soccer games unused in a corner, antiquated slot machines with rusty arms, the orphan girl perched primly at the till in her neat white uniform to take the shoeshine money and dole out change for the machines. He can remember every detail, how he kept his attention on the colonel, voluminous in his khaki shirt, his skin still damp and glistening from the bath, seated at the furthest of the shoeshine seats.

A glint from the thick lenses as he bent his razored head to peer with the meticulous scrutiny of the half-blind at the shine on his shoes reached Jilguero from the gloom of the cave. He could also see the patched shirtback of the old man who, absorbed in his work, expertly tossed the brush from one hand to the other behind the shoe box without slackening speed for a second, and above the colonel's head, the painting on the wall showing a distinctly masculine mermaid raising a bottle to her lips:

"YOU AND ME" SOFT DRINKS
no danger to your health

And then, recalls Turco, we both clearly heard above the hooting of the traffic, the yelling of the lottery sellers, the bawling of a kid squatting with its Indian mother on the pavement selling shawls, the single short tap of the brush against the crate that announced the shine was finished.

Yes, Jilguero says, untying his bootlaces, the cigarette still dangling from his lips, I tilted my dude's hat and set off across the street as fast as I could, dodging the cars, squeezing in front of the overheated grille of a bus pulling in to the kerb, and reached *El Jardin de Italia* just as the colonel was struggling down from the chair, tipping himself out onto his feet, feeling for change under the flap of his loose shirt.

His magnified, blurred eyes sought out my features from behind the pebble glasses as I bowed in greeting.

"What can I do for you?" he snapped.

"It's about those performers—don't you remember, Colonel?" He took out a Vicks inhaler and poked it into his nostrils while he looked me up and down, sizing me up.

And you, scared he might recognise you, eh, damn fool that you are, Jilguero, says Turco, laughing and jostling him affectionately, sitting now in the ring of khaki-uniformed men, their bright faces like schoolchildren at a camp. Turco goes on: we'd dressed him up for the occasion—a flashy tie, pork-pie hat, two-tone shoes, Ray Ban shades, a plastic briefcase and, do you remember? the best trick of all, to have you put on the voice of a Mexican nightclub tout.

Jilguero had followed him to the darkest part of the room, where the orphan girl sat hunched over her till under a portrait of Saint Vincent de Paul.

> Do not tamper with these machines
> Property of the needy children of Guatemala
> under the auspices of Monseñor Giron Perrone

The colonel paid the girl and made for the door, Jilguero still in tow. Out on the pavement, he turned again to look this sport over suspiciously.

"Is that where you have the photographs?" he asked, jabbing a finger at the briefcase.

Jilguero told him his colleagues had the artistes' portfolios, and that they were waiting for him in *El Portal*. Grasping his arm, Jilguero leaned over him to look at the time on his watch, so he would understand that they were already late.

"And just where is that?" he asked, still in two minds. The daylight out in the street must have hurt his eyes because they started to water; he wiped them under his glasses.

"A popular bar right near here, just round the corner from your hotel, sir," and I pointed with the briefcase to show him we only had to walk a few blocks down the avenue.

He acquiesced with a grunt. We started off, Turco on the far side of the street keeping to the same slow walk as us, me watching carefully his every step, because the colonel found it hard to make anything out properly—I guided him along slowly so he didn't bump into passersby, cleared a path for him, and helped him across the street at corners—there wouldn't have been much point if he was knocked down by a car, would there?

When he saw we had got beyond the point of no return, that I had led him past the Panamerican Hotel and that the colonel, oblivious to his destination, had made no attempt to enter, Turco broke into a trot to reach *El Portal* before us and warn Indio.

He dived out of breath into the bar, full of the lunchtime hubbub of customers greeting one another, pushing tables together, carrying chairs, sorting out the first round of drinks, the smoke from their cigarettes already drifting in layers under the bamboo ceiling hung with fishermen's nets, where the fans' black blades hung motionless. Indio was glancing at a newspaper when Turco slid onto the stool next to him. He's on his way, we've hooked him. To hide his feelings, he got out a comb and began nervously to comb his hair in the bar mirror, with its multicoloured bottle reflections.

Indio threw his cigarette butt to the littered floor. As he stretched the tip of his shoe to stub it out, his sockless, skinny ankle appeared; he took off his glasses, folded the *Imparcial* under his arm, and turned on his stool to face the entrance; his face no longer proud-featured, the strain of age already starting to show.

Office workers, travelling salesmen, bank clerks, were still thronging the door, trying to spot a free table or to catch the waiters' gaze as they rushed past with their trays above their heads. Half-past twelve by the Alka-Seltzer clock above the liquor shelf.

We tried hard to stay calm, Indio facing the door and me staring into the mirror, waiting for Jilguero to show up with his captive, but that walk along Sixth Avenue seemed eternal. Although he let himself be led, the colonel leaned on Jilguero with all his flabby weight, stirring at times to put on the semblance of a soldierly gait, while Jilguero steered him along, keeping up his patter, rousing his interest with the tale that the girls from the imaginary troupe were dying to meet him, especially Tania the Devil

Woman, the shooting star of striptease, who had seen his photograph in military uniform among the mourners at the funeral. He chuckled encouragingly: think of me when you're having your fun with Tania, Colonel. If you take the girls to Nicaragua, Tania's reserved just for you.

"Where is this Tania from?" he rasped at me, as harsh as possible to show that in no way was he bringing himself down to my level.

"No country in particular, Colonel, nobody knows where she came from or where she's going to, only that she's a goddess in human form. That funeral turned out lucky for you."

We had reached the awning of Eichenberg Photos, we were passing *La Gafita de Oro*, we were going into the arcade, we'd almost reached *El Portal*. At this though he came to a halt on me, annoyed.

"Lucky? Why's that?"

Terribly upset, squirming with embarrassment, I explained that if he hadn't been his country's delegate to the funeral he wouldn't be taking the little ladies with him, would he? No disrespect meant to the memory of President Castillo Armas, of course, sweeping my hat off in exaggerated courtesy; and though his wooden face registered no reaction, still offended as he was at my mentioning those sacred remains in the same breath as the strippers, I knew he would remember Tania the Devil Woman as I had conjured her up for him, and he did not utter a word of reproach. He leaned all his weight on my arm again, and we reached the bar doorway. We passed the cardboard king cut-out on the threshold, with his drawn sword and the slogan that Indio always hailed the barman with in mock-pompous fashion:

Halt! No man may pass
Who refuses to greet
The King of the Portal
Offering you a treat.

We had made it inside—Pedro Infante booming out from the Rockola *Soon we'll be in Penjamo, see its bright roofs shine*—I got worried when I couldn't spot you, Turco, and elbowed my way through the crush of people, but finally I saw you at the bar, and Indio signalled to me with the glasses in his hand to get him into the back room. You can't imagine how hard it was steering that whale between the tables, excuseme's all the time to the grumbling customers we forced to stand up as we pushed through.

But you did it, Jilguero. You fought your way through the bar, you made it to the corridor and out to the back room, a polite name for the hole next to the urinals, piled with crates of beer, mops, and broken chairs, but also with a table for any overflow from the saloon.

Swollen with damp, the door stuck in its frame, and I had to heave it open.

"Take a seat, Colonel." I drew up a chair, blew the dust off it, and guided his rear end towards it. He refused the cigarette I offered: a drink?—nothing doing, he turned everything down with a curt gesture. He spread his elbows impatiently on the table-top with its huge picture of a Gallo beer-bottle top, and peered at the dial of his watch. There was no bulb in the socket hanging from the green cord above his head, and more noise than light reached us from the bar down the corridor.

"What's keeping your associates?" he asked, wrinkling his nose at the stink of disinfectant from the toilets. I soothed him: they were just finishing with another important client, from Panama, they would be here any second, and at that, as if my words were magic, you appeared.

The colonel turned his head to follow the shadows that had slipped into the room and moved into the empty spaces around the table. He started in alarm when he heard the door scraping across the dirt floor, the shudder of the frame as it was banged shut, and the drawn out rattle of the bolt.

Jilguero paled as he bolted the door and turned back to face him; the colonel pressed his hands to the sides of his face in an effort to make things out more clearly, trying to focus on their faces, to pick out Indio as he took up position to his right and laid his *Imparcial* on the table, where it slowly unfolded; Indio, who coolly struck a match, took his time lighting a cigarette—and the flame must have finally enabled the colonel to make out who Indio was because the smile vanished from his face and, startled, he swung round to look at Turco instead.

He was straining to make out the taut, proud profile of Turco on his left, but in response to his desperate enquiry Turco only went on staring straight in front of himself, at Indio, as though waiting for instructions, while Indio gazed down at the match-stick writhing in his fingers. When finally he blew it out, Jilguero slipped behind the colonel. That was the signal.

Suddenly recovering from his shock, the colonel made as if to stand, pushing swiftly at the table in his attempt, but his weight made it a useless gesture, and when he felt Jilguero's urgent hand searching him and removing his revolver, he let his arms fall to his sides, all hope gone.

"What are you going to do to me?" he asked hoarsely, his head sinking to his chest.

The fishermen would have seen him silhouetted against the sun, paddling closer over the still water of the sandbar, would have watched him drag the canoe from the velvety waters and ground it on the sand, clamber out cradling a baby in his arms, whom he protected from the glare of the sun with a parasol, then walk up the avenue with its lines of withered palms and buried tracks, Trinidad trotting along behind, a bundle of clothing balanced on his head, all three of them silent in the heat, making their way up to the park. Perhaps even some of the men from the jetty would have followed some distance off as he climbed the steps of the band-stand and, snapping the silk parasol shut, took possession of the ruins, destined for the next few years to be home to him and his two boys, Trinidad the elder of them, and he himself, carried that day to San Juan del Norte in his father's arms.

Because he was born possibly in San Carlos and that is where they had come here from, further upstream, down through the rough water and into the calm waters of the lake; or perhaps in El Castillo, or in Sabalo, anywhere along the banks of the San Juan river, but he doesn't remember; or perhaps Taleno his father (R.I.P.) never told him anyway; nor did he ever describe his mother for him, beyond that she had a serene face like that of virtue itself. Taleno took his children from his wives early on, to bring them up in his own way, and that was why he can remember nothing of his mother, though perhaps on occasion he has glimpsed her in dreams, a girl with unformed breasts playing with a rag doll in a sleepy yard beyond which there may have been a river because there is the sound of water flowing. Taleno has said it was unlikely, the girl in his dream was not really like her, because when he'd left she was still so young that even though she had given birth she had no breasts to give milk.

San Juan del Norte, with the sea roaring in the distance beyond white dunes like polished glass; the ruins of stores and banks, hotels, casinos, and brothels, steamship agencies and consulates, mansions with the bare bones of their algae-encrusted towers exposed to the wind, their owners' names or effigies carved in crumbling pediments, the thick knotty roots of eucalyptus and tamarind trees from once planned groves now thrusting up through the cracks in marble slabs, heaving them up; branches pushing their evergreen fronds in at French windows; a bar once upon a time *La Maison Dorée* now open to the sky like a walled garden, slender Viennese chairs still clustered around its iron tables which in the mists of dawn look as though they have just been vacated at the end of a party; a safe as tall as a man thrown in the middle of the street, a semicircle of golden letters on its door: *F. Alf. Pellas and Co.*; tombstones from the foreigners' cemeteries with their

Hebrew, German, Italian names, washed by the rains down to the beach, where the women use them to dry their clothes on; in the mouth of the river a dredger, towering immobile above the clumps of weeds swaying slowly with the tides, like a green plain, bending before the Atlantic wind, herons from the jungle that swoop down with raucous cries onto the oily beach, clouds of mosquitos and gnats swarming round the oil-lamps at night; the growling of pumas and the chorusing frogs, and in the darkness, the breeze wafting all round the harbour the whispers of the men who are squatting down at the quayside piled high with caged monkeys. Sometimes he wakes in the bandstand, terrified of their howling, their cages strewn now not only all over the jetty but along the coast at the rivermouth, on the dunes, and inside the ruined houses, more hunters emerging from the jungle every night with their captives in wicker cages, the monkeys' cries rising from every corner of San Juan del Norte.

Old sheets hang down from the bandstand rafters to provide some shelter from the wind that sweeps across from the dunes. The bandstand has a zinc roof supported on slender iron columns, and a wrought-iron balustrade around its base. On its platform there are still some rusted music stands; and there is a dais where the children sit hidden among rambling yellow weeds run wild from the park beds, with clouds of flies hovering above the clumps of undergrowth, and pigs rooting in search of rotten gourds or the reddish, black-speckled mangoes. In his mind's eye he sees himself standing on the steps of the bandstand because his father isn't there, off yet again on one of his hunting expeditions, and Trinidad is helping the dark-skinned, silver-haired woman who cooks for them to blow the flames of the fire they've made with brushwood from the park. Taleno's father has disappeared as though they will never see him again; the first sign of his return is the vulture bobbing opposite the bandstand as it tears bits of flesh from the hides of the wild animals drying in the sun.

Then one day they leave San Juan del Norte on a tugboat to go to Puerto Cabezas, taking with them the rest of the inhabitants who, at his father's insistence, leave their hovels and follow him in search of a place known as La Misericordia near the river Macuelizo. There is talk of discoveries of gold there so magnificent that the sand of the riverbed gleams yellow in the distance, and when anyone treads in the water, their feet are covered with sticky gold dust; so the procession of villagers descends the tree-lined avenue to the jetty carrying all their belongings, oil lamps, stools, statues of saints, mattresses, grain sacks, here and there a kitchen stove on someone's back, a few hens, their dogs bringing up the rear. Once they are heading in their canoes out to meet the boat, they start to sing to the music of mandolins, and the song gets taken up from canoe to canoe as they paddle towards the mouth of the estuary as though they were going on a half-hour pleasure trip. The wild animals take over their huts on stilts, and only roaring, howling, chattering, and the beating of wings are left to be heard among the toppled walls. As they are sailing down the coast, Trinidad goes to the side of the boat and asks if the country they can see is the same as the one they have left, and nodding, Taleno's father points and says that all the distant outline is in fact the same: Nicaragua.

But neither they nor their band of followers have any luck in their prospecting. Gradually the spikes and thorns strip them of even the clothes they stand in; sullenly furious at the shame of showing his bare backside, Taleno pans the dirt for months on end without ever seeing the glint of gold; not in La Misericordia, or in Animas de Alamicamba, where also there are more rumours of mineral wealth. When the others lose all hope of a fortune and drift away, the three of them are left to wander through the desolate regions of the Atlantic coast, Taleno already embarked on his new trade of a roving pedlar. They travel the length and breadth of the land, weighed down with battered suitcases and cardboard boxes, not that his father prospers in this rough journeying either, that takes them to the upper reaches of rivers, jungle clearings, tiny hamlets of wooden huts, offering clothing, hats, lengths of cotton, hand mirrors, ribbons, perfumed cakes of soap, quinine, Solka rouge, cholagogo, purgatives. He can still remember Prinzapolka, Kukra, Waspam, Wambla, remember endless strips of charred tree trunks, the never ending drone of saws toppling pines which, chained together, bump their way downstream to the open sea. They spent whole nights in dugout canoes tied up to river banks roofed over by the jungle, then trudged along tracks, his father carrying the suitcases, the boys responsible for the cardboard boxes, for night to overtake them in abandoned shacks where they had to beat the floor with sticks to scare away the snakes before they could lie down to sleep. They came across the most unexpected villages where Moravian pastors the image of the Bristol calendar man had built churches with no bell-towers; Baptist missionaries dressed in black with Bakelite collars debating religion from one canoe to another with Franciscan friars perched astride loads of bananas. They bought and sold, slept side-by-side with the foresters, rubber workers, skin hunters, and migrant labourers, in shacks reeking of smoke and sweat, where on the same floor the travellers sought relief with prostitutes specially brought to these remote corners, or crawled across to women strangers and found happiness merely in the warmth of a thigh. The boys would lie wide awake, sharing the same cape as their father, having to go to bed or wake at dawn in the same fermenting stench of shirts and rags laid out to dry by the fireside, crawling on all fours to find their place under the hammocks taut with the weight of one body, or two, recognising in these cheap lodgings strangers they have run into elsewhere, identified by their hat or their clothes, watching them spread out their waterproof capes to sleep on, listening to one of them stammer out by the light of a candle pages from a battered copy of *The Count of Montecristo*. From the sleeping bodies every night came a chorus of heavy breathing and ferocious muttering, the rattling of their snores, the captive animals clawing at their wire cages.

Nights later, the far-off lights of sawmills, the distant clatter of mining engines, back up the rivers, a flat-bottom boat carrying the likeness of a Jesus of Silence amidst the bushes, blindfolded and with bound hands, his white tunic flapping in the wind. A burnt-out hut on the riverbank, a man standing among the ashes waving his hat, the sound of trees crashing down through the jungle, the chattering protest of birds wheeling above the spot where the treetop had been, and voices, which seem meant to guide them to a place they could only sense the existence of, ring out, lost in the denseness of the forest: General Sandino has been through here! and the answering cry, farther off: That's good news! Then the voices fading into nothingness. At another point on their trek they stumble upon an aeroplane's ruined fuselage on a hillside, and from among the trails of insects swarming over the cockpit, Trinidad pulls out a compass that he proudly keeps. A few steps further on, when the mist has lifted and they can see more clearly, they spot a skeleton dangling from a hawthorn branch, swaying limply in the breeze, green slime obscuring the US Marine uniform, a tuft of withered blond hair still clinging to the skull. Some golden, luminous worms crawl out along the fleshless limbs and drop off to the ground; the same worms glitter behind the airman's goggles pulled over sightless sockets. The three of them set off again, and that whole day it does nothing but rain on them, storm clouds and more rain.

When Chepito takes the guitar from under the counter and hands it to him, Jilguero stares for a few moments at his blurred reflection in its surface, as in the water of a still well, the black guitar incrusted with mother-of-pearl which has lain there silent ever since the death of Lazaro, its owner, such a delicate instrument that he would sometimes exclaim in wonder "it's like a woman", cradling it in his arms. Jilguero settles slowly, contentedly, round the guitar and begins to try it out, preparing himself for the sound of the chord that seems to come from a long way off.

Raul and Pastorita can't find anyone to take his place, that's why the trio *Los Caballeros* doesn't play any more, Chepito explains. He sweeps the stage, then the wet sawdust full of cigarette butts and packets and bottle tops that he's sprinkled over the dancefloor. He pushes the pile out to the gangway and as it falls in a cloud to the water below, he beats the broom against the edge of the planks. There are only two of them in *El Copacabana* at this mid-day hour, Jilguero with his feet up on the table, Chepito doing the chores. He spots Jilguero's cowboy boots through the planks of the bar, and the plinths of the music stands with their painted phosphorescent green palm trees. His gaze also takes in the corrugated iron roof strung with coloured streamers and the strands of red and blue lights along the beams right out to the gangway, which connects the nightclub built on piles in the lake to the shore. Next to the rail of the passageway are crates of Victoria beer, grimy bottles of Spur and Canada Dry, full of rainwater where drowned cockroaches float, silver-topped siphons, and a tin barrel for ice.

Chepito comes back in, puts the broom away, and discreetly covers his mouth as he laughs to himself as he hears Jilguero start to sing one of Raul's songs: *I don't know if you were real in my life or only a dream*. Jilguero accompanies himself on the guitar, repeating the line to work out the right key, then falling silent while he tunes the guitar, staring at it the whole while as if questioning it, then trying the song again. Chepito wets a rag in the dishwater and energetically rubs the bar counter, all his attention on Jilguero, weighing him up and trying to guess his reaction to what he is about to propose—if you wanted to, you could join the trio and replace Lazaro, the one who got killed; Pastorita is afraid to ask you because he thinks you might take offence.

Jilguero strums the chords, slaps the box of the guitar with his open hand, and looks up with a smile—why on earth should the idea offend me? What an idiot that Pastorita is. Then he bends to the instrument again, his hair falling into his face as he begins to play once more, cautiously, carefully, as if at last it will respond to his touch, while Chepito continues to polish the bar, its wood scored by knives and stained by drink and sweaty hands. When he speaks in a rapid monotone it is as though he is obediently repeating a lesson he has learned: it's because you're looked down on if you're a guitarist, and the last time Pastorita met your brother Carlos, at a party where they had gone to play, he warned him that they were ruining your life with all these nights of drinking and serenading.

It's my life, Jilguero shrugs, and picks out a fresh tune on the guitar. Chepito asks him why doesn't he play *La Moralimpia*, and Jilguero agrees, trying to recall the tune first by whistling, then on the instrument itself. There's a coincidence for you, you mention my brother and here I am waiting for him to come and pick me up for a leaflet we're going to have printed. He said he'd be here at two—what time is it now, Chepito? Chepito has no watch, but goes across to the window and leans out to look at the sky: it must be around one. Caught in the glare of the April brightness, he stands gazing out towards the spot where they laid Lazaro out, his body stretched on a sheet in the sand while they tried to scrape together the money for a coffin, the four candles stuck on the top of pebbles, Lazaro murdered early one morning in *El Copacabana*. Chepito returns to the bar, breathes on the glasses, wipes them, then puts them back in their places on the shelf, in this place which will one day sink just like the *Xolotlan* race track, thinking of the flooded stands visible from the same window. Jilguero slips down until the back of his head is resting against the seat, or like the ruined jetty, against whose still visible cement posts the scum now beats.

Were you here that time they killed Lazaro? Chepito nods, a look of sorrow at once stealing over his features, as it does whenever he's asked that question. I was standing right here, he says, and then it really was one o'clock because the firestation siren boomed across the town stilled by the heat, and Jilguero repeats that at two without fail his brother will be coming to fetch him. Chepito though has already launched into the story of how that night he had already taken off his Caribbean dancer's costume after the last show, and the musicians from the *Champu de Cariño* orchestra had packed up and gone some time earlier. *Los Caballeros* were doing the rounds of the bars along the lakeside looking for work, because it was the August holidays, when they ran into a stranger.

He got it into his head he must take them to Jinotega for a serenade, though the *Caballeros* said he was crazy, it was too far from Managua; but he swore that the woman of his dreams lived in Jinotega and not to go and serenade her that night would be a dreadful betrayal. He followed them from place to place, imploring them, ordering them, shaming them in front of everyone, with the money in his hand—they could name their price, he would pay for a taxi there and back; smiling to placate him, they told him not to be so silly, that if he was so desperate there was no end of other trios to choose from down at the lakeside. But he was pigheaded—it was the *Caballeros* or no-one.

They came on down to *El Copacabana* from a place called the *Flor de Azalea*, near the Parque 25 de Mayo, to leave their guitars with me as usual. They were still arguing with the man as they came in, and when Lazaro disappeared through the back door with an "excuse me, I'm just going to the toilet", he followed, and then going up to him with a smile and a gesture of putting an arm around his shoulder, for no reason whatsoever, in complete cold blood, he stabbed Lazaro in the back. "The *Caballeros* or no-one," he muttered again as he pulled his knife out.

Chepito recalls the crime, and the past plunges into an immense hangover tasting of vomit or spilt beer, the guitar with its broken, curling strings still lying on the scuffed dancefloor, and the murderer running through the bushes of the lakeshore still clutching the knife. He will never be able to forget the blood that covered Lazaro's face as if gushing from his eyes; or the faces of the other two *Caballeros* who still had not had time to register fear or even to drop their instruments, until all of a sudden Raul broke down in tears and kneeled to put his jacket over the body, which was twisted to the right so Lazaro's playing hand had been trapped beneath its weight, blood drying between the fingers. A little while later a magistrate appeared, his gown over striped pyjamas, and pushed his way through the crowd of curious onlookers who had come flocking at the news from all the nearby bars, and were being kept back on the gangway by some policemen. August 1952, almost two years ago, he sighs, sitting down with Jilguero.

Shame you never got to know him, or to see him when he was laid out for the funeral. There was no consoling Raul and Pastorita, above all because they felt they had been crippled, they would rather have lost one of their own limbs than had Lazaro killed like that. They spent the whole of that night reminiscing about all the serenades they had given; their gambling; the scandals they had caused and their bar-room brawls; the number of times they had been thrown in jail after singing and drinking and shouting "down with the government" right under the noses of the police; their week-long poker games; their guitar challenges to see who could play best—competitions that Lazaro always won, the best guitarist in the whole of Nicaragua. What more proof was needed than that time he got a secret summons to a deserted seaside hotel outside San Juan del Sur, because someone just landed from a ship wanted an accompanist to sing some tangos with. That person had been none other than Carlos Gardel, his body covered in burns, his face horribly scarred, leading a wandering existence up and down the continent, and in whichever country he found himself offering an invitation to the best guitarist to some and sing. In Nicaragua this honour fell to Lazaro; all night they spent shut up together, but Lazaro never got to see Gardel's face properly because he hid it beneath the brim of his hat. They said goodbye at daybreak, and that was the last he ever heard of him.

How it hurt to think that an artist like Lazaro had only a single pair of shoes to his name: the day after his death the *Caballeros* went to his room in a lodging house in Quinta Niña to get his best clothes to lay him out in, and there they saw his iron-frame bed, sagging right to the floor, his dirty clothes scattered all around, and hanging against the wall, protected from the grime by a sheet of newspaper, the gabardine suit he wore when they had a formal engagement, shiny like a mirror from the number of times he had ironed it, what they could not find was the spare pair of shoes, two-tone coffee and white, that Raul swore he had once seen him wear; they spent some time looking sadly at his mirror, covered with photos of international singers, and his own handwriting at the bottom of a photo of the *Caballeros* leaning on their guitars:

This is the best trio in all America. Plus one of Lazaro by himself when he was just starting out, a lanky youth bending forward with one foot on a chair to croon into the microphone, while in the background a furtive, downtrodden little boy looked on.

And the sleepless nights they spent on a dismal bench in the station square, their contests to see who could piss furthest without getting up or stopping whistling, tales of suicide victims they had toasted with the day these men had slashed their wrists, noting in them as they drank a sadness like a deep abyss; of men who gambled away their wives at dice after already losing their houses, of the sickly paleness of adulterous women's faces in the daylight; of the counterfeit money printed by the rich and powerful of which the poor have not the slightest notion; of secret tunnels from church vestries to convent schools for the priests to slip into the girl boarders' rooms without a sound; of the real burial place of Sandino's body, and how it was buried and dug up again so that nobody could ever find it; or they tried to imagine the crowds of fans there would be if one day *Los Panchos* were to visit Nicaragua, something they at once dismissed from their minds because it was too impossible to think of. Occasionally famous stars did pass through Las Mercedes airport on their way to other countries, as Augustin Lara had once, together with Maria Felix, but they had been surrounded by the police and nobody had been able to get anywhere near them, except for *el hombre* who went out to the runway to greet them in person. Sitting on the dismal bench, they composed songs, Raul being the talented one, and their voices would rise triumphantly in unison through the square where the railway linesmen were sitting up on their flatcars waiting to start work for the day; or their voices would waft out of their rooms in Campo Bruce, Quinta Niña, or San Judas as they practised during the day in silent neighbourhoods which seemed to grow even quieter out of respect for their art, without the *Caballeros* ever showing their faces, like thieves, spending their nights singing and their days in hiding. Religiously they wrote songs about women glimpsed one day and enjoyed only in dreams, proud women whose fickleness they scorned in music because they were forever getting married, and when they happened to meet in the street, these women who inspired so many boleros did not even bother to turn to look.

As they stood by Lazaro's body stretched out in the sand, they remembered The Flying Yolanda, the Salvadorean trapeze artist from the Gran Circo Atayde with whom one night the three of them had made off after the performance and taken along the lake to Lazaro's room, not far from the circus. As owner of the bed, Lazaro had the first turn, with the promise that he would whistle when he was done, and hand over to the next one; but no sound came through the closed door, almost as though Lazaro and The Flying Yolanda had passed away inside, until the other two, squatting on the kerb outside, saw the day coming up. The Flying Yolanda grew so fond of Lazaro she quit the trapeze to be with him; she would wake up and ask for dishes to wash, but he had never had so much as a spoon, let alone a plate, and when the three of them got together on the dismal bench he would complain to them that he did not know what to do with her stuck in his room, he could not turn round in such a small space without bumping into her, and anyway she was always in bed, like a broody hen, and constantly told him not to be back late, as if it wasn't precisely his job to roam the streets at night. The fact was that Lazaro wasn't the sort to live with a woman, sooner or later they always got pregnant; he could put up with them for a short while in the dark, but to have them hanging round him the whole day long was enough to shake the romance out of him. Even so, he had managed to father three children in his travels; Chepito had met one of them, a boy who was a shoe-shine under the dome of the Temple of Music in the Parque Central, but had only heard of the existence of the other two. Worried, Lazaro asked their advice: "What on earth can I do?" The Flying Yolanda spent the whole night sitting on the bed racked with coughing fits, and he even began to miss contracts so as not to leave her all alone. And what if the cough was tuberculosis? "Take her to the hospital for a check-up," the others suggested, but he did not want to hurt her feelings.

Then one day he turned up at the dismal bench grinning that he was a free man again. The Flying Yolanda had left for her home town, Sonsonate, leaving a note with her address saying if by any chance he should be touring that part of El Salvador he was to be sure to look her up. That adventure had been the inspiration for Raul's slow foxtrot beginning *Yolanda, Yolanda, everyone's flower, it was the wind which brought you, the storm that carried you away.*

What about Lazaro's dream? Lazaro once dreamt that the *Caballeros* had been abroad to sing, and that late one night in El Ocotal, Lazaro's home town on the border with Honduras, their voices came loud and clear on the radio in a programme from Cochabamba or Guayaquil. The next morning the legend of that broadcast spread throughout the town; when people opened their doors in the morning haze they stared at each other in amazement, as if a miracle had taken place in the night. Lazaro always wanted to be remembered with his guitar in his hands, not with them silent, as they were now, with him stretched out in the sand, dressed in his blue formal suit, his face washed with warm water to wipe off the blood, his only pair of shoes without laces, and no flowers for his funeral.

Jilguero nods absent-mindedly, that's what is so dreadful about being an artist in this country. Chepito, tears in his eyes, says yes, that's the great shame, but perhaps if you say yes the *Caballeros* can get together again. Do you think an hour's gone by already? asks Jilguero, anxiously picking the guitar up again, because Carlos is a man of his word, and he promised he'd be here at two o'clock sharp. Chepito goes over to the window once more—right, two o'clock it is. I would have loved the life, Chepito, I love the guitar, though I'm no more than a beginner, but it's easier said than done to replace Lazaro. Chepito comes over quickly to press the offer—but you play well, I swear you do, even someone as demanding as Pastorita, has said to me more than once: "I won't have anyone but Jilguero touching that guitar of Lazaro's."

Someone whistles outside, and Jilguero jumps up towards the door, but Chepito stops him, no need to worry, it's only the van with the ice, and goes out to get the day's supply. Disappointed, Jilguero sits down again, and from his corner watches the translucent cube being dragged along with a pair of black pincers across the wet sawdust of the platform, sees it cut on the spot with a saw that showers out a white spray as the blade cuts closer to the scored heart of the block. The two halves gradually split until one topples over and the man, wearing only trousers and a piece of sacking over one shoulder, heaves it across and drops it into the barrel, while a second man drags the other half away with the pincers and dries off the sweat with the back of his hand, sweeping off the bits of ice stuck like frost to his cheeks. Soon the truck has pulled away and Chepito comes back to join Jilguero who, shaking himself as if out of a deep daydream, starts to pick one more tune on the guitar; if he doesn't join *Los Caballeros* it's because of a delicate bit of business he's got involved in. At that, Chepito draws even closer, almost touching him now, and Jilguero has a close-up view of the lines on his middle-aged face, like an adolescent gone prematurely old from too much masturbating, as Lazaro used to say. What business might that be, Jilguero?

Jilguero hands the guitar back to him: do you know Captain Santiago Taleno, Chepito? And Chepito, his voice so deep and resonant that his delicate looks seem incongruous, tries to draw him out with his accomplice's whisper: of course he knows him, he's seen his picture in the papers many a time, standing behind *el hombre* at banquets. Isn't he the head of the presidential aides? And at that very moment he remembers something else, but takes care not to show the slightest surprise so he will not betray the fact that he had forgotten it until now: and I met him myself once, right here, in *El Copacabana*, and he was with your brother; have I told you about that, Jilguero? It was a strange thing; it was last November, when the Miss Nicaragua competition was being held, the one your sister was in. All the customers had left—it was past midnight, and I was just closing up when I heard shouts from outside down by the lake; I went out onto the gangway and all I could see was the shapes of two men punching away at each other, swapping blow for blow for a long time. First one of them would fall, then the other, they would get up without a word, without so much as an insult. They must have been scrapping for a good half-hour, when they stopped and began talking to each other. They saw that I still had my lights on and came up to ask me to give them a drink. They were Captain Taleno: I recognised him from the photos, and Carlos, both of them all cut and bruised, with blood all over their shirts, Taleno in his white dress uniform, and your brother in a lightweight dinner jacket. I didn't want to serve them because it was so late, and so odd that these two should have been punching each other silly a moment before and now wanted to drink together. But the army is the army—this place belongs to one of them, and that always makes you think twice, doesn't it? So I did give them a drink, and in the end they stayed here until six in the morning. To this day I haven't figured it out; to beat hell out of each other like that they must have hated each other, but then why get together for a drink afterwards? Jilguero stands up with a smile, and gently moves Chepito out of his way: that's how great friendships start, with a beating.

He said he was off to see what the devil had happened to Carlos, and walked over to the door. As he was going out, he halted for a moment, straining to catch a sound in the distance, almost lifting his hand in surprise, to call for silence in the silence.

He trips over a tree root hidden by leaves on the muddy ground, loses his balance and jabs the butt of the rifle downwards to try to stop himself falling flat, but Turco grabs him under the armpit, steadies him, and sets him off walking again through the curtain of rain. They grope their way forward in single file, and behind him he feels Raul clutch at his belt as he too stumbles. Turco is out in front now leading them through the downpour, the rest of them following him uncomplaining, coming to a halt every now and then, planting their boots as firmly as they can in the greasy mud before they start off again, for days leading them in search of a river they are supposed to cross. Once again it's the horseman with his three-cornered hat and frockcoat from the Putnam sure-fast dyes poster raising a defiant arm and shaking his fist at the posse chasing him down the steep hillside.

But that Saturday afternoon in August when his father, back from Managua on the five o'clock train, did not stop to take off the striped drill coat he always wore for visits of condolence or on trips to the capital, but went straight through to the back of the shop and locked himself in the dispensary without bothering to switch on any lights, the rider on the poster stuck on the door of the medicine cabinet had not yet begun to move. His legs were too short for the stirrups, and as yet he had not learnt to whirl the reins through the air to lash the horse's flanks as it reared up blindly, terrified at the darkness; but neither was there any reason for him to flee, because the troops of pursuers could not advance either, the dust cloud hung in the air as their horses' hooves rattled on the pebbles of the hillside.

Brushing past his wife who when she had heard the carriage ran out into the road to welcome him home, his father, bald and stocky in his crumpled jacket, the porch light shining off the bones of his forehead, had staggered between the living-room furniture with the looping step of a drunkard and shut himself in the dispensary. Only much later in reply to her incessant drumming on the door did they hear his hostile voice, muffled as always, as if from the dust of his medicinal powders, asking to be left in peace.

Now, as Jilguero listens to the rustling of the leaves in the squall, there also well up in him the distant echoes of the excited cheers that rang out in the quiet of the sunny Sunday afternoon the day after his father had shut himself in, a wave which carried to the room of crumpled sheets where his mother, who had spent a sleepless night, was watching over Liliana asleep in her cradle while she told the two brothers to peer through the transom over the door to see if they could make out any movement from their father among the dark shelves. But Carlos refused to go, and he himself, his face pressed tight against his mother's breast that still smelt of milk, could only concentrate on the waves of applause carried by the wind that Sunday, to reach him interspersed with shouts broken off by the sound of running footsteps as people fled from shots in the air, only to break out again a few blocks further on, this time as challenging yells.

At noon the cheering died away, then the street filled with the sound of hasty footsteps, a crowd of people drawing nearer amid explosions of rockets and firecrackers, a cloud of smoke spreading thickly to cover their whole block, higher even than the rooftops. Pressed up against the railings of their gate, they could see the crowd advancing, and when the demonstration reached them it was as if the walls of their house had been suddenly spirited away and the shouting flooded right into the room and made Liliana start to cry in her cradle.

Meeting in a cinema surrounded by troops specially brought in from Managua, the opposition parties had that morning proclaimed his aged grandfather as their candidate for president. Trainloads of departmental delegations had been arriving in Masaya for days, groups of strangers smelling of vinegar and barbershop perfumes, who wore stiff frock-coats, with fob watches and ties like napkins, and squatted on the pavements around the market to eat the lunches wrapped in banana leaves that the local committees handed round, or fanned themselves with their hats as they took a stroll around the bandstand or along the tree-lined avenues of the Parque Julio Cesar where, after all the available rooms had been let, many of them camped out in the open, gesticulating as they argued how they were going to kick out the dictatorship in free and fair elections. Now, arm in arm with the serious, stern-looking leaders of the convention, the old man approached the house, taking his place in the front rank of the excited procession which lifted banners that the sun had already bleached of colour. The candidate returned in triumph to his home, the doctor's consulting-room he lived in across the street from his natural son.

The evening before, his mother had sent Carlos to warn the old man, but it was not until late on Sunday night that he was finally able to cross the street, with the last of the party faithful despatched back to their regions with instructions for the election campaign, and those who had stayed behind, waiting for something more to happen long past there being any chance of it, eventually resigning themselves to the idea and drifting off down the street carrying their furled banners.

Followed by his daughter-in-law and the two boys, the old man went straight to the back room and rapped several times on the door. When there was no reply, he called for a rocking chair and positioned himself facing the locked door. He rocked gently to and fro and, as though his son were sitting there with him, began to tell him all that had happened at the party convention, how he had been chosen unanimously to lead the civilian forces in the election campaign; no-one could stop them, the opposition was going to sweep to victory.

Then they heard the scrape of a piece of paper being pushed under the door, and the old man leaned forward painfully to pick it up without rising from the chair. He put on a pair of spectacles, rocked well back to catch the light, and scanned the note thoughtfully. When he had read it through, he snatched his glasses off and turned to his daughter-in-law with a despairing gesture. Then he looked myopically at the top of the door, as if his son's voice would materialise somewhere in mid-air, and gently chided him for not having trusted him enough to come to him as soon as he felt the first pain, before the disease had taken hold; what was the point of going all the way to the capital for a useless diagnosis when he could have just crossed the road. The sudden sound of his son's abrupt voice cutting in from the locked room seemed to take him by surprise, as if he no longer expected any answer, the son caustic that what would have been the use of that, the old man had been completely ruined by his politicking, why didn't he go off and lose his election, if that was what he wanted. At that the voice stopped, at the end of its prophecy, and their grandfather, his hand criss-crossed with bulging blue veins trembling as he laid the paper on the crochet mat on the table near the rocking chair, left the house with an unsteady but proud step, left their mother still undecided whether or not to cry. Jilguero remembers watching Carlos help him down the step into the road, the flaps at the back of his eternal white linen suit folded like the pleats of an accordion, the shoulders far too big for his bony frame, his panama hat fresh from the press clasped against his chest.

Even more than his face as an old man he remembers the one in a youthful photo painstakingly reproduced in the opposition newspapers that always arrived in Masaya days out of date, his portrait in the photo-engraving edged round with the nails used to fix the block standing out from the dense sea of hand-set type of the front page of those four-sided broadsheets that left the reader's fingers smeared with ink. His grandfather's features, those of a serious, studious adolescent, smudged by the wear of the copper plate so they were only vaguely discernible, with the bulging eyes and half-open mouth, his oversize ears, hair parted in the middle and the prominent Adam's apple, the wide lapels of his coat and the skimpy knot of his tie lost in the starched collar of the spotless shirtfront; a photograph that had been taken out from its shelf and dusted off since the turn of the century, when, after his return from France with his surgeon's diploma from the Charcot de la Salpêtrière Hospital, his patients' relatives had gone round collecting signatures proposing him for President of the Republic, awed by the surgical operations he performed, the first seen in Nicaragua, and carried out with the same aplomb whether he found himself in a dimly lit stable or in a bedroom.

Frustrated by dictatorships, armed interventions by the US Marines, frauds and vote-rigging, his candidature had been upheld for decades in expectation of the day of reckoning, his supporters swelled by every patient who came round from an operation, with their family and descendants. In the towns, people never failed to rush to their doors to wave their hats whenever he passed by, tilted over by the weight of his black medical bag, on his way to answer the call of one of his patients. He also travelled out of town, perched up on the driving seat of his carriage, and in the villages too they would halt his horses to greet him, urging him to climb down and accept a drink. His portrait in the bars, cockpits and taverns was always garlanded with flowers, lit by candles in the niches of isolated shrines, ever-present on the altars set up at wakes in shacks and on the poor farms, offered for sale in markets by the vendors of holy relics, miracle cures and lucky charms.

Shortly after her arrival in Masaya, his French wife had died of marsh fever in one of the rooms of the corner house which forever afterwards remained shut. Despite the pomp of her funeral, when her flower-bedecked corpse had been mourned in an open coffin with violins and recitals in the drawing-rooms of the local club, and her funeral procession had been able to reach the cemetery only late at night because of the endless speeches pronounced at every street corner, nobody could now recall the small plump foreign girl, whose name the council had chosen for a park down by the lake that somehow never got built. To everyone it seemed that the old man had always lived as a confirmed bachelor in his consulting-room, a real lay saint, looked after by a dedicated band of women volunteers, who took it in turns to sweep the house clean, wash his clothes, and prepare his food.

He slept at the end of the passage, his hat and his bag beside him on the bed. He never bothered to undress, and the women, held back by a feeling of respect, never went in to clean up the filthy, untidy room; pages from old medical magazines got wafted to and fro on the floor, surgical treatises piled up in its damp corners, and the walls were lined with a collection of lacquered urns with ground glass tops that bore solemn engravings—malignant tumours, foetuses of Siamese twins, the viscera of famous men that he had removed at autopsies, outstanding among them the extraordinary, colossal brain of Ruben Dario.

Jilguero remembers how he often used to creep into the room to stare at the dust-covered recipient through whose glass he could dimly make out, floating in an amber-coloured liquid, the huge mass of shrivelled brains that his grandfather was in the habit of bringing out into the patio to show off to any stranger who had dropped in to wish him well, or to groups of schoolchildren in uniform, pointing proudly to the convolution of Broca, where the spirit of the muses had been located.

The only one of those devoted women who had dared to conquer the barrier of respect around the room to sweep it out was one day discovered to be pregnant; and although his supporters immediately leapt to defend him against any slight on his honour, particularly from his political adversaries, he himself took the decision to present himself at the registry office to recognise his son, gave him his own name, Desiderio, and then handed him over to his spinster sisters to be brought up.

Often over lunch, his father's glistening bald head bent over the steaming plate as he stirred his soup, Jilguero had heard him cursing that pair of miserly aunts who had forced him to eat in the kitchen and used him as an errand boy as though he were an orphan, and when he was older, had fought tooth and nail with his father to hand him over to the Salesian fathers. Fortunately they lost that battle, and he was sent to Leon, his trunk and his campbed labelled beside him in the train, to study medicine.

Year after year he failed his examinations, until he became a well-known figure in the faculty with his heavy features, the perpetual sprinkling of dandruff on the shoulders of his medical apron, his sudden outbursts of anger and his misanthropy. Cantankerous and anti-social, he would shut himself up in his room in Laborio and leave it only to give injections in patients' houses, to do his periods on duty at the hospital, or to visit the washerwoman who lived down by the abattoir and who both washed his clothes and slept with him.

After a succession of failures, a telegram from his father, convinced by now that his son would never follow him in the profession of doctor, instructed him to study pharmacy instead. When finally he returned to Masaya with his chemist's degree, the house opposite his father's surgery where he was to set up in business had already been rented. At about the same time his father also proposed him for membership of the social club, and he was duly accepted, despite several blackballs against his name due to his elopement with a young dressmaker from Nandaime, where she was to have been the queen of the local saint's day. The whole village was celebrating as they were married in the registrar's office that was filled with curious onlookers after the bride's father had got a court order to have them taken there.

And that was one of his mother's commonest complaints, one of those she appeared merely to let slip as she was unpicking the threads of her sewing—the fact that she had been forced to get married in such a rush, had signed the register not in her own home but in the judge's office, and had been shamed into walking across the square with head lowered in disgrace while the bells were ringing out for the celebrations: to have got married in that dark corner whilst fireworks for what should have been her coronation ball exploded all round, not to have swept grandly through the main doors of the church in veil and coronet, not to have any wedding photographs to treasure.

He had provoked that unnecessary scandal just to annoy the old man, and it was for the same reason that gradually, despite his feelings of shame, he let himself be drawn in to becoming a supporter of the regime. He began to sign whatever pledge of loyalty to *el hombre* he was asked to, volunteered to work as a teller for the government in the elections, and went up to the capital to attend banquets in honour of *el hombre* without anyone being aware he was there, squashed as he invariably was at the end of a table in the midst of departmental delegations of tax inspectors and primary school teachers, who could never get enough to eat.

CHAPTER 2

"What do you mean, what are we going to do to you?" Indio asked, pocketing the gun that Jilguero passed him. "Nothing at all."

The colonel's glistening jowls were quivering slightly; he looked beyond Indio to the door, also carefully avoiding looking at Turco, though their elbows were practically touching. He shook his head several times at the offer of a cigarette from the packet Indio was waving in front of his face.

"How about a drink then? A beer perhaps?" Indio put away the cigarettes. Jilguero, still standing behind the colonel and struggling to undo his garishly coloured necktie, pointed out he had already offered, but without success. Hearing Jilguero the colonel started as though bitten by a snake.

"You—you brought me here on false pretences. And you've got a lot of nerve taking my gun from me."

He was so furious that all Jilguero could think of to do was fold the tie over and over before stuffing it into his shirt pocket. He left the talking to Indio, who was still smoking with a thoughtful air. After all, he was the one who was supposed to take the lead.

"No, Catalino, let me explain," Indio drew his seat closer. "There's no reason for you to get so upset."

"All I want is to get out of here, right now. And where's my gun? Give it back to me at once," he ordered Jilguero, his composure regained.

"But you won't even give me a chance to talk; it's been such a long time since we last met, and this is how you greet me, Catalino." Indio stretched his hand out to lay it on the colonel's arm, but he pulled away. He was sweating so much it seemed he had just bathed with all his clothes on.

"Well then, what's all this about? What do you want with me?" he snapped.

"Just to ask you a favour," Indio raised his arms, begging to be believed. "I'm sorry about the way we got you here, but I told the others—didn't I? I said 'I know Catalino, he's so suspicious that if we simply invite him here, he won't want to come.'"

"But you tricked me into coming here—this fellow here did. You deceived me, you lied to get me here, and then you had the nerve to search me."

Indio had got through one cigarette and was tapping another on the packet before lighting it. Turco was still quiet as a mouse, like none of this had anything to do with him.

"Don't blame Jilguero," Indio pointed to him with the still unlit cigarette; "it was all my idea."

Taking this as a kind of official introduction, Jilguero lifted his hat in greeting; and when he heard this name, in spite of his anger the colonel also seemed saddened.

Indio took advantage to try a second time to lay a hand on his arm. This time the colonel did not pull away.

"It won't take long to explain, Catalino. The others have asked me to be their spokesman. Who could be more suitable than an old comrade-at-arms, eh?" He accompanied this with a flourish of the arms to indicate there could be no refusing this appeal to past friendship. "Before that though, I want you to promise me you'll have a drink with us. We can't talk like this, completely parched."

"Have a drink? What the hell do you mean?" the colonel asked, shifting in his chair. His jowls were suddenly firm: "I'm a prisoner here, and you say—have a drink!"

Indio would not take his hand off his arm despite his struggling, trying to calm him down.

"A prisoner? Only you could have such a crazy idea, I swear. You haven't changed a bit."

Indio's eyes shone as he looked them over lengthily from behind the cloud of smoke masking his features.

"Jilguero, open that door," he ordered.

Jilguero immediately drew the bold with military smartness and pulled the door open with a single tug.

"There you are, now the door's wide open for you. Who's keeping you a prisoner?"

That was the moment when he could have tried to push the table back, throw himself out into the corridor, cry for help. But he did nothing, and sat there pensive, without saying a word. He did not even ask for his gun back. So then Indio pulled his chair closer still, and draped his left arm round the back of Catalino's seat. Suddenly he plunged his other hand into his own mouth and carefully removed a set of false teeth, which he placed on the middle of the newspaper.

The colonel stared first of all at the saliva-covered dentures—it took some time for him to register what they were exactly—then peered quizzically at Indio's puckered face.

"See? I'm just a toothless old man," he said, lowering his voice, whispering to the colonel with the voice of someone reassuring a child in the dark; "so there's no reason to be afraid of me, is there?"

"Afraid—who's afraid?" the colonel retorted gruffly.

"That's the spirit," Indio slapped him on the knee, picked up his teeth, and put them back into his mouth so recklessly that he seemed bound to swallow them. "Now you'll have that beer with me, won't you?"

The colonel merely undid his jacket, and the flaps fell down across his thighs, but Jilguero left the room like a shot to fetch the round of beers.

Indio, with the cigarette still dangling from his lips and smoke drifting into his eyes, busied himself serving the colonel. He placed the full glass in front of him, then raised his own arm in a toast that came rather too late since the colonel had already grabbed the mug with both hands and was gulping it down quickly, wrinkling his face like a man swallowing medicine.

"I must admit you've upset me,' Indio said, wiping his mouth with the back of his hand. "How on earth could you think that I'd want to harm you?"

He was still sitting right next to him, his arm wrapped affectionately round the chair.

"It's because you lied when you brought me here," the colonel repeated, but his tone was calmer now. He pushed the empty glass away. "And I got mad at the way you manhandled me."

"Well, so you won't be angry any more, here's your gun." Indio pushed it across the table towards him, but the colonel did not so much as try to pick it up. Jilguero stood alert in the doorway, ready to rush out to the bar again: "How about another beer?"

"No," the colonel replied hastily.

"One on its own doesn't count; we haven't even begun to discuss the matter yet," Indio said, and despatched Jilguero for the second round before he had time to protest. When the glasses were full again, Indio stared at his as if he might find strength or inspiration in it, while his cigarette burnt down in his motionless fingers.

"Well, not to beat about the bush, Catalino—it's simply that we want to go back to Nicaragua."

The colonel's jaw dropped in disbelief. Then he frowned at them as though the brightness of a light in this lightless room was hurting his eyes.

"Return, that is, perfectly legally, not secretly. You yourself have to admit that even if I've been a bit violent in the past, I've always been completely honest with you. The fact is, we're fed up killing ourselves just to make ends meet . . . and that's the truth of it. Do you know what I do for a living? I make children's party favours, believe it or not."

He searched through his shirt pocket stuffed with cheap ballpoints and crumpled papers, then pulled out a card with red and green printing on it. He put his glasses on, and read out in a lugubrious voice:

COME ONE, COME ALL

> Our special service for your children's birthdays: chairs, trestle tables, a magnificent selection of drinks and hygienic ice creams, and the most colourful piñatas. Be sure not to miss our new attraction: film shows with full sound equipment.

Listening to Indio reading this out, the colonel kept the rim of his glass to his lips, obviously trying to hide a smile, most likely conjuring up in his mind Indio in an apron heating up the starch to make the piñatas. But Turco jerked him out of his amused reverie when he abruptly got up and stood to attention as though in the presence of a superior officer, clicking his heels.

"Permission to speak, Colonel?" he asked curtly.

Although he knew Turco was there, this was the first time he had heard him speak; spluttering, without going so far as to look at him, the colonel made it clear that he was in no position to give permission or otherwise, and that Turco was free to speak if he felt like it.

"If I am allowed to go back I am prepared to face a court-martial," was all Turco said, still standing at attention.

"See, Catalino, we're putting our lives in your hands," Indio said, filling the colonel's glass again.

"But that's nothing to do with me," he argued, taking his glasses off and rubbing them on his jacket lapel: "I'm not in immigration," closing his bleary eyes while he wiped.

"But you give the orders and others jump," Indio said, sweeping his arm across the table, almost knocking the bottles and glasses off. "You're surely not going to tell me that you don't have any influence down there these days?"

Turco asked the colonel for permission to sit down, as if he had kept him standing there all the time. Confused once more, he could not make up his mind whether to answer or not, but finally nodded his consent.

"I know that *el hombre*'s sons up on the hill are told that I'm here planning an invasion, and that it was me who had their father killed. Fairy tales." Indio shook his head disconsolately: "You can see how down-and-out I am; can you get a revolution for a dime? And as for me being innocent of the death of *el hombre*, I won't even bother to swear it to you—here, look at my hands, they're clean," and he thrust his hands out, turning them over for the colonel to inspect.

He was hunched over, deep in thought, so Indio, seeking to seal their bond of friendship, pulled out another cigarette, lit it from the tip of his own, and stuck it between the colonel's lips. His mouth twitched in surprise, but Indio would not relent until he had begun to puff on it.

"Look, Larios . . . " he started to say very sheepishly to Indio, but Indio cut in, thumping the table so hard the bottles shook.

"What d'you mean, Larios? I've always been Indio to you; I'll be deeply offended if you don't call me that now."

A smile spread across the colonel's face. "Well then, Indio" he corrected himself, and the latter nodded with satisfaction, as though freed from a slur: "I promise you I'll do whatever I can; maybe they'll listen to me."

"Thank you, Catalino! I knew you wouldn't let me down—didn't I say so, boys?" Indio stood up, beaming.

"I can't promise anything though," the colonel said, flattered.

"You don't have to promise a thing, having you on our side is guarantee enough," and Indio sent Jilguero on his way for a third round, so they could drink a final toast to the success of the colonel's efforts.

"Why don't we go into the bar and have it there? Most of the customers have left, and we'd be more comfortable," Jilguero suggested.

"Okay, but this will have to be the last one, then I must be off," Turco said: "I've got a lot to do."

"We've all got lots to do—but it's true, let's get Catalino out of this hole: we only brought him here because of the noise in the bar."

Jilguero stepped behind the colonel to help him to his feet, bracing himself as he did so, because once again Catalino flopped on him with his full weight.

"Don't forget your gun." Indio picked it up from the table and put it back in the colonel's pocket.

The lunchtime throng had departed by this time, and only a few solitary drinkers were left in the room. The coloured lights of the Rockola spiralled upwards in the gloom, and the barman, absent-mindedly wiping the rows of glasses with an expert flick of the wrist, smiled in greeting from behind the bar at Indio, making as if to unsheath the cardboard king's sword.

They didn't settle down in their seats this time, to give the impression they were about to leave; Turco asked the time in a worried voice, and Jilguero did not put his briefcase down. When Indio stood up to make the toast, he did not bother to sit down again. They downed these last drinks and sat in silence waiting for the bill, as though there was nothing more to say or ask. Indio took a few steps around behind the colonel, rubbing his back to take the stiffness out of it.

"I won't feel right with myself until I confess that the idea about the dancers was mine, Catalino—but didn't he play his part to perfection, eh?" Indio said, grasping the back of the colonel's chair. "That's because he's always hanging around nightclubs."

"He certainly fooled me," the colonel admitted.

"Jilguero knows every single one of our ladies of the night here in Guatemala," Indio went on, laughing. Meanwhile Jilguero had gone over to the bar to pay.

"I bet he doesn't know some I know," Turco said with a yawn. "Housewives, girls from convent schools who meet in very discreet, intimate places. Places you wouldn't even dream of, Colonel."

"Do you still like a good eyeful, eh, Catalino?" Indio said, suddenly seizing him by the shoulders.

"What's that?" he stammered, pretending he had not heard properly.

Coming into Siuna on the coast one afternoon in the month of March, outside the village meeting room gutted by Yankee planes they find an old man stretched out on the charred remains of a door, dying. His head is resting at the level of the shuttered window, and one of his bony hands, the hand of a country saint, lies by the side of the round hole for the shutter-crank. A small group of onlookers is gathered around him, amid the blackened, slime-covered ruins of the building, one of them a lad of about fifteen who is sitting on a pile of rubble fingering the keys of an accordion as if about to start playing, and another a plump, dark-haired woman wearing an enormous wide-brimmed hat dyed in several colours that range up in circles from the base of the crown. She is on her knees in the dust, settled for once in this windless hour before dusk, and squeezes out a wet handkerchief into the old man's toothless mouth as it opens like a dark gash to receive the drops of dirty water.

They would have continued with their search for a place to stay if they had not noticed, leaning against one of the burnt walls, a strange bundle covered in a weather-beaten sheet, its ghostly octagonal shape lying there like a huge kite, and giving off a smell of dampness and paintwork, the smell of filthy hands, of bets with grubby banknotes and coins, of candles, the frying smell from countless fairs and firework processions. Without opening his eyes, the old man raises his left hand to point to the wrapped wheel, and says something in a faint gurgle which only the woman crouching over him can understand. She repeats it dutifully word by word for the others: that the thing over by the wall is a portable stall for the fair, a poor man's wheel of fortune. His whole life he's carried it on his back from fair to fair, even slept beneath it; the two of them even had a child under there once. With it he has seen downpours, droughts, the horrors of war, train crashes and flooded rivers, knife-fights in gambling dens and cockfighting pits, the wheel always rolling out its fortune, bringing luck, taking it away, on all the saint's days in Nicaragua. Was there no-one who would do him the favour of buying it so that his wife could go back to her village, Malacatoya, from where they eloped such a long time ago, so that she wouldn't have to keep wandering in a life ruled by chance?

The woman leans over him to catch any more words he might say, but he has lapsed into silence, so she carefully places a bundle of rags behind his neck, then straightens him again, gently rubbing his side. She turns her head to the newcomers: poor thing, his hour has come and still he thinks of me, she says in a voice that is both sad and shrill, the voice of a fruit-seller.

Taleno's father puts down all his packages, wipes his hands on the seat of his trousers, and kneels by the side of the couple, craning his neck forward to speak into the woman's ear beneath her hat-brim. He whispers so that no-one else can hear, perhaps ashamed of bargaining with a dying man: how much do you want for it? And the woman, in the same high-pitched whine, they can have it for next-to-nothing, thirty cordobas and it's theirs. Taleno's father studies the dying old man for a moment then, almost on all-fours to press his mouth close to the woman's ear, forming the words in an exaggerated fashion as though this might help convince her: that's a bit pricey, isn't it? Why, you can buy wheels of fortune like that brand new in Masaya for only forty cordobas. The woman bends even closer to the old man's chest as he gasps out: but look what a fine piece of work it is, carved from a single piece of wood like the old-fashioned Christs you used to see. Taleno's father, anxious not to offend, flaps away the flies from the man's forehead, but still offers him only twenty.

Let him have it for that, then you can get back to your village, the old man says to the woman after a pause. Without more ado Taleno's father pays, counting out the coins on the ground by the light of the storm-lamp Trinidad has brought because it is almost dark by now: shiny, worn coins in a little pile, which the woman scoops up into her damp handkerchief and tucks away in her bosom. With Trinidad's help, their father hoists the new possession onto his back, and between the two of them they cart it over to the lodging-house, leaving him to look after their other belongings. They are already on their second trip, this time all three of them loaded with boxes and cases full of their wares, when the woman catches up with them, panting: she had forgotten to give them the chute that goes with the wheel, and the roulette balls, the tiny tube with its supports to fix to the centre of the wheel, and the big, milky-coloured marbles kept in a round tin of Para Mi talcum powder, with streaks of yellow and light blue spiralling down into their translucent depths, blood red swirling out. The woman smiles at them as if expecting some response, her hat tied under her chin with a shoelace that seems to be cutting into the fat of her sweaty jowls. Now she can be off to Malacatoya, there was nothing more to keep her here, and anyway the money would be barely enough to buy the old man his coffin when he breathed his last.

They sit on a bench at the table in the rooming-house, facing the fire where the three sisters who run the place are busy cooking, their faces ruddy from the flames. None of them can take their eyes from the canvas-wrapped treasure lying there in the corner as yet unexamined; while they are waiting for dinner, their father goes to ask for a bit of soot from the pots, which he mixes with water on a bit of broken tile from the yard; he roots among his things and pulls out a toothbrush, the bristles yellowed and worn with use, and spreads the black paste on the tile. Then he writes on the canvas:

Property of Jose Asuncion (Chon) Taleno
Purchased in Siuna, April 1934

While their father eats hastily, stuffing his cheeks with steaming pieces of boiled plantain, he explains he has done it so that nobody will steal it from them, because they will be taking it among crowds at all the fairs. Trinidad, sipping his bowl of coffee: they could take the wooden junk and leave us just with the cloth, Dad. He swallows and turns on him angrily: you're always coming out with the same garbage, aren't you?

That night, bedded down on the rough unscrubbed boards of the dining table, which smells foul doubtless because of all the other children that had previously slept on it, they often start awake and peer through the darkness to make sure the wheel is still there, wrapped in its winding sheet, while their father slumped alongside it against the wall, is finally overcome by sleep, but continues to protect it with his body.

From that day on, they sleep on park benches, in church porches, in the doorways to village halls. When it rains they seek shelter beneath the wheel itself; they tramp through the night with devotees on pilgrimages, ford rivers with the lines of people on foot and on horseback or in caravans of carts, joyful shouts and laughter greeting each fall into the water; surprise meetings in the dark, perched high on the back of trucks or in railway wagons. The wheel always goes with them, careful to arrive at each village the night before its saint's feast, because at dawn music erupts in the square, fireworks explode and cartwheel through the skies, and giant reeds of gunpowder spit fire. Taleno's father, alert as ever, sits gaunt on his stool beside the wheel, the tattered brim of his earth-coloured felt hat patchy with dark sweat, his face streaked the colour of tobacco leaves, his grey worsted shirt buttoned tight to the collar. His sharp, tiny eyes, occasionally obscured by a satisfying drift of smoke that brings a smile as he chews his cigar, dart to and fro. His voice is hoarse as he takes the bets, then all his attention is fixed on the ball as it drops from the chute, jumps the black numbers and the red, then bobs on until finally it comes to rest. He plucks the ball out again with a deft movement of the hand, a sharp tap of his knuckles signalling the winner or picking up his own take.

Dawn and dusk are all Taleno sees of these days as they travel with their father up and down the Pacific coast from fair to fair. Day is breaking as he leaves his night's refuge and already there is the blare of music and the whiff of gunpowder from the first procession's fireworks, the mist rolling down from the hills or rising up out of the valleys and closing around the tented merry-go-round, the horses' iron rods beaded with dew and immobile; the Ferris wheel, the stall for other wheels of fortune, the food huts, the fencing for the improvised bullring. Then the first bonfires are lit in celebration, the fairmen stumble behind the church to relieve themselves and start the day. Or it is getting dark, and amid the rows of gambling booths set up along park pathways or in a main street the lights glow dimly from overhead branches, and the wandering crew of stallholders, conjurers, fortune tellers and cardsharps begins to gather, one of them an itinerant preacher who baptises in church porches during the day and then at night packs away his cassock and busies himself inviting passersby to try their luck on the waste ground where the women he is always accompanied by lie waiting on their mattresses.

It is at nightfall too that Trinidad always falls prey to an overwhelming desire to become rich, because he can see plainly enough by now that their father will stay forever poor with his wheel of fortune. He wanders among the gaming tables until it begins to rain, or until finally the raucous music from the scratchy records ceases, pushing his way in among the tightly packed circles of sad-faced gamblers, all of them beaten before they start, before they open their fists and let the sweaty notes uncurl on the damp cloth. Trinidad watches as eagerly as any of them as the calendar numbers of the roulette wheel spin in a blur of colour, hearing the spike on the support catch on the nails of the wheel with its sharp intermittent rasp, like that of the fifth string of a guitar, and how he longs to be able to decide when it will land odd, when even, so that one morning he might wake his father, drag him out of his cave under the board, and thrust pocketfuls of banknotes at him, having bankrupted the roulette wheel, or beaten the adults at dice, tilting the tumbler with masterly flicks of the hand. This was Trinidad's dream, despite his father's repeated warning that he was in for a good thrashing the day he so much as went near the forbidden den that was always to be found tucked away behind the walls of some ruined house far from the main square, because the bone dice carry with them the memory of a knifing, a suicide from ruin, a friendship lost forever through gambling.

Taleno's father has set up his wheel outside the church in Comalapa, perhaps the one dedicated to San Pedro of Lovago, hoping to attract people as the procession leaves the church, when someone comes to ask if his son is the twelve-year-old who has been gored by a bull he was trying to dodge. Someone with more money than sense had waved a five cordoba note from the seats at the bullring, daring someone to challenge the bull which was already kneeling at the post in the centre of the ring, and the boy climbed as best he could over the rails, went over to the stand and accepted the man's challenge. Though at first he just laughed and made fun of him in front of the other spectators, in the end he agreed, and Trinidad was handed the red cloth, which was so big for him that he could barely lift it from the ground. The very first thing the animal did when, in an uproar of music and firecrackers it found itself freed from the post, was to lunge straight at the boy without even noticing the men on horseback trying to attract its attention. It ripped open the boy's stomach, and tore out the bag of his intestines, which splattered out over the ground as he fell. They had been asking at all the fairground booths, but nobody knew for sure whether or not the lad had any family.

Taleno's father spits on the ground among some spilled grains of corn and leaves him to look after the wheel until he gets back, then heads off for the bullring following the man who has brought the news. On his way he spots the slow procession coming towards him in a cloud of dust, carrying the gored boy on a four-poster bed with its curtains flapping in the breeze and its four columns like the masts of a ship sailing down the street. When they meet, the bearers lower the bed so that he can see whether it is his son, while people who had been strolling in the park push and shove to catch a glimpse of the encounter, and the band in the bullring is playing: "Let's see the dappled bull, son of the black cow, to try my luck before this fair lady'', the men on horseback reining in their mounts to keep in step with the music.

Trinidad, his face grazed and smeared with the dirt of the bull-ring, raises his head painfully to look at his father, his fingers feebly twisting the crucifix given him by the owner of the bed. He manages a faint smile. As they lift him up again, his father begins to shout furiously at him, wanting to know if he thinks he's a stray animal without an owner to be going off like that while he is working himself to the bone to earn a bite to eat. He is still scolding him when he takes the bowl which contains the huge flower of bluish-pink intestines so that he himself can carry it the rest of the way, holding it out to one side and taking great care not to stumble, as if it were a holy relic, until one of the men carrying the bed asks where it is they are headed, and the father sees that the mass of intestines is no longer pulsing in the water and replies, nowhere.

They were aircraft, Chepito shouts, spreading his arms wide to imitate wings, fighter planes that zoomed in, crossed the Managua sky, then headed off south; and Jilguero said goodbye again with a wave of his hand from the gangway, running so fast he almost tripped as he jumped up onto the concrete. That was the last he saw of him.

Pastorita carefully spreads a handkerchief on the chair before he sits down because he has just changed into clean clothes: yes, some planes drop bombs, others just drop bits of paper. He tells them he had gone down to Diriamba that Sunday to lead the fun at a baptism party, and early on Monday morning he had been waiting outside the station for a truck to bring him back to Managua when the planes had appeared, spraying out the sheets of paper, which drifted down in clusters over the roofs then into the streets, where gangs of children and even some adults chased after them excitedly. I saw them swirling around my head and at first I thought it was another silly advertising stunt by La Mejoral, but then I got curious and, keeping a tight hold on my accordion case, I launched myself into the crowd and grabbed one, all damp from the drizzle:

WANTED
DEAD OR ALIVE

with row upon row of tiny photographs, the whole sheet covered with the faces of civilians and military men. I was already worried by this when in a bottom corner—good God, isn't that Jilguero? It was him, that photo of his graduation from high school he always carried in his wallet.

Without taking his eyes from Pastorita, Raul shuffles the pack of cards nervously—and there was a picture of his brother Carlos too, wasn't there? Pastorita nods, but he hadn't recognised him at first because he didn't know his features very well: someone he had spotted at once was that Indio Larios whose courage you're always going on about, Raul—it was that old photograph of him when he was a National Guard officer, the one they fish out every time there is an uprising.

Raul lowers his voice, and surreptitiously beckons them to bend their heads closer together: Larios got into the country clandestinely from Guatemala, and went round Managua as large as life in different disguises while he was plotting, dressed sometimes as a beggar, at others as an elegant lady, in satin gowns and bedecked with jewels. He had even chatted to *el hombre* once at an official function, hiding his face behind a fan, and, would you believe it, though they searched for him everywhere, he was never recognised – yes, the same Indio Larios who used to be such a friend of that colonel of yours, Chepito; both of them played a big part in getting rid of Sandino on *el hombre*'s orders, but then afterwards Larios began to feel sorry that he had spilt a fellow freemason's blood, so to atone for it, he went over to the other side. Did you know, Pastorita?—he's in league with spirits, they tried to shoot him as he was escaping, but he got clear away from them, bullets couldn't touch a fellow like that! So how on earth did they expect to capture him with these ridiculous bits of paper?

Pastorita pulls back from the circle of listeners and says doubtfully, you don't really believe those stories that he can get into prisons to plot with the political prisoners, do you? Or that his spirit haunts the Campo de Marte, or that he is able to get right next to *el hombre* despite all the bodyguards? No, that would be impossible. Why should he be frightened, if bullets can't hurt him? Raul asks, no longer whispering, but Chepito is not really interested, he wants Pastorita to go on with his story about Jilguero.

There's nothing more to tell, Pastorita hesitates, trying to pick up the thread of the story, except that all the way back I was thinking about him, that now he was really in for it, and perhaps it had been his brother's fault for getting him mixed up in those things. I kept turning the piece of paper over in my hands; the others in the truck said that the revolutionaries had been on the run through the coffee plantations since the previous day, chased through the estates at Carazo in the direction of San Marcos, at La Concha, near a place called Las Pilas. Las Pilas? Raul interrupts him. He motions them closer again, that was where they captured Jilguero's brother before they killed him, that's something I'll tell you about later on. Yes, tell us afterwards, Chepito cuts in annoyed, let's hear Pastorita first.

When the truck reached Las Esquinas we ran into a dreadful roadblock, steel-helmeted men everywhere, stopping all the traffic at gunpoint; they made us all get down and searched every last one of us. I was trying to make sure they didn't do any damage to my accordion, but I couldn't get Jilguero out of my mind—could he be hiding out in the hills there somewhere? I even imagined I saw his shadow in the coffee plantations by the side of the road.

But he was nowhere near there, Raul butts in knowingly. His brother was, but he was six feet under by then; Pastorita nods and goes on, how could he have imagined that when he reached his place in Campo Bruce the National Guard would already be in the street waiting for him, the whole block surrounded as though they were expecting a battle, when the only person they had come for was him, a poor musician. "You're to come with us," they ordered, and bundled me into a jeep with my accordion and all, and who should I see at that moment but Chepito, in his underclothes and handcuffed: we were both so scared we didn't even greet each other.

Did you get your accordion back in the end? Raul asks anxiously, but Pastorita says no, they told me to go and collect it on Monday, but if they lose it or damage it I've had it, it's not even mine, and how on earth will I pay for it? Chepito here can get his colonel to pay, Raul cuts in sarcastically. But Chepito winces as he shakes his head incredulously, it was the colonel himself who came to take me prisoner. He sits down painfully because of his aching ribs.

He had been fast asleep when he realised the light had been switched on. He was sure someone with a knife had come to kill him, as they had done with Lazaro; instead, there were soldiers with rifles standing there, and detectives with revolvers who crowded in. There were so many of them they could barely fit into my room: it was hardly big enough for anything more than my bed as it was, every night I used to be terrified that if one of the rotten planks gave way it would tip over and I'd end up in the water. It wasn't even a proper room, more of a space the colonel had got cleared of crates and rubbish so that I could sleep on the premises.

He tried to shield himself from the glare and protect his nakedness by lifting an arm across his face and turning his head to one side, away from the soldiers. Now that he was not so dazzled by the glare he could make out the colonel, his bulky form blocking the whole doorway, standing there in his fatigues with his arms folded across his chest, the red stone of his ring shining like the eye of a wild beast among the hairs of his fingers. He was giving silent orders, pretending he was not involved as the men searched the room, tipping out the drawers, strewing his clothes over the floor, rummaging among his few possessions, some huge paper flowers, his dancing shoes, his rumba costume with its concertina sleeves and sequined shirt front, the hat he wore for dancing the *jota*. "What's all this fancy dress?" guffawed a lieutenant by the name of Quesada who was leading the search, picking up the gypsy's hat in the tips of his fingers as though it was something filthy. Chepito found Jilguero's words coming back to him: "In this country there's no respect for art, Chepito." He explained that the clothes were his wardrobe for the floorshows he put on. Lieutenant Quesada looked over towards the colonel to check if he was telling the truth, and from the door came a weary nod—yes, he was a dancer, it was something that could not be helped.

The men completed their search and handed the lieutenant some photographs they had found at the bottom of one of the drawers. As he remembers, Chepito smiles to himself: they weren't much use to them, one was of my mother, who lives in Catarina and looks after the colonel's estate El Corozo, the other was of Tuzo Portugues, the boxing champion. And don't trample on the flowers, my mother made them with her own hands: but the lieutenant did not pay the slightest attention. "Do you know someone by the name of Lazaro?" he asked me, reading from a typewritten sheet.

Raul draws a card from the pack with a languid movement of his hand, mine's the highest, I'll deal; so they were looking for dead people too, just fancy that—that's exactly what Chepito had told the lieutenant, Lazaro is dead, sir, he was killed in this very nightclub, but he wouldn't believe me, the bastard, and he sits down again, wincing at the stab of pain. But the colonel confirmed it was true, there had been a guitarist called Lazaro killed in *El Copacabana* during the August celebrations, "Lazaro Cordero, claimed to be dead", the lieutenant wrote on his list. "What about Raul Guevara then? Do you know where he lives? Or is he dead as well?" Raul lifts the edge of his cards to see what he has, then drops them flat on the table again: your turn, it's you to play, Pastorita urges him.

Chepito's gesture of helplessness got him nowhere, so he spread wide his skinny arms with their bulging veins and, how should I know, he doesn't really have a home, he sleeps wherever night finds him. The lieutenant carried on scrutinising his list, marking the replies with a ball-point. "What about Jose Asuncion Pastora?" Well, he was another member of *Los Caballeros*, he did know where his house was, but it was too complicated to explain. "Don't worry, you're going to come along with us and point it out, and also where that fellow Guevara may have spent the night."

They came to fetch me at my work in Bataola, Raul says, scooping up the money he has won. I hadn't even been there a week, and when I went back today after they had let me go free the foreman comes up and tells me they don't want any subversives working in the quarry. Of course he didn't bother to pay me for the days I worked, that's justice for you, shuffling the cards then dealing them out again.

The colonel motioned the lieutenant out of the way so there would be room for him by the bed. "You know how fond I am of you, Chepito," he began, "I brought you here because you were always dreaming of the good life in Managua, all there was for you to do out in the country was to help your mother make paper flowers, right?" He looked from Chepito to the lieutenant, the other guards and detectives as if he really were introducing them to a friend. "I set him up as manager of *El Copacabana*, he dances in the show because he likes that sort of thing, and he's a first-class barman, plus his accounts are always on the level", praising me like that in front of the soldiers, although they were just itching to give me a good working-over without so much chitchat. Naked and scared stiff as I was, I had to thank the colonel for what he'd said, but then he went on with: why didn't I tell them where that fellow Jilguero was hiding, "and take care you tell me the truth and don't mess us about, this is a delicate matter, he's one of the leaders of a plot to overthrow the government".

Chepito sat up straighter on the edge of the bed, tidied his hair with a sweep of his hand as if in an invisible mirror, and began to move his jaw up and down as though chewing gum: it was ages since he'd seen Jilguero. When he said the word ages, he dragged it out to convey the vast length of time. At that, the colonel turned on his heel and had them cart me off, in my underclothes, muttering as they dragged me past him that what they were going to do to me served me right for being such a fool. Just a friendly beating, laughs Raul, and picks up the winnings a second time.

Raul here's going to clean us out, he's hit a real winning streak, Pastorita says in mock complaint; we'd better play chequers so at least I might win one game. Chepito makes to stand up to fetch the chequerboard, but Raul stops him and goes himself to get it from under the bar where it's kept alongside Lazaro's guitar.

He would have been willing to let them kill him for Jilguero's sake, and they very nearly did, Chepito says, kneading his aching chest. They forced him to drink canteen after canteen of salty water, then set to work on him with electric shocks. Have you ever had that pain in the balls when they burn them with a metal prod, Pastorita? I wouldn't wish it on anyone. And for good measure they cracked his ribs with their rifle-butts, but there was no way he was going to let on about Jilguero's visit that Sunday, when he'd been waiting for his brother so that the two of them could go off and do whatever it was they were mixed up in.

Nor was he going to tell them that Jilguero's brother Carlos had spent a whole night here with Captain Taleno, the other one involved in the conspiracy, after first of all they had been beating the hell out of each other! Now he came to think of it, he had never even managed to finish telling Jilguero that particular story. "It may be more than you're worth if they find out you've been drinking with someone who's against the government," Carlos had said to Taleno at one point; but the latter did not reply, simply downing his drink: "Don't you believe it, I've been thinking along the same lines as you about what you insulted me with the other day," he said slowly. "It's true, it's a lousy job emptying out other people's chamberpots, even if they are gold-plated." What was it all about; why the insult in the first place? Pastorita wants to know. It seems what happened was that Taleno had wanted to dance with Jilguero's sister in the International Club gala ball, and Carlos had stopped him, saying: "Our sister doesn't dance with guardsmen, especially those whose only job is to empty chamberpots."

When the two of them were alone here in the early hours that morning, Carlos listened carefully while Taleno explained that he agreed that he was little more than a flunkey, Carlos might not believe it, but he had often seen that clearly enough, and he hadn't been born just to be someone's valet. Carlos paused before raising the drink to the side of his mouth that was less bloody and swollen and replied: he might find himself emptying out chamberpots for a good while longer, because after the father's there would be the son's, and maybe after that the holy ghost's as well; here's to you. "We'll have to talk about that—here's to you," Taleno lowered his voice. "Whenever you like," Carlos replied. I heard every word, pretending I was busy with my clearing up.

In the interrogation that bastard Lieutenant Quesada got nastier and nastier when he stubbornly refused to talk. He shouted at him to stop chewing, set two of his men on him to pry his mouth open and get rid of the chewing gum. "There's nothing there, it's just the faces he pulls," they told him, wiping the spit from their fingers; so the lieutenant took his revenge by sticking the electric prod in him again: "Do you still think you can go on fooling me, you faggot bastard?" The colonel, busy questioning other prisoners, could hear him shrieking with pain at the electric shocks but made out he was deaf, as if they had never met in their lives.

In the end they had to let him go, and only then did the colonel call him into his office, asking him to excuse them, but sometimes that kind of tough questioning was necessary, there was no point in his being resentful about it, he needn't worry about his job at *El Copacabana*, he even sent him back there in a jeep. Who the hell wouldn't be resentful, Raul grunted, slapping himself across the knees. What about us two, who never even had the time to set eyes on Jilguero—didn't they take it out on us just for the hell of it? They loosened all Pastorita's teeth with one punch: and Pastorita opens his mouth wide to show his teeth, feeling them gingerly one by one; and they stripped me and threatened they would start on me next, but praise be they never got round to it.

The west-bound train to Miraflores goes by, the second class passengers staring sadly out of their windows, the peasants standing crushed together in the final freight cars; as the train skirts the lake it leaves a grey column of smoke hanging in the sky above the yellow bushes of the shore.

For a long while I sat there smoking in the darkness, stretched out on my campbed in the projectionist's cabin. Before I put my last cigarette out I groped on the floor to make sure I knew exactly where the revolver was in its holster, my fingers bumping first against my soaking boots, which I knew would be bone dry by morning, with layers of mud caked around the soles. I also felt for my flashlight under the pillow, then turned on my side to get to sleep more easily. I was drifting off when from the cinema hall where my troops were bedded down I heard laughter and the sound of benches tipping over; I got up and asked what was going on. "These men are trying to rape me," the serving boy the mayor had left us shouted. Randy bastards, I smiled to myself as I lay down again.

After that all I could hear were the snores of the soldiers and their regular breathing, but then a little later came the sound of strange bird calls from outside in the rainy darkness, answered by others further off; that's strange I thought, a chorus of dawn birds and it's not even midnight; well, strange things happen in the mountains. A little while later, there was the sound of the scraping of tiles above my head on the roof, then of some four-footed creatures—lizards perhaps? But there weren't any big enough to make such a noise. Foxes? I felt under my pillow for the flashlight, but I did not draw my hand back out, because by now it was plain it was footsteps which were descending the roof, and a trickle of dust fell on my face.

I wanted to shout an order, but my voice caught in my throat and I couldn't utter a sound; or perhaps it was because by then I had heard the first rush of footsteps into the cinema, and the shouts and screams of my soldiers as they tried desperately to grab their weapons or to escape, but in the midst of the sounds and flashes of fierce gunfire all they could do was mill around like cattle, herded into the pile of benches in the middle of the cinema by these enemy shadows which seemed to spring out of the walls themselves. In fact I could see through the half-open door of the cabin, that they were swinging down from gaping holes in the roof, then dropping behind the shelter of the rows of seats at the back of the hall to fire their guns point-blank, shouting their battle cries. Above that I soon heard the street door giving way and the venomous spitting of a machine gun. All the rifles stopped firing at the same moment as the machine gun, as though it had been directing operations, then shortly afterwards I heard the machetes being put to work, smashing through bones, splintering the benches, raising sparks from the floor.

The screams for help had died away almost completely by now, and a thick acrid smoke hit me in the face, bathed in a sticky sweat that also covered my shoulder blades and ran down the inside of my thighs, while a nervous itching paralysed my fingers, still stretched out towards the revolver. Face down on the bed, the last faint voice to reach me in the uproar of the attackers' cries was that of my cousin Mercedes: "They've killed me," he called out to me over and over, until the sound faded away completely.

I let myself slip down under the shelter of the bed, and lay flat on the planks of the cabin floor without stirring an inch. Now I could hear the snorting and neighing of horses out in the street, people shouting orders, and the jangling spurs of those who were going round taking my men's weapons, packs, and cartridge belts, stripping the bodies of their uniforms, chortling: "It's all brand new," and laughing gleefully, "What dudes those Yanks sent us." Then the footsteps moved away, and I heard galloping hooves and more shouts: "Long live General Sandino! Long live General Pedron Altamirano!" and as the band got further off, some wild singing in the distance.

It took some time for me to feel the warmth coming back into my body, the blood surging again down from my head warming my back, flowing through my limbs and bringing sensation back; and it was at that moment, before I hauled myself out from my hiding-place under the bed, that I realised it was not sweat that had soaked my pants but my own urine, which had lost its heat and become icy in an instant. I crawled over to the door like a frightened animal, and was confronted by a spectacle of darting flames which were consuming both benches and the naked bodies that writhed as they began to burn and stared at me with hideous grins; the blaze leapt up to the roof and at moments between the flames, patches of clear night sky were visible through the gaping holes. An oven-like heat was already singeing my eyelashes, and before the wall of flame completely blocked my way to the exit I snatched up my revolver and threw myself towards it, stumbling over the butchered bodies and the seats. At last I found my way out into the street, firing my gun into the air, and the villagers who had crowded round outside ran off in terror. As they edged their way back towards me, the mayor, wrapped in a blanket, with plugs of cotton-wool in his ears and smeared in Vaporub, came forward. "Put your weapon away, we're all friends here, Sergeant, sir," he implored me.

Now they stood clustered around me, but still very warily, either because they were afraid of my revolver or more likely because of the stench I gave off. Shivering, defenceless and naked, I let the dogs lick my bloodied feet until they were shooed off by the mayor, still standing next to me wrapped in his blanket, staring at me and at the flames, which he pointed to with a big Bible he was carrying: "That was the work of Pedron Altamirano, Sergeant, sir." Then he invited me to his house to clean up.

The cinema was still burning at daybreak; the smell of charred flesh spread through the whole village, and no sooner was the sun up than the vultures moved in, first of all circling high in the sky, then flocking to the trees all around, the branches of the papaturros outside the cinema bowed down with this black fraternity. "There's nothing we can do against such a blaze, everyone's been helping with bowls and pails of water, we even brought in a fire tender, but it was no use." The mayor came back to his place every so often to inform me what was happening with the fire; I couldn't bring myself to go out, but sat on the bed wrapped in the blanket he had given me, trembling with a heavy cold sweat, whilst his seven children, his wife, mother, and mother-in-law all looked on. The mother-in-law even brought her rocking chair in and rocked to and fro silently staring at me while she cradled her youngest grandchild. At lunchtime, the eldest children brought their food in and began to eat on the floor in front of me. Neighbours also dropped in and out, whispering in the doorway for a while before disappearing and being replaced by others.

At mid-day, though the fire had burnt itself out, there was still a tall column of smoke, and the cinema had been gutted. The smoke must have been visible from a long way off because a column of troops on the march had spotted it and came on in to the village. The officer in command came to the room looking for me, and stood to attention when he saw me. Although I was shivering I stood up as well and saluted him in return, noticing that he was a higher rank. He asked me my rank and number and for a report on what had happened. The mayor stepped forward clutching the Bible to his chest and removed his hat: "I expect the sergeant finds it impossible to talk after going through such an ordeal, Lieutenant, he's the only one we've got to show for the whole company." But the officer shut him up, and ordered him out of the room with all his brood, his relatives and his neighbours.

Because when we were alone I collapsed back onto the bed without asking permission, he asked if I was too badly wounded to remain standing. I shook my head sadly. "Well then, get dressed" he ordered me, but in a gentle voice: "Where are your clothes?" "They got burned," I told him. He went off to find the mayor so that he could lend me a change of clothes that would do at least until we reached the barracks at Ocotal; and eventually the mayor found me an old pair of flannel pyjamas that smelt of sickness.

He didn't even take off his campaign hat when he came back into the room. He helped me carefully to put on the pyjamas, and he was so near to me as he buttoned up the jacket that I thought I caught him sniffing at me, though he tried not to show it, because of course as soon as his column had entered the town he must have heard what had happened to me. Once I'd got the pyjamas on, I gave him my report: that I had been on my way to my first mission in the Segovias, that Lieutenant Hatfield of the U.S. Marine Corps at Ocotal headquarters had given me the task of making contact with a settlement of about fifty squatters on the El Dulce Nombre estate beyond San Fernando, breaking up their camp because they were all hostile elements, and relocating them in different scattered hamlets. My orders had also been to destroy their crops and burn all their huts; that we had made an overnight stop in San Fernando, where the mayor had put the disused cinema at our disposal to sleep in, and that was where the battle had taken place.

I would have had to be blind not to notice that he didn't swallow the story about a battle; after he had heard me out without a single interruption he sat down next to me on the bed, offered me a cigarette, and then we smoked together for a while, drawing in the smoke in a leisurely way. "I've come from Palacaguina where I've been involved in a very strange affair," he said, flicking the ash to the floor. "We had a report that the Sandinistas had got into the town secretly two months ago, and like mountain foxes, without anyone noticing they began to strip the houses of all the well-to-do people, all those who in one way or another had helped the Marines, by taking in officers or giving food to the troops and so on. They took all the tiles from their roofs without anybody hearing a thing, tile after tile the whole night through, until they had left the rafters completely bare; then they lifted out the doors and windows and threw them into a gully. And, just look at the strange coincidences in life, as soon as day broke it started to pour down with rain, and it went on all that day and the next. The people who had lost their roofs were caught in their beds by the driving rain, just as though they had been sleeping in the middle of the road. There was nowhere for them to run, as they splashed about on flooded floors, watching all their belongings, furniture, chairs, pots and pans, being carried away by the torrents that poured through the houses. Palacaguina became a circus: the other people could not care less about getting soaked and ran laughing fit to burst from one roofless house to the next so as not to miss the sight of desperate respectable ladies clinging to the top of wardrobes as their husbands struggled in vain to keep the water out, the floods sweeping branches, chickens, everything, in and out of the houses. Each time that one of them tried to stop a piece of furniture being swept out into the street by the current and fell on their backside in the water, a huge cheer would go up from the onlookers. That was why we were sent in—the Marine Command ordered me to break up the demonstrations, force the curious people back into their houses—and we had to beat them back with our rifles to do it.''

He sat there for a few moments caught up in his thoughts, with his legs crossed and an elbow resting on one knee, smoking a fresh cigarette. ''They all thought it was the funniest thing in the world. They were convinced that Sandino gets help from above: 'God is on the side of the Segovians,' they said. 'Sandino takes the tiles off, and Papa Jesus sends the rain.' '' He chuckled to himself, and either that or the smoke in his lungs brought on a cough, a dry rasp which he could only stifle by lifting his fist to his mouth. ''So you see, Sergeant, the worst thing one can do is to become a laughing-stock,'' he said, and then, suddenly serious: ''How do you expect the Marines to swallow your story? The Yankees may be a bit simple, but not to the extent that they'll believe that a patrol leader loses all his men in a battle while he himself turns up without a scratch, naked in a room; you'd be offering them a court-martial on a silver plate.''

My mouth dropped open in dismay as he began to pace up and down, talking to me not reproachfully but as though he wanted to give me advice, appearing to show real concern that the Americans were not going to believe that I had fought with valour in a deadly combat. He sat down on the bed again and said gently to me: ''Perhaps you won't credit this, Sergeant, but as soon as I got in here and saw you huddled in your blanket like that, I said to myself—there's someone who's right out of luck; and from that moment on, I have felt sorry for you. That's why I'm asking you to tell me the whole truth, to see how I can help you. Think it over,'' and as he stood up he smiled his cunning smile.

He left me then to go and supervise the burial of my soldiers. Their charred remains were to be put in a common grave in San Fernando itself: the only bodies taken out of Las Segovias were those of the US Marines, who were shipped back to the United States. New as I was to the war, I only found that out then, and I couldn't help but feel sorry for my aunt in Catarina, where I had recruited most of my men, because she would not be able to give my cousin Mercedes a decent burial, and she had seen us off so enthusiastically, convinced by my father that the Marines would be paying us our wages in gold.

As I waited in the mayor's room for us to move out, I thought about his offer of help. He was right, the Americans would not swallow the story about a battle, and maybe even my godfather President Moncada would not be able to save me from a court-martial: he would probably be too ashamed anyway for recommending me for recruitment to Colonel Cummings of the USMC. So even though in my moment of despair he was a complete stranger to me, there was nothing else for it but to trust myself to him. Make your choice, he was saying—his beckoning arms or a court-martial.

CHAPTER 3

At that moment Jilguero came back and, pretending he was completely in the dark, suggested that we have some real fun, that this chance meeting should not be wasted, that we had to look after the colonel, make sure he met some girls who would treat him well. We must help him get rid of the taste of the funeral. And by now more men have drifted in from other parts of the dark camp, their curiosity aroused by the laughter they can hear from time to time from the smouldering campfire, Turco's relaxed full-throated laugh standing out from all the rest.

"That's just what we were saying," and Turco stood up in a rather disappointed way: "but it's hopeless today—on Monday even hens don't lay."

"But what you say goes at Lasinventura's, Turco," Jilguero said impatiently. "The doors there will be open like magic if you give the word."

"That's the out-of-the-way place we mentioned," Indio reminded the colonel, his hands still pressing down on his shoulders.

"I'd like nothing better, but I have to see some new clients about insurance. And it's already getting on."

"What can you do with a guy like Turco who's so much in demand?" Jilguero complained.

"Wait a second—let's hear first of all what Catalino thinks of the idea," said Indio cautiously. "Would you go, Catalino?"

The colonel took out his inhaler and without a word put it in his nose.

"Are you still mad at me, Colonel? If it's because of me that you don't want to go—you three go, and I'll stay here, don't worry!" God, you were servile, Jilguero!

"No, don't think that, friend," the colonel said, turning his head awkwardly in the direction of Jilguero's plaintive voice; "that's all been explained"; and he concentrated on the Vicks once more.

"Why don't you phone Lasinventura anyway?" Indio suggested to Turco.

"You don't think they have a telephone in such a discreet place, do you? If you want to go, we'll have to take a taxi and drive straight there."

"What are we waiting for then? It'll soon be nightfall, and we'll still be stuck here like idiots," Jilguero implored each of them in turn.

"Is it a long way?" the colonel asked, as though he were still protesting, but behind him Indio could hardly contain his delight.

"Fifteen minutes at most by car," Turco replied, still appearing undecided.

"Fifteen minutes is nothing," Jilguero coaxed. "Are you going or not, Turco—make up your mind."

"The problem is I'd be losing money on the policies."

"Do it for Catalino," Indio said, straightfaced now. "You can't let him leave Guatemala without having tasted its delicacies."

Turco hesitated a few moments more, looked at Indio with a frown, asked what the time was.

"Okay, I'm with you," Turco finally said, with a resigned shrug, and the others congratulated him. Only the colonel was still seated, and as had become the custom Jilguero went over to help him up.

"Are you really in the mood, Catalino?" Indio asked as he made room behind the colonel's chair. "If not, we can leave it for another day—you're in charge here."

The trio stood stock-still around him, like toy figures whose clockwork had run down, and as he sat there rigid, time seemed to stretch out endlessly; then suddenly he pushed back in an effort to get to his feet, and triumphantly Jilguero pulled the chair back to give him room to stand up.

"Let's be sure that we're not there too late, boys," he said, adopting his gruff protesting tone once again as he stood up: but that last word was a token of friendship, and the three looked at one another, not knowing whether to be pleased or scared, unable as yet to believe their eyes, to believe that Indio had really done it. He was going.

The perfect master of ceremonies, Indio took the bill from Jilguero and insisted on paying himself, casually peeling off one of the ten quetzal notes we had struggled so hard to collect for the operation. It was already around five o'clock in the afternoon; as we went out into the shopping arcade, some shop-keepers were drawing down their metal shutters, and the street-vendors were busy packing up their bags and bundles.

The bells of the cathedral were ringing for Castillo Armas' memorial service. People in mourning were congregating outside the entrance, groups of officers with black armbands over their uniforms, official cars that drew slowly to a halt. Though it was still daylight, golden chandeliers shone behind the windows of the presidential palace, where as ever sentries with machine guns stood on guard, the light reflecting off the greasy, damp pavements.

But Jilguero cannot remember that much, perhaps the call of a bugle from the military academy behind the presidential palace, and yes, he remembers the chill wind that ruffled Indio's hair as he ran stooping into the street to stop a taxi and settle the fare.

We bundled the colonel into the taxi until he was wedged in with his knees pressed against the back of the front seat; Jilguero and I sat either side of him, with the springs jutting up through the tartan blanket on the seat. Indio sat in front.

The dilapidated blue and white taxi pulled off down Sixth Avenue. The two of us, separated by the colonel's bulk, did not even dare to look at each other, frightened we would give everything away with an indiscreet smile, as we left the Panamerican Hotel behind us, and the neon sign of the *Jardin de Italia* which had just come on with the others in the dusk, their vertical lettering twinkling or gloomily static: *El Cielito Papi K Listo de la Luz y Fuerza La Casas de los Abrigos N. Polanski*, the poster announcing *The Holy Shroud* at the *Lux* projecting out into the street, the lid of the glove-box tied up with a piece of wire rattling constantly, and every block we travelled meant he was that much more in our hands. We were suffocating on the gasoline fumes, but at least we had passed the police headquarters, the Parque Concordia, and the neon lights were getting fewer and fewer; we reached 20th Street, still worried because even now he might suddenly say—stop, I want to get out; but we arrived at the avenue by the cemetery with no problems, its interminable white wall still bright, though above it the cypresses were gradually losing their outlines as night fell; the shadowy forms of headstones, crosses, and the statues of angels littering Jose Esposito's stonemason yard, tiny eaveless houses with yellow skirting, blue doors and narrow gardens glimpsed through cement block walls; corn mills, butchers' shops, dimly lit bars, the rain-streaked figure of the goddess of luck on an adobe wall

10 centavos and you'll be poor no more
Chica lottery offers you the chance of your
LIFE

Then out onto the Antigua Highway, past the windows of the Roosevelt Hospital, the lights of the city further and further behind us, the air streaming in through the badly fitting windows cooler now as we rattled along, until with a loud backfiring explosion the driver slowed down for the 13 kilometre police post.

Soldiers with machine guns came out of the shelter and surrounded the taxi, shining their lights in our faces: where were we going at that time of evening with the state of siege in force: didn't we know it would soon be curfew time? The driver was too terrified to think of a reply, and turned to Indio.

"Nicaraguan military personnel," Indio snapped. "Colonel Catalino Lopez, official delegate to the president's funeral, and his escort."

"Sure we aren't squashing you, Colonel?" Turco asked him casually, but loud enough for the soldiers to hear.

"No, no, I'm very comfortable, thank you," he replied, sitting back, co-operating with us.

The soldiers lifted their hands to their helmets in salute, then stepped aside to let us through.

"Why the roadblock? Are we leaving the city or something?" the colonel asked, leaning forward to speak to Indio, as the taxi began to gather speed again down the highway.

Nobody answered. Jilguero wanted to be as attentive to his needs as Indio had been, and tried to light a cigarette for him, but the lighter only whirred uselessly.

"How come we are on a highway?" the colonel insisted. Small hills, clumps of pines, darkened hedgerows flashed by, and the mounds of a sawmill:

mahogany cedar teak
Antolin Cerezo and Sons

At last Jilguero handed him the lighted cigarette.

"We're coming into Mixco, it's just around the next bend," wheezed the driver, speaking for the first time in the whole journey. He was about to add something more, but had to concentrate on a group of people standing at the roadside around a broken-down truck. He passed them carefully.

For a moment the headlights picked out the immobile passengers clustered around the truck as it was being repaired, then they were swallowed up by the darkness once again, together with the names painted on its side:

"Did I hear that you're from Nicaragua?" the driver asked, peering into his mirror to make us out.

"Yes, thanks be to God, as the song says," Jilguero answered, crushed by the colonel's weight as the taxi rounded the bend. We passed the sandpits and finally come in to Mixco. Indio told the driver to carry on to the far end of Calle de la Amargura.

"Well, in case you've a mind to know, I buried my wife in your Nicaragua," the driver said as he pulled to a halt and took off his woollen cap. Perhaps he was expecting one of us to ask him more details, because he sat there holding on to the steering-wheel. Nobody said a word though.

By the time he had switched off the engine, even the barking of dogs that had pursued us right from our entry into the town had stopped; the only noise to be heard was a woman somewhere screaming to be let out as she banged on a door. Or was that another time, Jilguero?

"How much do we owe you?" Indio who had got out first poked his head in at the driver's window.

"You must know Masaya—we used to live down by the station; I buried her there and then made my way back as best I could to Chiquimula, trailing our little kid with me. Some of the time we walked, sometimes we rode on trucks; we slept out in the middle of nowhere, or underneath bridges, but the boy was tough, he didn't cry even when he was hungry. That'll be five quetzals."

"But we agreed on four," Indio claimed.

"Well then, have it your way. I called in all my poorest neighbours and told them: 'share out all these things, I'm not taking them with me—my hammock, my carpenter's tools, the boy's cot, everything. I'm going back to my own country and I hope never to set foot in this desolate place again,'" as he took the notes that Indio, who had put on his spectacles to be sure, was counting out one by one.

Turco had reached the house and could hear, as from a distant street, the colonel complaining to Indio about how late it was, and

Indio's reply that it was not even seven o'clock yet, and anyway why be worried about a silly thing like time when he was on the threshold of paradise, gloating as he pronounced the word. Further off still he could hear Jilguero telling the driver that he himself came from Masaya, and of course he knew the area around the railway station, and the wheezy delight in the driver's reply: fancy meeting someone from Masaya so far from home. Then at length the clatter of the taxi down the street, its headlamps creating a tunnel of light along the walls and picking out their crudely painted slogans:

Los amores de Tecun Uman, Alma Chapina, La Rondalla,
Aqui esta tu son Chabela, Noches de Xelaxu

A succession of restaurants, bars, brothels, garbage dumps and butchers; and at the very end of the Calle de la Amargura, Lasinventura's place, which had no sign outside and looked more like a school chapel or a police barracks than a brothel because of the anonymity of its grey cement front, relieved only by the decorative ironwork on the windows.

Turco used a coin to knock several times, and the sounds were like rifle shots in the silence.

"It would have been better if that taxi had waited," the colonel complained as Indio and Jilguero hauled him up onto the pavement.

"The problem is they're all rogues, they charge a fortune for waiting," Indio said, then, worried because there was no reply at the door, went up to Turco, who had begun to knock again.

"There must be somebody in," Turco said, stepping back to survey the door.

"We're not open today, everything's closed," a woman's bad-tempered voice called from the other side.

"Don't you recognise me?" Turco said, his mouth pressed to the door.

"Why, if it isn't my little Turco!" came the cry a few moments later, upon which Turco triumphantly turned round to the others.

The door opened with a rattle of bolts, and Turco gallantly stepped aside to let the others in before him. It was Lasinventura herself who greeted them, and Turco almost swept her off her feet in his embrace.

"Where have you been all this time, Turco? And you, Jilguero? You're a real sight for sore eyes—I thought you had abandoned me, you devils."

"A pleasure to see you again," said Indio, taking her hand and raising it delicately to his lips.

"Goodness, if it isn't that fine gentleman Don Indio."

She passed quickly from her delight at Indio's graceful manners to a sighing complaint about her dreadful aching bones which had kept her wide awake for nights, it had been like trying to sleep in a thorn bush, but all the while her curious gaze was fixed on the imposing figure of the colonel, who was standing silently behind us.

"Allow me to introduce you to Colonel Catalino Lopez, a fellow countryman of ours," said Indio, ushering him forward.

"Another Nicaraguan! Well, that means the whole colony is here!" she said, going up to him with an inquisitive smile.

Indio launched into a pompous oration in praise of the colonel, who responded to every compliment with a respectful bowed head, no stranger to this kind of flowery speech.

"We promised to show Catalino the best bit of nightlife in the whole of Guatemala, so here we are."

"Don't believe a word of it, Colonel: they're the ones who bring some life to the place, they're so merry." But in spite of her denials, her face puffed with pride.

"What's become of the Girl Prodigies?" Turco asked, hugging her again, then laughing and whispering, as he led her behind the bar. Once his private chat was over, he came back to join us, while Lasinventura set about getting out some glasses and crushing some ice.

"It's all arranged, gentlemen; the Schoolgirl, Fatal Fatima, and the Rosemaid just happen to be here this evening—it's our lucky day!"

"Did you say the Schoolgirl?" Indio asked admiringly. "She's the one for Catalino, Turco. No doubt about it."

And you, Turco, the soul of generosity: of course she was.

"But you mentioned only three girls," the colonel calculated.

"Don't worry," Turco encouraged him: "one of us will make the sacrifice." He went over again to Lasinventura: "and make sure that nobody else gets in—I want the place locked and bolted!"

"The house is all yours," she grinned, then disappeared to look for the girls.

"I can only stay for a while," the colonel insisted in a whisper to Indio.

"Turco was only joking, don't pay him any attention, we're not going to stay shut up in here all night, don't worry," Indio soothed him, then passed him over to Jilguero, because the party was to take place further inside the house.

Jilguero led him through the empty room, bare apart from the pockmarked bar-counter and a painting leaning against the wall; they had to stoop to pass under a red canopy stained with white bird droppings, and then they came out onto an inside patio off which branched the rooms of the house. Lasinventura's contented cackle came from somewhere deep within as, in their honour, she switched on a set of Christmas lights, most of which had already burnt out, that were hidden behind the leaves of an ivy which climbed the walls and sent out dusty feelers along the rickety wooden struts of a pergola.

"Locked and bolted," Turco's voice echoed, and from the concealed recesses came the sound of the Girl Prodigies flinging open wardrobes and drawers to get their clothes.

The boy's father leads him across the square to pay their respects to the woman whose four-poster bed Trinidad had died in, to thank her for her kindness. The huge house stands opposite the bullring, its thick walls patched with mud and sparta-grass, white beneath a layer of dust, built on a base of cemented stone blocks, and on its green-encrusted tile roof lie the sticks from the spent rockets of the fiesta. There is a beaten earth staircase up to the open gallery which runs along the front of the house, with wildflowers still growing on it despite being constantly flattened by the tread of visitors, wretched villagers in heavy sandals who lean on their relatives' arms to climb the stairs, old men with bandaged heads under their palm hats, barefoot women giving suck to rheumy-eyed children as they sit on the gallery floor.

Standing at the bottom of these stairs on the last day but one of the village celebrations, Taleno's father cannot make up his mind to climb them. He gazes in silent wonder at the horses cropping the grass in the street as they wait for their owners, at the carts left unattended by the rails, their oxen dozing in the sun. He stands aside as a man wrapped in a blanket is carried in on a stretcher, then takes hold of his hand once more, and they set off back the way they came. It is only the next day, with his hat freshly pressed and his armpits carefully washed in the municipal washroom, that they do finally go up the steep steps which seem to be ushering them into a church, climbing them with heads bowed down, like two pilgrims, hoping that at the top, outside the main entrance, they will be able at last to free themselves of their burden of blame and hunger.

Once they are in the gallery, his father hesitates on the threshold of the corner room piled with sacks of corn, sawn planks, dark demijohns, the blade of a plough, farming tools, and the smell of plantain vinegar seeping through the whitewashed walls. He makes no attempt to go any further, or to call to see if anyone is there; instead he spreads his red handkerchief on one of the benches and sits down to wait with the others, staring out over the square. Taleno stands next to him, frightened of climbing up beside him, not wanting to infringe on his silence; and they stay like that a long time, hearing from inside the house the humming sound of a grinder, the patter of the toasted corn cascading down the funnel, the voices of the tortilla-makers as they wait for their flour. By now the rest of those waiting have all gone, and it is getting dark; the screeching of the parrots in their cages in the courtyard dies away, and Taleno's father sits impassive as dust swirls in clouds around his face, swallowing it without so much as blinking.

First they hear the clink of keys coming in their direction, and when the woman's face, red from her chores, appears in the doorway, Taleno's father still does not budge, but studies her out of the corner of his eye while he contrives to look even more dejected and down-trodden, his doleful gaze fixed on the dull glow of the lights in the square which have just come on after an engine has sputtered to life somewhere in the distance, and is now beating out with a steady throb. Only at length, with a calculated slowness, as though the effort of moving his head was an act of penance, does he turn to look at her, and there she stands, wearing a white sacking apron that is tied round her waist with a rosary of thick black beads from which hangs a bunch of keys; spectacles with no stems balance on the bridge of her aquiline nose, the only exuberant note in her face the high cheek-bones, her hair parted in the middle and anointed with an unscented oil falls in bushy curls to her hips, a rustic angel fallen from grace, for though perhaps once beautiful, her body has now grown heavy as it yields to encroaching age, as though with the blessing of pregnancy. Demure but concerned, she approaches them, and in the tone of someone praying, invites them to step inside. She has to repeat the offer since his father, sly and sad, pretends not to hear, and Taleno has to go over and help him up from the seat. Do they really hear the music of a carol, a hymn, welling up somewhere? It is not Christmas, so perhaps he only imagined it, the festive notes ringing out as, with contented hearts, they enter the house, like two wandering souls at last finding shelter.

Now they are dining at her table, and she is attentive at his father's side, listening to him recount his life's adventures while he eats, as though he had set off on a journey one morning without ever dreaming he would be out so long, and was still trying to find his way home. Later, after all the lights in the square have gone off, they ask her permission to instal themselves in the courtyard, and bed down under the quelite tree, dragging in the wheel of fortune and all their other belongings. Next morning, his father hangs his mirror from the tree trunk to shave, whistling as he does so; he spreads their blankets to air over the branches, and anyone seeing them at that moment would have thought they had been made homeless by some flood or fire which forced them to sleep on the ground with the tree for a roof over their heads. On the Monday night, when all the stalls and sideshows are being dismantled ready for the move on to other fairs, his father leaves him to sleep alone under the tree and disappears into the house.

The next morning, the women who arrive early for their corn to be ground watch him emerge from the bedroom, sure of himself and with a contented air, jam his hat on his head and set about working the levers of the corn-grinder as though he had been doing it all his life, joking in whispers with the women, pinching their backsides on the sly, his cheroot stuck in his mouth the whole time, adjusting the controls and taking their money for all the world as if he were still at his wheel of fortune. And when with the sun already high the woman comes out to fetch the boy inside to give him breakfast, his father shouts at him as they go by, telling him to get a broom and set to work sweeping instead of just sitting there moping.

La Milagrosa, as she had been known since her youth when she dedicated every Friday to travelling to help the sick in memory of Christ's passion, would ride out in her ox-cart full of bandages, medicine bottles and bowls that clinked together as the cart rolled on, setting up a furious clanging in the lonely silence of the countryside. When she blew a horn into the wind of the plains to announce her arrival at the entrance to estates, the sound would bring flocking from horse and cattle trails, from corrals and milking parlours, all the sick who were carried on stools, the wounded brought to her on stretchers, those with axe-wounds or stomachs ruptured by falls from trees or threatened by something evil buried inside them, their innards bulging with reptiles, or sent off their heads by love charms. On the floorboards of the cart she would deliver babies, lance festering knife wounds, ease out splinters and thorns, soothe the highest fevers, her hand appearing out of the cart's leather canopy to give a blessing or to heal, selflessly dispensing relief or bringing comfort to those at death's door, listening patiently to those who begged her for a cure, and to long stories of chronic illnesses. The only sound in the awed silence around her came from the prayers that her patients repeated in chorus on their knees in the dust. They laid flowers at her feet, candles by the side of her blood-stained apron, or sometimes simply burst into tears, for surrounded by flowers and lights as she sat back, sturdy, in her chair under the canopy, to them she seemed a shining soul in purgatory, giving off a glow from the Mercurochrome daubed on hands she used both to heal and to take the coins proffered in payment—unless of course they paid in kind, with bunches of plantains, bags of corn, boxes of sweet biscuits, honeycombs, jars of vinegar, bundles of firewood, or even ploughshares, all of which they would load onto the cart where she also carried back the shrouded bodies of the dead.

But by the time they arrive at her house she has already abandoned this roving healing mission, and now sees people only in her room, cloudy with incense, the walls crammed with pictures of archangels disembowelling dragons, flaming sacred hearts pierced with daggers and crowned with thorns, martyred women saints with their breasts lopped off by a sword, or whose eyes stare up from pewter dishes. Later on, during afternoons when there is no grinding to be done, an occasional breeze stirring the bloodstained bandages on the floor, Taleno's father sits and watches her at work, marvelling as he learns, out of sight beyond the range of the oil lamp she uses to do her healing by. He comes mournfully to regret all the time wasted in his travels at fairs or as a pedlar when he imagines he could have made his fortune as a healer.

At other moments he goes out into the streets to admire the house, thinking that maybe there were still new things for him to discover about its construction in spite of all his previous examinations. He strides around it, goes into the courtyard, back to the corn-grinder and with the same happy disbelief sits down to eat at the dining table with its clean tablecloth where La Milagrosa serves his food piping hot. Though he chews each mouthful contentedly, he almost seems afraid to swallow, as if he were recovering from a bad illness and did not want to run any risks. And when they are installed in the four-poster bed, he spends the whole night trying to persuade her they ought to go and live in Managua, to convince her that in the city they could make their names as healers, women ailing from their husbands' wayward romances or given up for lost by their doctors would come to them for a cure—it would be like owning a gold mine if they could succeed in looking after the rich, and they would not have to work so hard.

She always pretends to be asleep, and lets dawn surprise him talking out loud to himself, but then one day luck forces her to let him have his way. A carpenter's wife dies in childbirth, and word gets round that La Milagrosa had put a spell on the poor woman to make her die. One night a mob appears, threatening to set fire to her house, and the bells of the church peal out; wrapped in their blankets they flee to seek shelter under the quelite tree, and La Milagrosa, shivering, barefoot, runs to join them. As the shouts from the street grow louder, and the light from the torches leaps above the roof, his father presses her to make up her mind once and for all to go, to sell everything and leave. That very night, sobbing disconsolately, she finally agrees.

She sells the corn-grinder and gets what she can for the house, gives up her different jobs, shuts her consulting-room, and they set off, just as another fiesta is starting in the town. For the first time they are not arriving as part of the wandering company, but are leaving, saying goodbye to that life forever. Perched high on a pile of bundles and pieces of furniture, his father is busy checking that the ropes are fastened properly, and as she locks the doors of her empty house for the last time, he grumbles at La Milagrosa: why doesn't she let him carry the bag with the money, why doesn't she trust him?

She must want to get down the steps as quickly as possible to escape from his outburst, because there is a guileless look of urgency on her saintly matron's features (the money tied securely under her arm); but in fact she descends the stairs cautiously, setting her heavy shoes carefully on each step, impeded by the weight of her belly that the buffeting wind blows out even rounder under the white tunic and which seems to bend her forward, now truly heavy with the grace of pregnancy.

The chequerboard is still there on the table, and Raul is looking on the floor under the bar-counter for bottletops to make up the number of pieces. And who do you think gave me strength in the last part of the interrogation? Chepito asks them as if it were a guessing game—Carlos' wife; she was always so serene, not even the threat of throwing her into a cell with the prostitutes frightened her, all she ever asked was permission to breastfeed her little boy who was screaming his head off at being left on a bench in the barracks corridor. When they promised her that if she told them where Jilguero was she could see her husband, all she replied was: "You've already killed him. Why desecrate his memory by talking of him like that?"

They brought her from the room where they were holding her to confront me face-to-face, but we had never even met before. I knew of her existence only because every Friday when Jilguero dropped by here, he would say without fail as he left: "I'm off to Claudia's to collect our wages." She financed the brothers' attempts at farming by selling popsicles, pastries, and cakes at the teachers' training college, and also took care of all their debts, because they had about as little luck with agriculture as they did with revolution: their beans got burnt by the sun, their tobacco plants rotted from too much rain, locusts devoured their corn. Carlos always insisted to her that it was a lottery, that every once in a while you struck lucky—didn't she remember the year of the bumper harvest, when he had managed to start building the house in the Calle Colon which afterwards never got finished. "That's why the walls always smell of wet cement," Jilguero used to tell me; but despite all their failures, they refused to give up. "The only thing we're not going to try in this life is our patience," that was Carlos' motto.

Raul finally announces that all the chequers are ready—black are the Spur tops, and white the Pepsi, and makes sure they are all in their proper places on the board. Well now that you've mentioned Carlos, Chepito, at last I can tell you how he died, tell you about the conversation I overheard once in my cell in the middle of the night when I couldn't sleep. There were two guards talking out in the yard, and what they were saying caught my attention, so I stood on the bed to reach the skylight and hear them more clearly.

He reaches for his glass, drinks slowly from it, wipes the beer froth from the corner of his lips and savours the taste: one of them was telling the other that on Sunday the fourth of April he had been sent off in pursuit of the rebels, and at about eleven in the morning his patrol was making its way back from the La Boquita and Casares area to the National Guard barracks at Las Esquinas when they heard the sound of heavy gunfire coming from over towards San Marcos. They immediately got orders to reinforce the other patrols in that area. The firing was coming from an estate known as Las Pilas, Raul explains as Pastorita crowns one of his chequers. That one's a crown, he shouts excitedly.

They arrived at the place, and the commanding officer explained how they were to spread out, then they all began to move forward towards the fighting, advancing cautiously so they would not accidentally fire at each other. Chepito studies the board and wants to warn Raul that he'll be crowned again unless he moves.

They edged forward for about half an hour, but the shooting had stopped by the time they had reached the spot. The only thing they noticed was a heavy silence; the wind rustles the paper streamers on the ceiling of *El Copacabana*; Pastorita is watching Raul intently, but Raul does not move any of his pieces. Then from somewhere out in front in the scrub they heard a voice ring out, as the commander of the combat troops ordered the others to surrender in the name of the Nicaraguan Army; and Raul cups his hands round his mouth like a megaphone, but his voice still comes out softly, and seems to trickle away between his fingers.

Pastorita goes back to the game and moves a piece forward. "There is only me here", they heard from the far side of the gully: "I will surrender, but only to an officer from the military academy, otherwise you'll have to kill me first." The officer, still crouching down under cover, shouted back: "I am a graduate lieutenant and I guarantee your life." Then Carlos told him to stand up slowly so that he could see his rank-badges. "Let's both stand up at the same time, I'm not afraid," the officer said. "If I had been afraid, I wouldn't have got into this in the first place," was Carlos' reply.

There was a snapping of twigs and we could see his head in among the dried canes as he slowly stood up; and Raul himself rises from his seat. The two men were facing each other, machine guns at the ready; Pastorita pulls the board out of the way so the pieces will not get knocked out of position. Carlos looked carefully at the officer and must have seen the bronze badge on his shirt glinting, because he threw his weapon to the ground and put his hands up. Sit down, someone might see you Chepito says, glancing anxiously at the closed door.

Then the officer ordered his troops to advance, and when they got to Carlos they handcuffed him; Raul sits down again and puts his hands out in front of him, his fists together—this is how they took him to the barracks at Las Esquinas, handcuffed and sitting on the floor of an army truck. Chepito asks him to wait a minute, he's just going to get some cigarettes, and climbs painfully to his feet: oh my ribs, I can hardly breathe. Pastorita fills his glass again with beer that is tepid by now, and looks down at the board, but they have given up playing some time ago, and he still has only the one crowned piece, lying there in his opponent's first row.

So you see, according to this soldier, Carlos was fighting all on his own when they captured him at Las Pilas; the others had all run away, trying to find ways to escape, or they had already been taken prisoner. They kept him until dawn the next day in the Las Esquinas barracks, sitting on the floor tied hand and foot, though they had taken the handcuffs off, and there were strict orders not to give him so much as a drink of water. At around three in the morning a party of high-ranking officers from the presidential palace in the capital arrived. Raul looks with a mocking smile at Chepito: do you know who was in charge? That colonel of yours, no less—our great friend. Chepito lowers his head.

They spoke quickly to the lower-ranking officers in the barracks, then called to some of the prisoners to come out; Carlos was the last of them, he was tied so tightly he had not even been able to stand, so they ordered the knots on his feet to be slackened; Pastorita absent-mindedly moves a chequer. Where were they taking them? Raul finishes off the last drop of drink in his glass: well, from the direction the trucks took at first they thought they were headed for Managua, taking the prisoners for interrogation up there—and jerks his head backwards, grim-faced, to indicate Tiscapa hill; but when they reached the entrance to the Brasil Grande estate they were told to turn down its main avenue, and Chepito nods in acknowledgement, he can remember where the estate is along the southern highway because he picked coffee there with his mother as a boy.

In an open patch in the middle of the coffee plantation they picked out Carlos from the other prisoners in the jeep, made him get down, and untied his ropes. The soldier who told the story was the one who undid them, and so he saw him close up for the first time: scratched with thorns, covered in insect bites, barefoot, with only a scrap of his battle fatigues left across his back. He was given a spade and ordered to dig a deep hole, and when it was the depth of a man—Raul raises his hands, measuring—a man standing up, they told him to climb out. It was still night, he reminds them, but none of them has forgotten that, and the headlights from the jeeps dazzled the prisoner standing at the edge of the pit.

The colonel stepped forward from the group of officers who

were talking outside the ring of lights. "Listen, we want you to be honest with us, we would like to help you. Tell us all you know about the plot: you were one of the leaders, so go ahead and tell us everything"; and Raul encourages the invisible prisoner to speak. Carlos said he was a prisoner of war and therefore was obliged only to give them his name, his age—twenty-nine—and his profession—a farmer; married, with one child. The colonel swished his foot impatiently through a clump of dried grass, and the group listening feel Raul imitating the action across the planks of the floor. "There's been no war here, this was just a crackpot escapade a handful of you dreamt up. Tell us what you were supposed to do."

At that a calm smile appeared on Carlos' face. "All right, I'll satisfy your curiosity, I'll tell you what I was to do. Yesterday April fourth 1954 at 2.30pm I was to proceed at the head of two hundred men up Tiscapa hill and take the presidential garrison in a lightning raid. Sunday was chosen because it's visiting day in the barracks, and so the guard is relaxed, and that particular time was chosen because the off-duty soldiers are all asleep in their huts after lunch"; and Chepito nervously grasps Raul's arm—You see? That's why Jilguero was here waiting for his brother that day. Then he slumps right back in his seat.

Raul waits for Chepito to let go of his arm, then continues. Carlos also told the colonel that those of his men with machine guns were to have been issued with a dozen magazines and four grenades each; the others were to have long-range light arms: Raul shuts his eyes, pauses, then corrects himself: some of them were to have assault machine guns, the rest automatic rifles. The colonel exchanged satisfied glances with his colleagues. "And what part of your plan went wrong?"

Carlos took a deep gulp, finding it hard to take in air despite the breeze that swept down from a valley running through the plantation, rustling the leaves. "The opposition politicians had promised me two hundred young, fit, well-trained men. What they sent me were forty old peasants, and a few young boys straight from their farms. I told them all to go home;" and Raul dismisses the peasants with a wave of his hand, let them go back to their homes with their wives and children, there's no point them dying senselessly.

Until then, the colonel had been gentle in his questioning, talking to the prisoner with the air of a priest; but suddenly his tone changed, and he raised his voice unnecessarily loud, since the only sounds to be heard were the crickets and the leaves quivering in the sudden gusts of wind: he wanted Carlos' list of contacts; "Tell me the names of the officers who were going to help from inside the palace barracks." Carlos smiled to himself again, but his lips moved so quickly that no-one would have seen him but for the glare of the headlights. The colonel pointed to the pit; and Raul points to a pit over by the dance floor, beneath the orchestra platform with its green music stands, and then to the jeep: if Carlos wanted, he would take him safe and sound to Managua—the jeep parked out beyond the gangway, somewhere in the sand of the lakeshore. Blinded by the headlights, Carlos took some time to make out the colonel's gestures, who pointed and offered him the choice: "Which do you prefer?" His only reply was to go on smiling, and now the broad grin on his battered face was clear for everyone to see.

The colonel wanted to give the impression he was sincere, a man of his word. "Although you won't believe me, I'll vouch personally for your life if you give me the names of your contacts. Tell me straight out that the chief link with the palace was Captain Santiago Taleno, and you can save your life." But Carlos merely kept on smiling, as though he found such insistence amusing. Why did the colonel insist though? Pastorita asks, shifting nervously in his chair. Couldn't he see he wouldn't get another word out of him? Chepito nods. Not another word.

"Why are you laughing?" the colonel asked, getting annoyed; and Raul sweeps all the pieces from the chequerboard. "Because I'm no coward, I'm ready to die," and Carlos walked a few steps towards the hole, still facing the lights; the pit is the table now, and Carlos a token pushed to the edge of the old, tattered board where the black and white squares have almost completely faded away. The other prisoners did not move or say a word. The colonel ordered one of the conscripts to step forward out of the darkness, and the soldier lifted his sub-machine gun to shoot.

"Fire!" came the command in the darkness; Raul knocks a beer bottle over and warm drops spill onto the board. It's nothing, Chepito says, not bothering to stir from his seat, I'll clean it up later. "Long live free Nicaragua!" Carlos shouted, in the midst of the same silence that had accompanied the order. The hammer of the machine gun clicked as it fell, but the weapon jammed, would not fire; the soldier cocked the trigger a second time, but again nothing happened. A sergeant was called out and the gun handed to him.

"Fire!" the colonel ordered again.

"Long live free Nicaragua!" Carlos repeated.

The words echoed from the hills; and the three of them seated at the table can hear more sharply the sound of the waves lapping on the lonely lakeshore. This time a burst of gunfire did thunder out; after the shots everything in *El Copacabana* is quiet. Carlos fell on to the pile of earth at the edge of the hole, and seemed to be making an effort to stand up. It took several shots at close range finally to still the body.

It was day by the time the convoy reached Managua, because at other points on the way they stopped and branched off into other coffee plantations to execute more prisoners. When they were all back in the presidential barracks, one of the sergeants who had gone over to Carlos to finish him off kept repeating as he undressed and lay down on his bed: "Balls like that on him," and Raul cups his hands to show them.

Where on earth do you think Jilguero is at this moment? Chepito wonders; Raul goes to the window and they hear him say that he would follow Jilguero anywhere. The grey waters of the lake continue lapping quietly.

They are trying to cross a river but find it impassable; Turco puts his ear to the ground and motions them to stand still while he listens to the distant roar in the jungle from the torrent that will soon come down the river, sweeping uprooted trees and drowned animals along in its tumultuous rush, so they help each other up to a ledge above the bank out of the way of the flood. Once they are safely up Jilguero sits down in the mud, and manages after a struggle to heave the stiff boots from his swollen feet, which stink as if they belonged to a week-old corpse. The skin of his ankles has a soapy bluish hue, as though a poisonous water were flowing through his legs; legs that had been too short once to reach the stirrups of his mount which, not being spurred to flight, was placidly grazing the grass free of its bit, and the horseman in his three-cornered hat and frock-coat sat firm in the saddle grasping the pommel, the horse's tail whisking his chaps as unworried he stroked the dry silkiness of the horse's mane, unworried because the posse of pursuers cannot break out of its immobility as it descends the far-off slope, dispersed in the cloud of dust against the glass door of the medicine cabinet, while outside the locked dispensary the street was still swept by the storms of the elections, and there was an endless stream of supporters to the old man's house, its whitewashed walls still pitted with bullet-holes from the civil war where spiders now strung their webs, and the painting of a doctor's wand of Mercury standing out over the door of the corner room, supported by a carved pillar, the door always open even when his grandfather was away on one of his trips and there was nobody to wait for him in the row of wicker chairs that alternated along the wall with china spittoons.

Inside the house, an open verandah gives on to an enclosed courtyard where doves pecked at grains of rice on the brick tiles and an aged, sluggish peacock with tarnished plumes sauntered up and down, and whenever it had to drink flapped awkwardly the short distance up to the rim of a fountain under the branches of an almond tree; constantly falling red and yellow leaves floated to the sides of the slimy pool, which the women helpers used to water the garden with its straggly plants, beds of heliotropes, star jasmine, begonias and jalacates, their stems bare and dry, a rose bush turned briar thrusting up like a barbed wire fence, and on the hard earth around the plants, white patches with dried-up bubbles which were the traces of where the old man rinsed his mouth after cleaning his teeth. With a toothbrush in one hand and a tin mug in the other, he would spit the water out onto the ground as, his body shaken by violent but mute gestures, he rehearsed his speeches to a wall overgrown with ivy.

During the months of the campaign this oratory, practised for so long in the confines of his courtyard, spilt out into public squares all over the country. The old man would embellish his phrases with a self-accusatory beating of his chest that brought on fits of senile coughing and left the crowds waiting in respectful silence under the burning sun while he was doubled up with spasms on the platform. Eventually he would resume his harangue, his voice hoarse and wheezing as he strove to air all the accusations from his prison days against the thieves in public office, speaking without removing his panama hat, his linen jacket folded over his arm, and his shirt sleeves rolled up as if he were attending a patient. He would turn out his pockets and repeat as he had done so often in the past his litany against corruption—this was how he would walk down Tiscapa hill when his period in office was over, with his pockets turned out for everyone to see that not a single nickel had got stuck in the lining.

He remembers how early every Sunday morning he would hear the hubbub of the old man's supporters as they came to fetch him to catch an express train and then ride out to villages where noisy throngs eagerly awaited his arrival. Fragile and tremulous he would be swept from his railway carriage and escorted jubilantly along streets lined with coconut palms and plantain fronds: the village squares bustling with festivities as during their saints-days, with sideshows and roulette wheels and gambling games, rowdy bands striking up bullfight parade tunes or military marches amid the wild explosion of firecrackers all around the old man as he advanced, with everybody trying at least to touch his coat sleeve; greeted by clattering horsemen in villages the railway did not reach and led in a cavalcade, mounted on a docile mare which someone would lead by the bridle so that he could wave without worrying about the reins, dragged into bars improvised in the street where toasts were drunk in his honour, to platforms erected on the front steps of village churches, or clambering up onto tailors' tables set up in the diamond of baseball fields, or in the circle of a crowded cockfighting pit to deliver his speeches from the fine dirt floor crawling with fleas. He remembers too his slow and measured exhausted voice speaking to the country on the radio between interruptions of romantic music straying in from other stations on the dial, or disappearing altogether in a crackle of static, interminable civic speeches on the night air that invariably put his listeners to sleep, though no-one dared, out of respect for the old man, to switch off their sets.

Also during those campaign months he heard night after night stones being thrown at the consulting-room, a hail of pebbles bouncing off the roof, cracking tiles; bags of excrement bursting against the walls, hens and other dead animals tossed over into the courtyard. The posters showing his grandfather's blown-up youthful photograph were smeared with tar, his supporters' cheers were silenced with rifle butts, there were riots in the street with people arrested and wounded, rumours that a gang from the San Miguel market in Managua was on its way to set fire to his house, and all this time his father remained locked behind the silent door, oblivious to the tumult in the streets.

Following the Sunday in February when the voting took place, he and his brother again stood on tiptoe at the door to peer through the iron lattice-work and watch the growing crowd of indignant people who from early in the morning had filled the street with their shouts of Fraud! Fraud! Fraud! The first trains from Managua on the Monday morning brought with them rumours that *el hombre* had forbidden the electoral officers to start counting the voting papers and had ordered that the ballot boxes be locked in the cellars of the National Palace.

The old man appeared at the corner door of his house to a swirling mass of flags and supporters. They suddenly hoisted him onto a chair, from where he spoke to the crowd beneath their waving banners. He raised his mangey hands clutching fistfuls of telegrams pulled from his pockets, and tried over and over again to convince the worried faces that there had been a landslide victory for the civic forces in every constituency throughout the republic, as all the telegram messages confirmed—sent to him by the opposition scrutineers at the voting tables, sworn witnesses to the elections. He carefully put on his spectacles and read over and over, with failing energy, the tally of votes.

As incredulous shouts went up, he put the telegrams away and leaned back in his chair to pull a copy of the Political Constitution of Nicaragua from his breast pocket with a triumphant magician's gesture. He held the little leather-bound book up to the gaze of the suddenly silent crowd, and straining his voice, declared that this was their country's magna carta, that in its commandments lay their guarantees: the constitution was the sovereign power which would defend the people's electoral victory against any machinations by those who sought to continue the present corrupt regime; and his last words, his final gesture, holding the book aloft as at the moment of consecration in a rural mass, led the crowds, though still suspicious, to begin to drift away towards their homes. For some time after though, small knots of people lingered on, and then larger groups began to form once more, and started to chorus for him to come out again, so he would re-appear in the chair under the sun-bleached banners and repeat his explanations, the constitution yet again in his hand. Then one last time he came out to beg them to return home peacefully, because he had heard from the supreme electoral council that the recount of votes could not start until the demonstrations that were taking place in every town and threatened to turn violent, were dispersed; he himself was about to leave for the capital at the head of a citizens' committee so that he could be present when the ballot boxes were opened.

They cheered him on his way when he got down from the chair to walk to the railway station; and although the crowd broke up obediently, some groups followed him at a respectful distance first to the station and then to the telegraph office, after the station master had informed them that all trains to Managua had been cancelled for that day and for the rest of the week; but the telegraph operator could not get through to Managua because torrential rain had brought down the wires. "What rain?" the old man's followers, crowding noisily into the office, wanted to know: "it never rains in February." The operator shrugged—if *el hombre* gave the order, it rained.

Days later, the government newspapers arrived from the capital to put an end to any uncertainty; the banner headlines proclaimed an overwhelming victory for *el hombre* in free and fair elections supervised by observers from the Panamerican Union, and carried photographs of the re-elected president having his hand shaken in congratulation by the visiting American envoy. Then the military ordered the closure of all the cinemas and billiard halls, and threatened to jail anyone found on the streets. Squads of soldiers sealed off the streets leading to the old man's house, and when at dusk he tried to climb onto his chair at the house-corner to declare to the deserted road that it was true that he had been robbed of the elections and that the constitution had been flouted, the soldiers forced him back inside, and told him that he was under house arrest until further notice, so that now he was shut in his room just as his son was locked in his dispensary on the other side of the street.

It was the old man who first broke what seemed to be a fresh challenge between the father, defeated by electoral fraud, and the son, gnawed by cancer. One morning a few weeks later he stepped out into the street displaying a taffeta presidential sash over the bony cage of his sunken chest, while in front of him marched a barefoot boy beating ceremoniously on a drum. He strode down the centre of the town streets until his tiny procession reached the market, a large building fortified with thick walls like a cathedral or a castle. Then he paraded through the passageways of the market, followed by a trickle of people who left their stalls and work, the drum in front of him clearing a path through the maze of fruit and vegetable baskets, heaps of sweets, corn-sack rags. When he came to a halt on a carpet of plantain leaves soaked from the drains that crisscrossed the market, he began his acceptance speech as President of the Republic. He read with a sparing solemnity, veiled behind the haze of dust from corn husks which rose like incense or gunpowder among the blackened pillars, enveloped in a confusion of smells from dried herbs, rancid cheeses, reheated slices of bacon fat, clutching in his trembling fingers the faded yellowing sheets of paper with their purple writing that he had kept ever since he had first stood as a candidate in the days of his youth.

The speech over, he withdrew, bestowing a ceremonious wave left and right to the unmoved onlookers. As he strode off majestically to the sound of the drum, the market women pressed round him as if to hold him back, wanting to protect his nakedness, to throw some scrap of cloth or blanket over him, but he ignored them serenely and moved on, making his way along the muddy, foul-smelling alleyways to repeat his words in other corners of the market. On the days that followed he would make his appearance at noon and be the last to leave the market as the attendants were locking the gates, walking back to his house pursued by gangs of children who crowded round happily at the sound of the drum. As the ceremony was repeated day after day, this beating took on a funereal note, so that everyone would shut their doors in compassion as the old man passed in his lonely procession, barely raising his hat now to salute around him, no-one wishing to offend the nobility of his misfortune, or so they said as they reverently drew the bolts, not opening up again until they heard the drum in the distance.

Only after their mother had begged him for days, scraping at the door of the dispensary, did his father finally agree to abandon his sanctuary to go and fetch the old man. When he opened the door, a filthy, emaciated figure stood before them, the striped drill suit he had worn all those months before on his return from Managua completely unrecognisable. Shielding his eyes from the mid-day glare, he walked barefoot to the market, where he found the old man surrounded by leather straps and cords, strands of garlic and onions, piles of jute sacks and bales of tabacco, delivering his speech yet again, though by now there was no audience, and the boy with the drum lay asleep under the table. He let him finish and then went up to lead him away; but the old man, showing no surprise at all at seeing his son there, motioned him back, and declared in a final impromptu message that since the investiture was now complete he would withdraw to govern peaceably in his own house, as befitted the head of a true civic state, without military fanfare or the adulation of court followers. At that he did allow himself to be led docilely back home, the two of them walking silently through the brilliant glare of the streets.

Now, with his bare, swollen feet resting in the mud, Jilguero can hear the rushing of the approaching torrent, and recalls how ever since that day, his grandfather would pace up and down in his house, can see him hunched over, his arms gesticulating or clasped behind his back as he talks to the shadows, a puzzled look on his face, the presidential sash smeared with swallow droppings still draped across his chest.

CHAPTER 4

"Here come the Girl Prodigies," laughed Turco, who clapped his hands and stood up to welcome them. When he heard this, the colonel broke off his talk with Indio and also tried to stand up, craning his neck to make out the three women who were fighting one another noisily to get through the door into the hall of mirrors, as the back room was still known. Turco brought them over one at a time and presented them to Catalino; they greeted him politely, stretching out the tips of their fingers, according to the instructions Lasinventura had given them. The last to come up to him was the Schoolgirl, her white poplin uniform stained with yellow patches, the blue of her sailor collar washed out. She curtsied so low that her knee brushed the floor.

"This is the Schoolgirl we've told you so much about, Colonel," Turco said, propelling her into his arms; he fell backwards into the chair with her on top of him, pretending to gasp for breath in her embrace, his cheeks already black with her eye-liner.

"Catalino, all this is in your honour!" Indio shouted , as if at a bullfight, then pushed the other two girls on top of him as well. They sat astride him, stroked his shaven head, jostled him playfully and tried to catch hold of his penis under the folds of his belly, kissed him and covered him in saliva. Sprawling back, he made half-hearted attempts to push them off, but then drew them back to him, taking advantage of the confusion of bodies to grab handfuls of whatever he could.

At Turco's signals, the girls calmed down, and left the colonel to the Schoolgirl, who settled on his lap, and made sure he drank his glass of rum to the very end. He flailed his arms about as though drowning, while the drink dribbled from his chin onto his hairless chest and down to his stomach. He might have been waving his arms, but he couldn't hide how much he was enjoying it, surrounded by Prodigies and with one dressed up as a schoolgirl right there on his knee.

Lasinventura looked in one last time to see if they needed anything more; she was leaving her young ladies to make sure the men's needs were attended to; she thought she had better go off to bed to see if she felt any better in the morning; everyone chimed in with their thanks for her kind attention, and she went off satisfied. Soon a guitar appeared out of nowhere and on Indio's prompting Jilguero began to tune it. Glass in hand, Indio walked up and down trying to remember songs to sing, asking the colonel what he would like to hear; Catalino, his head buried so deep in the Schoolgirl's hair he could hardly breathe, said yes to whatever Indio suggested.

Jilguero struck up a tune on the guitar and the singing began. Indio finally persuaded the colonel to join in, and though he mixed up the words, he did help with the choruses. The girls brought food and more ice, lemons and soft drinks from the kitchen, really looking after them while they were still sober; one by one the bottles fell dead to the floor.

At some point Indio leapt up onto the table and started to dance a jig, whirling his handkerchief above his head, his stamping heels scattering glasses and bottles alike. The colonel guffawed at his cavorting, and began to beat out the time on the Schoolgirl's knees; at that moment, just to cause mischief, Jilguero abruptly changed the rhythm, and began to play a slow romantic bolero, stopping Indio in his tracks. He tried to steady up, then jumped down first to a chair and then to the floor, without daring to look at the others for fear they would laugh at him; angrily, he wiped the sweat from his forehead.

After he had forced Indio down from the table, Jilguero went on playing sad ballads, songs that were so old no-one could remember the words, romantic serenades that Fatal Fatima and the little Rosemaid danced along to barefoot with their eyes shut, pressing themselves tightly against the bodies of invisible partners. The conversation meandered to an end, everything got stranger the more they drank; the men just lolled there like idiots watching them dance.

"Back to our Nicaraguan jigs," Jilguero shouted, and the din started all over again, the bottle going round from hand to hand, and more dead men on the floor, except that Turco and Jilguero were now beginning to fill their glasses with Pepsi Cola, because they knew that if they got drunk they were done for.

"This is the life, eh, Catalino?" Indio said, leaning over him, swirling the ice around in his glass: "but you're not drinking, what's the matter?"

"Of course I'm drinking, ask her if you don't believe me," he replied, raising his head from between the Schoolgirl's arms.

"Let's drink together then," Indio suggested. Both lifted their glasses and downed them slowly, without pausing for breath.

"There you are, Indio, shoulder to shoulder like in the good old days," the colonel spluttered, pushing his empty glass back onto the table. Indio opened his arms wide and leaned over to embrace him; for a while they stayed hugging each other, cheek to cheek.

"The two of us, like in the old days."

"You were a fool," the colonel's hot breath wafted into Indio's face.

"What makes you say that, Catalino?" Indio pulled back to look at him quizzically.

"If you hadn't done what you did, you'd be loaded by now," and the colonel, an edge of pity in his voice, cupped his hands while weighing imaginary bags of gold.

"What became of Calzones, Colonel?" Turco asked as they straightened up; the colonel started in surprise.

"Who do you mean, Calzones?"

"Your adjutant, Lieutenant Quesada."

"Lieutenant Quesada is in the Canal Zone, in Panama, on a counter-insurgency course," he replied, serious all of a sudden.

"Well, what a coincidence. At the military academy we always used to call him Calzones, because all he ever talked about was the Canal Zone—that's why we baptised him 'Calzones'. His great ambition was to go there to study war with the Yankees—so now he's made it."

"Three times I've tried to commit suicide, if anyone's interested," the Schoolgirl sobbed gently, still perched on the colonel's fat thighs.

"Why kill yourself if you're happy with life?" Fatal Fatima tipped her glass over in her haste to attract attention, the honeyed brightness of her cat's eyes marred by the mark of a blow she had received on her right cheek bone.

"Don't pay any mind to the Schoolgirl and her suicide stories, I've heard them all before," Jilguero laughed, stopping playing the guitar. She struggled out of the colonel's grasp, and slipped down until she was slumped at his feet. She rubbed her eyes, and the eye shadow, loosened by her tears, started to trickle through her fingers. At a loss, the colonel tried to haul her back up, looking to Indio for help; but when Indio went over to beg her to stand up, she looked at him choking back her tears, and asked him whether they wanted to listen to her or not.

"Cry—why should I cry?—when I left a Panamanian millionaire stranded on our wedding day?" Fatal Fatima cackled.

"Let the Schoolgirl speak, or we'll never get her up off the floor," Indio said, helplessly.

"I spurned him at the altar, yet still he comes in his private plane each and every Saturday and begs me on his knees to go to Colon with him, where he owns a big perfume factory. 'Fatima, never shall I forget your kisses'—that's what he says. Is that a reason for doing away with myself? I'd rather laugh at life."

"Fatima, the Schoolgirl wants to tell her story," Turco said to shut her up, but she was so lost in her own thoughts she didn't even hear him.

Very stiff and correct, the Schoolgirl allowed Indio to sit her down in a chair set apart, then bent over, chewing the hem of her uniform. All at once she stretched her hand out into the dimly lit room.

"As if it was today I can see myself washing clothes at the sink in the courtyard of our house in Zacapa, dazed by the sun's glare"; her hands fluttered around her face to protect herself from its rays, or to drive away the shadows. Jilguero knocked the guitar as he reached for something on the table, and the strings reverberated. Indio sternly motioned him to be quiet.

"Standing on a block of stone because I am too small to reach the sink; under my feet the water runs out warm and tinged with blue, the dogs drink from the puddles and find it has no taste."

Indio tiptoed over to serve another drink to the colonel, who was all on his own now that the Schoolgirl had gone into her trance.

"Look at my raw red hands—from inside the cane shack that's our kitchen, my mother can only shout at me for being useless and ungrateful—can you hear her fury? She says I can never do anything properly, and attacks me for taking the washing off the line before it's dry, just so that I can go and play, and that's why it goes mouldy. Without her noticing, I take my little rag doll from a hole in the wall behind the stones, and begin to play with it, safely out of her sight."

"If I ever escape from this life, I'm going back to Cartago with my parents—you should see the tearful letters they send me, forgiving me for my mistakes," Fatal Fatima turned to Turco, who took her in his arms to keep her quiet.

"Now it is another morning, the Wednesday before Easter. I have lost all love of life, it is only an obstacle to me. My mind is made up; I go up to my mother and say to her: 'Mama, it would be better for me to kill myself.' Look—she takes the blunt knife she has been chopping onions with and gives it to me, opening my hand as though she's offering me a sweet, or something nice as a present, and then goes on with her work, shouting at me that it's a good idea, I ought to go ahead and kill myself, that would make one less mouth to feed. All I can do, standing there with the knife in my hand, is to burst out crying. I cover my face with my blouse, and I cry. I am eight years old."

The colonel gave a nervous laugh and, thinking she had finished, reached out to pull her onto his knees again. She opened her eyes and pushed him away.

"In their letters they offer me a fine house with servants, a cruise round the world in a liner, they say they will find a place for my daughter in the Sion College in San Jose—what more could I ask? They're things to make me glad, not sad, aren't they, Turco?" and Turco soothed her, of course they were, then pulled her close to him once more.

"From that day on I have had this wish to cut my wrists, but I haven't had the courage to do it," and she gripped her wrists, astonished at herself. Beating her knees with her fists, she plunged her head down between her open legs, overcome with laughter.

"Crazy woman," the colonel said, relieved as she climbed back onto him.

"Colonel, did you know my grandfather on my mother's side, Don Chico Garcia de Nandaime?"

He was as taken aback as when asked about Calzones, and hesitated before he answered Jilguero.

"By sight only," he said, flapping his hand as if to ward off the question.

"But why should I accept their offers—I prefer my freedom to a golden cage; and anyway, I have my jewels to console me. I have put the smallest pieces in pawn, and I never bring the most brilliant ones out into the light for fear of them being stolen."

"What a pity you never really got to know my grandfather, he was a great one for living it up—but your father knew him well, didn't he? My grandfather bought that farm of his, El Corozo, from him—to give you some idea of how much he liked a good time, as soon as he got back from the cockfighting on Sundays he would shut himself in his room and, drunk as a lord, would send for all the musicians from the procession band to come and play for him—carols, pasodobles, even funeral marches. What he loved most of all were Jose de la Cruz Mena's waltzes."

"Ah, Mena the divine leper," Indio cried out passionately; "if he hadn't had leprosy, he would have been famous the world over as a composer. He was a musical genius, the Ruben Dario of music!"

"Who gives a damn about waltzes these days, waltzes are old-fashioned," Turco mocked him, without letting his attention slip from Fatal Fatima.

The first house they had in Managua stands exposed to the sun in an island of bushes, on the far side of a rainwater stream that is also a garbage dump. A sad neighbourhood with empty plots of dry vegetation, weeds pushing through fences, adobe houses with high pavements, bar signs, the sounds of quarrels; old tyres and broken pieces of glass hot in the dust of the street, at the end of which there is a glimpse of a grey curve of water beyond a gap in the shrubs along the shore. Women go by with bundles of washing on their head, men drive horse-drawn water tenders, or pull squeaking handcarts, kites fly in the afternoon sky.

Cars nose their way stealthily to the edge of the stream, let out discreet hurrying ladies in high heels carrying big patent leather handbags. They cross the plank over the stream, leaving as they pass a trace of expensive perfume, that soon fades in the pervading smell of dried excrement. Taleno's father welcomes them at the door with a knowing bow, gallantly sweeping off his trilby as if it were a courtier's plumed hat. Once inside he sits them down by the blue curtain decorated with an aluminium foil crescent moon and stars, beyond which is the room where La Milagrosa foretells the future and prescribes the potions that he hands over to the women as he collects the payment for their visit. The idea of curing people by fortune-telling is his, and so that the seances will seem more realistic, he teaches La Milagrosa to talk to her clients in a voice from beyond the grave. She submits to the rehearsals unprotesting, asks him exactly how the dead speak: his father rolls up his eyes until only the whites are showing, and draws out his words until they echo lugubriously: "like this, like you were speaking from six feet under."

She cannot keep up the imitation however, perhaps because with her swelling belly she has lost the inclination to indulge in these magic trances, and now she reponds to questions only half-heartedly, and can be heard having attacks of vomiting in the middle of the sessions. When the clients depart (they are getting fewer and fewer anyway thanks to scenes like these), she timidly points out to Taleno's father, who is furious at her for not trying, that it is no easy matter to be pregnant at her age, that perhaps her innards have lost all their suppleness, like old leather. It was probably when his sister Alma Nubia was born that the magic cures stopped altogether. He remembers a wooden cot and one morning hearing a child bawling; or it may have been that La Milagrosa had a miscarriage before that, because his father is burning some blood-stained sheets in the courtyard and tells him to keep away.

Once her daughter is born, La Milagrosa cannot take her eyes off the cot; when his father tries to push her into starting the seances again, she pretends not to hear, walking to and fro cradling her child with a pained look, that of a fallen saint, her thick hair slovenly now, and the apron of her tunic hanging in tatters to the floor. Only later does he realise, seeing it hanging from the line, that it is made from flour sacks, because against the light he can see "Gold Medal" printed in the wet garment.

Since she is unwilling to continue, and he is tired of begging her to let him have the money to start up a business, his father begins to search every nook and cranny in the bedroom. He peers behind the religious paintings, lifts the saints' statues to look under their pedestals, is determined to find where she has hidden her money, even feeling between her breasts for it while she sleeps. And his desperate searches culminate in his crawling under the four-poster bed, brought along with the saints from Chontal, complaining on all fours from the floor, perhaps to disguise his feeling of shame, that the only thing she had contributed to the healing seances had been the scrap of curtain, and that even then he had had to move heaven and earth to get her to buy the two rolls of blue cloth; she had not so much as given a penny for the advertising, nor for the set of red lights. Hearing him scratching around under the bed, she took the opportunity to launch into a loud defence of herself, speaking as if he were not in the room at all, as if she were justifying her caution to complete strangers. Who could guarantee that she would not be abandoned with her poor daughter in Managua, robbed of the few wretched pennies she had?

At that, Taleno's father pokes his cobweb-covered head out from under the bed, stands up, brushes his knees, and strides out of the room, angrily pushing the veil of mystery aside, and puts on his hat as if to leave the house. Instead he starts to pace up and down, bumping into the furniture and complaining that if it had been up to him, he would have gladly sat behind the curtain and told people's fortunes, but women like that wouldn't dream of being cured by a man, they had faith only in women healers.

At the end of one of his indignant sweeps through the house, he announces that he is going out to the east of the city to see if at least he can't find some patients to give injections to; and now he does go out into the street, clutching his medical bag full of medicines and a syringe. Three days later he has still not returned, and La Milagrosa looks at the boy sitting silently in a corner and thinks to herself that his father is not likely to run off and leave him, so begins to wonder whether he has been arrested.

So La Milagrosa, with the girl in her arms and Taleno clinging to her dress, goes out to look for the army officer who rents them their house—Catalino Lopez, the owner of theirs and all the other houses, shacks, snooker clubs and bars in the neighbourhood. They wait a whole morning for him sitting on a step outside the hut in the Campo de Marte which is his office. They finally get in to see him and he listens, an electric fan blowing over his gleaming face the whole time. He telephones an order for the prisoner arrested for practising medicine illegally to be brought to his office. They sit there waiting across the desk from him, while he ignores them and continues with his paperwork, until some soldiers push the handcuffed prisoner in at the door.

After a talk lasting until nightfall, the officer lets his father go—it is six in the afternoon by the time they leave the barracks, they are lowering the flag to the sound of a bugle. Back at home, he has been so crushed by his stay in prison that La Milagrosa is defeated by his victim's face; she realizes that the only way to cleanse him of his sense of guilt is to hand him over the money he needs to be able to return to the officer, Catalino Lopez, and put to him his ideas for a business, because this is what Catalino had tempted him with in their talk.

That is how he came to set up his stall in the San Miguel market. Thanks to the officer he had no problem getting his licence. At first he sells a few things retail, but in a short while with good luck and above all due to the protection he receives, he is able to build up a wide range of goods. From that moment on he works without stopping, even on Sundays—he has lunch at the counter and supervises the people coming in and out with a nervous jerk of his head. He keeps tally of the goods sold with a scarcely perceptible movement of his tongue, tyrannises the porters and errand-boys, argues with truck drivers about their charges, will not let them get away with a single mistake in their change. The following year he can afford to greet his clientele with his very own calendar:

JOSE ASUNCION (CHON) TALENO
WHOLESALE AND RETAIL GOODS
White and yellow corn—the finest sorghum and
wheat—Rexoro and cracked rice—Momotombo and

Estrella matches—El Porvenir denim—candles and candlesticks—leather for soles and uppers—heels for men and women—hobnailed boots—ropes by the gross—genuine pig's fat—Chontales cheeses—machetes and knives—nails and rivets.
Eastern side of the San Miguel Market
Opposite 'Tropical' Pharmacy
WISHES YOU A VERY MERRY CHRISTMAS 1939
AND A PROSPEROUS NEW YEAR 1940

By now his father has put on weight, keeps two or three hats on the top of the wardrobe, wears a gold chain, and dark glasses with triangular tortoiseshell arms that become so typical of him, crimping his face as though he had received blows to each side of the head. He dines alone at the dining table always spread with its cloth, La Milagrosa having decided to withdraw to eat in the kitchen, and when he throws the plates to the floor in a rage if ever the food is cold, she simply sweeps up the broken crockery without a word.

It is about this time, coinciding with his first success in business, that the portraits begin to appear. New ones pour in constantly, until they cover a whole wall of the room where before La Milagrosa's clients would sit at the blue curtain, a cluttered collection that reaches right up to the ceiling, photographs cut from newspapers or posters, postcards whose colours fade behind their glass frames that sweat with the heat, all of them of the same man, his pudgy white face taken in countless poses—giving a speech in evening dress with a sash across his chest; the guest of honour at a banquet, in military dress uniform, weighed down with medals; staring out ecstatically at the ocean from under the peak of his baseball cap; climbing down the steps of a plane, lost in a crowd of people in formal dress or uniforms; smiling as he dances a folk dance with a girl dressed up in Indian costume; at the head of a military parade, wearing high boots and riding a thoroughbred. Dried flowers adorn the portraits, their stems and faded artificial roses poking out from behind the black and gilt frames; every day when he gets back from school he stares at them fascinated, wondering who the man in all these pictures can be. Until one Sunday when he learns the answer for ever.

His father gets him up when it is still dark, shines his shoes, puts a red flannel cap on his head, and takes him through the early dawn streets to the main square, the Plaza de la Republica. All alone, they take up position in the centre of the deserted square, and as the sun climbs in the sky they can for a while hear some carpenters hammering as they erect the framework of a grandstand on the steps of the National Palace. Afterwards they watch as the faithful leave the cathedral after mass and go their ways; it is almost midday by now, they have been there for more than two hours and the asphalt is starting to burn the soles of their shoes, but they do not move; as always Taleno's father sits and waits, never getting impatient. Later, the musicians from a military band arrive, and then trucks begin to appear which must have come from a long way off because their grilles and mudguards are spattered with mud; groups of peasants are told to jump down from them, and seem to lose their balance, bewildered by the glare of the sun, as they land on the pavement of the square.

The band strikes up a march, rockets and fireworks go off, the noise increases all the time, buses draw up, disgorging barefoot women, adolescents, and children who are carrying rolled-up banners. They come over shyly to the other groups that have already been brought in, and are pushed towards the crowd in the centre of the square, where all the streams of people converge, waving their cardboard posters with their painted slogans:

Barrio Riguero greets you
Sabana Grande—present!
Los Brasiles united behind you
Here's the red heart of Nagarote
All Tipitapa is with you
ORDER, PROSPERITY, PROGRESS
Hail the Sentinel of Peace
FOR EVER we love you

They are jostled from all sides, but Taleno's father defends his place like a tiger, standing firm and gripping the boy by the shoulders to resist the surge of people, all the time joining in the choruses of cheers which answer the monotonous panting voice exhorting them from a loudspeaker van. His father shakes him so that he will shout with the others, and he cries out in his tiny voice: Hurrah! or when told to, Death! also, Death! Death to the ungrateful sons of the fatherland!

Then the pushing starts all over again, and there is more shouting as above the strains of the band a wailing siren is heard approaching the square, the roar from motorcycle exhausts drowns their voices, and his father bends over him—"Can you see?" but he cannot see anything at all, so his father lifts him by the waist for him to catch a glimpse of *el hombre* himself as he gets out of a black limousine and, surrounded by bodyguards, walks to the stand, waving his military cap. It is the man in the portraits, he tells him sternly as he drops him to the floor once more, and whispers it in his ear a second time so that he will never forget: *el hombre de Nicaragua*, that same Nicaragua he had once pointed out to him from the boat, hazy in the distance.

They leave soon after, because there is nothing more to see; on the backs of the empty trucks lined up under the trees of the central park, government employees in charge of distribution dip into grimy barrels and hand out liquor and tamales to the crowd; a fat little man, probably a ministry clerk, grotesque in a tie that reaches down past his trouser fly, trots anxiously after a man who is walking off with a list under his arm, refusing to listen to his plea: "I came and they haven't put me down, I came and they haven't put me down!"

They hear shouts thick with rum, and cheers from the last of the crowd as it disperses into the streets by now too dark for them to make out properly. They trip over the bodies of drunken demonstrators lying in the gutters in pools of vomit; there is still a mingled smell of liquor and gunpowder in the air, as the wind sweeps up plantain leaves and forgotten hats. Some peasants lie fast asleep on the benches of a narrow little park cut in the diagonal of two streets, propaganda handouts covering their faces, and the red ink mixing with their sweat and running down their necks; others wander about disconsolately, bundles on their backs, lost among the avenues of shuttered shops, complaining bitterly that they have no idea how to get back to their villages now the trucks have left without them. And do they really hear a voice, someone shouting: "Come on, run, *el hombre* is throwing handfuls of coins from his car in the San Miguel market"? Anyway, Taleno's father is scornful, and tugs him along to hurry him up, what a lot of nonsense, as if *el hombre* were such a fool as to throw his money away like that.

A few blocks further on, his father whistles contentedly; he cannot see the expression in his eyes because they are hidden behind the black squares of his glasses, but he can sense his enthusiasm when he snatches off his flannel cap, runs his fingers through his hair, tousles it, and tells him: "Always follow the one who's in command, that's what I say."

And sometime later, perhaps when they are already entering their own neighbourhood, walking down the middle of the street, he confides in him: "My greatest wish is for you to become a military cadet. I want you to be an officer in the National Guard one day."

Pastorita is copying the new songs from April's *Cancionero Rayo* onto sheets of lined paper, tracing the words diligently between the fine blue lines like a schoolboy. He whistles the tunes to himself as he follows them, while Raul peers over his shoulder from time to time to check what he is writing, as if something that might affect his own future could appear at any moment in the words. "Do you think the chorus is repeated at the end of this part of 'I saw myself in your eyes'?" he asks, and frowning, Pastorita reads over what he has written. They had better listen for the song on the radio, these songbooks often get it wrong.

At that moment Chepito comes in from the town, wearing dark tortoiseshell glasses and a baseball cap with the inscription Cinco Estrellas, and carrying a greasy paper bag containing tomatoes, green plantains and a piece of bacon wrapped in a newspaper, to cook for his lunch. Without moving from behind Pastorita, Raul follows him with his gaze, his big, odd-shaped hands still resting on his knees, hands so large that as Lazaro used to say, the guitar always looked like a limp rag doll between them. We were waiting for you to get here so we could clear something up, he says, letting Chepito put his purchases on the counter, unbutton his shirt, and blow to cool himself.

He can dance to music well enough, but he doesn't understand a thing about melodies, he warns them, pleased all the same, and goes over, taking off his cap, which leaves an angry red mark stamped on his forehead. Pastorita does not look up from his writing but tells him it has nothing to do with melodies, it is about last month's election fraud that Raul wants to ask him.

Chepito winces exaggeratedly, remembering the pain in his ribs, and rubs his chest with both hands, sitting down on Pastorita's right. What elections? Raul straightens out his trouser legs, hitches them, stuffs his hands into the front pockets, and starts to walk up and down the dance floor—stop playing the innocent, the elections for Miss Nicaragua of course, when they robbed Jilguero's younger sister Liliana of victory. Pastorita refuses to believe there was any fraud.

Chepito sighs heavily, still massaging his chest, and says, without taking off his dark glasses—what's the point of lying, in the Miss Nicaragua contest I was on the side of the winning candidate, the colonel's adopted daughter. "Adopted"? queries Pastorita, still busy with his writing. How did he adopt her?

He won her in a raffle. I don't like to go telling people that, because the colonel doesn't want anyone to remind his daughter of her past, but that's how it was. The nuns at the girls' orphanage in Ticuantepe used to run charity sweepstakes on Sundays where they would raffle off the girls to the Christian families who attended, families willing to take the little angels in and adopt them; it was one way of getting rid of them as they grew up, or when the orphanage was full to overflowing. Sent by *el hombre* with other officers to show his face, the colonel turned up at one of these celebrations—it was just before the re-election in 1941, and *el hombre* wanted to keep on the right side of the religious authorities.

The colonel bought some tickets for the raffle without realizing what the prizes were, and was startled when just as he was about to leave the nuns presented him with the girl, clutching her bundle of belongings, and congratulated him because his had been the winning number. The other officers laughed at him, he looked so bemused with the girl sitting up among them in the jeep. They went from bar to bar in their usual carousing, and the girl sat in the jeep until dawn waiting for him, still fiercely holding on to her bundle.

He kept her though. He was a single man without a house of his own, so he kept her in the barracks for several months; she would creep about like a frightened deer, and climb dishevelled up into the almond trees for protection; soon however she began playing friendly games with the soldiers and the more favoured prisoners, so his great friend Indio Larios warned him that one fine day he would find his daughter's honour had been compromised in this messing around—why, her breasts were already beginning to show; he should either take her out of the barracks or give her back to the nuns. Indio's words must have had their effect, because he took his advice and moved her out of the garrison, sending her to stay with some aunts of his in Catarina while he found her a place to study abroad. And she is still in the United States, learning to type on a government grant. Whoever would have imagined an orphan like her ending up speaking English.

Raul continues to stride up and down the dance floor: Chepito is beating about the bush, the point is you knew very well they were fixing the contest, didn't you? Pastorita goes on writing, as though he were taking down everything they say. How did he know?

Because he himself was helping them with their fraud, that's how. Raul knows that Chepito, his ribs cracked from his recent beating, will not be able to deny it, and he does not; shamefaced, he stares at the empty glass still lying on the table from the day before, with the dried froth around its rim; he hasn't bothered to clear away the bottles either, there is no rush now that *El Copacabana* has been closed under the state of siege. It's true he was mixed up in it, but only because the colonel ordered him, and he turns, shifting the weight of his body towards Raul, who has come to a halt looking out at the lake through the white opening of the window: don't think I feel sorry about going against Jilguero's sister, he didn't care a bit about the contest, he told me so at the time: "I couldn't give a damn about this nonsense, it's all my mother's idea." His mother had not only got into debt with all the moneylenders in Masaya to pay for the gowns and pairs of shoes, she had made her sons contribute too, and forced them to act as their sister's chaperones at the balls—though Jilguero managed to get out of that with the excuse of having to go and plant tobacco in Tisma, so it was his older brother, Carlos, who had to do that job: which is how he got into that argument with Captain Taleno I was telling you about.

He falls silent as though that was all he had to say, and makes to stand up and to cook his lunch, but Pastorita points at him with the pencil: "Where does the fraud come in then?"

Well, the voting slips for the Miss Nicaragua competition were in the newspapers, and at first his job had been to go from door-to-door buying up old copies. He would appear on people's doorsteps with his little leather suitcase, and no-one would understand what he had come for, thinking he was either an evangelical preacher or a travelling salesman; but after he had explained his mission to them, they not only gladly gave him their newspapers, but also tried to dump all their old magazines on him as well. At that time nobody had the slightest interest in the contest. Afterwards he would take the newspapers to the colonel up at Tiscapa barracks for the soldiers to cut out the voting slips; and the scissors flew tirelessly, the barracks had the air of a tailor's cutting-room, as all the soldiers snipped at their copies.

But then all of a sudden everyone wanted to vote, the public began to take it very seriously, and a single copy of the newspaper was worth its weight in gold; any soldier who carelessly destroyed a voting coupon was likely to end up in the punishment cells. It was *el hombre*'s fault that things were upset for the colonel in this way. One morning on his return from a military parade in the Plaza de la Republica, he stopped his cavalcade at the International Club to cast his vote for the colonel's orphan in the presence of some photographers—doing what he could, as he saw it, to help the publicity for her. But it had the opposite effect, because at the din of the motorcycles and sirens, the crush of soldiers and body-guards, a lot of passersby gathered outside the club, and when they saw *el hombre* emerge and learning what he had been doing inside, they started to jeer loudly: he simply laughed and gestured rudely at them with his hand in his pocket.

From then on Jilguero's sister started to surge ahead in the polls carried out every Saturday on Radio Mundial by the Colgate-Palmolive Electoral Tribunal of the Airwaves. Of course, says Raul, going up to Chepito and waving his hands in his face, you don't need a crystal ball to know that, people fought over newspapers so they could vote for her, and there were huge queues outside all the places with voting boxes—stores, cinemas, ice-cream parlours, the Managua Club, the International Club; and since the lines were slow-moving, they would all start enjoying themselves, chanting merrily over and over again on the sun-scorched pavements

> The opposition is voting
> in this line here;
> Anybody in the other one
> must be a queer.

Pastorita erases something as carefully as if he were treating a wound, and bends over to blow off the bits—he still can't see where the fraud came into it. Chepito, self-reproaching, accepts the criticism in Raul's glare: since there was no way for the colonel's daughter to win enough votes, more slips were printed at the government printers. And they filled the ballot boxes with those counterfeit votes.

Raul stands triumphantly in front of Pastorita to judge his reaction—but he quietly goes on erasing, and doesn't even raise an eyebrow at the news, so Raul resumes his pacing to and fro, and suddenly imitates Chepito in a high-pitched childish voice: "And I'll keep to myself exactly what I got up to!"

No, I won't keep it to myself: Chepito stands up spiritedly, right there where you are standing, the colonel came panting in, his jeep waiting with engine running on the shore, and thrust the bundles of counterfeit votes at me, still smelling of printer's ink. "Only a man I can completely trust like you, Chepito, who has nothing to do with the army, can do this job for me." He went on that it was a life-or-death struggle, if his daughter lost, the opposition, the government's enemies, would be the winners.

I grabbed the packets and put them under the bar. On the days after that, I would take out bundles of the voting slips and turn up at different stores in the late afternoon, when nobody else was voting; bathed in sweat, I would take them out from under my shirt and when the assistants were busy with something else would stuff them into the slits in the cardboard boxes, scared stiff that someone might catch me at it. I needn't have worried, nobody knew about the fraud, but it was the colonel himself who put the wind up me by making me report back to him every evening. "Anything happen, Chepito?" he would ask nervously as soon as he saw me, then, pleased that everything had gone smoothly, he would tell his maids to serve me a good dinner in the kitchen.

He went on filling the boxes for several days before the final count, which was to be held after a horseback parade of the candidates—though in fact this involved only Jilguero's sister, since the colonel's orphan would come from the United States only for her coronation, and leave again the next morning: she doesn't like life down here any more. The parade ended in trouble, as you remember.

"How did the trouble start?" Pastorita asks, curious, but Raul is indignant with him for wanting such trivial details. Have you just come back from abroad or something? The triumphal procession made its way along the Calle 15 de Septiembre, with a mounted escort of her supporters behind her, and Liliana Rosales riding proudly out in front, elegant in black, with high boots and hat tied under her chin. She concentrated on the trotting of her horse, its hooves echoing hollowly on the asphalt, and waved rather nervously to the cheering crowds lining the pavements.

As her horse came out into Roosevelt Avenue, opposite the College of the Holy Virgin, someone on a second floor balcony shouted "Hurrah for Liliana Rosales, the opposition candidate. Down with the dictatorship!" Applause rang out from all sides, and she shyly raised her hat in thanks, looking up towards the balcony. And that was when it happened—a string of firecrackers went off under the horse's hooves—the crowd could see the old man who threw them, and the fuse burning, but there was no time to warn her. At the explosion, her terrified mount broke free, climbed onto the pavement, then plunged with rider and all into *La Casa del Lagarto*. The plate glass crashed in as the horse backed through the window, trampling on shoes and handbags, but Liliana did not fall off. The fearful animal was still rearing and kicking among the fragments when the other riders finally managed to grab hold of the reins for her to dismount. She was crying, white as a sheet. Chepito, you claim that Jilguero would have nothing to do with the whole affair, but it was he who helped her down from her horse and comforted her. The old man who had thrown the firecrackers had disappeared into the maze of the San Miguel market, and nobody could catch him.

That same night, with everyone out on the streets already stirred up by the explosion, the Colgate-Palmolive Electoral Tribunal of the Airwaves gave the final results of the voting—it was an obvious fraud, who was going to believe that the colonel's daughter could have won so many more votes? Spontaneous demonstrations broke out soon after the results were known, which the National Guard broke up by force, arresting lots of people and injuring many more. It was a criminal offence to have Liliana Rosales' picture in your pocket, and worse still to shout support for her; gangs of prisoners were taken from the jails that night to cover over her name on walls and posters; trucks of National Guardsmen patrolled Managua day and night as though it were under siege.

Pastorita rolls up the sheets of paper, taps them on the table to straighten them, then puts them in his pocket: all that fuss over a rigged contest like the Miss Nicaragua competition, whose idea was it in the first place?

It is only now that Chepito takes off his dark glasses, licks one of the stems, and begins to suck it thoughtfully: they go on to compete at the seaside in Miami, and whoever wins as Miss Universe becomes a famous movie star. The colonel didn't want his orphan to miss a chance like that.

Pastorita bursts out laughing, his beaming screen idol's features spoilt, as Lazaro always used to say, by the tell-tale marks of hunger. "You don't believe that, do you? All those Yankees do is screw them naked on the beach."

For the trip back to Ocotal they lent me a mare, also borrowed from the mayor; I was given a waterproof cape to cover my pyjamas, and joined the column weaponless. He never said as much, but I knew I was in his custody. After we had ridden a few miles out of the village, I caught up with him at the front of the patrol and, trying to summon up pride out of nowhere, I told him that if he had really meant it as a friend, I was willing to tell him the truth. He again looked at me with his priest's face as if from the other side of a confessional, a face in which his bleary eyes showed plainly that he had not washed for days. "That's right, tell me everything straight out, man to man." So as we rode along I told him the true story of what had happened; he nodded sympathetically from time to time, and occasionally closed his eyes as though he had gone to sleep in the saddle, which made me fall silent, but then, scarcely moving his lips, he would ask me to continue. At other times he would remove his hat to straighten a kerchief he had wrapped inside the headband, or to smooth his frizzy hair, drawing his fingers through it like a rake; as I was reaching the end of the story, and all I had left to tell him was how I had fired some shots in the air after the enemy had already ridden off, he reined in his horse, pulled out a bottle of Agua Florida and doused his temples with it. After all I had been through, the smell brought to my mind at once an image of people fainting, of the commotion around my poor aunt fainted on the floor when the news of the disaster reached Catarina: and to think she had even had her photograph taken with my cousin Mercedes dressed up in his uniform and with a rifle slung over his shoulder.

When he realised I had finished, he sat for a long time deep in thought, pleasurably sniffing the Agua Florida in each nostril, then he put the bottle back in his saddlebag, and when I was least expecting it, suddenly asked me if I knew how to read and write, in the same sorrowful tone he might have asked me: "Sergeant, are you a queer?" That was a bit too much, even though I was feeling so despondent—of course I knew how to read and write, how could he ask such a question? He spurred his mount on and made light of it—he was only asking because if I wanted him to, he could help draw up the report, which would take a lot of careful thinking. He said it in such a way that he was suggesting he knew just what was to be done: "First of all, you mustn't write that you gave the order for everyone to go to sleep without posting any guard outside the cinema," shaking his head in sad disbelief, "and secondly, if there were sentries (and we had better put that there were), they all had their throats cut, and were thrown on the fire with the other bodies after the battle. And you mustn't write that the Sandinistas calmly took the tiles off the roof and jumped down on top of you —no, someone opened the door for them from inside, and that person must have been the mayor's lad: thank goodness, his body was never found, or at least, it couldn't be identified." At that he thumped the pommel of his saddle gleefully, going through all the details as though it was he who would escape punishment by making all this up; and he said it all so clearly that it almost seemed as if he had had it all worked out in his mind beforehand. To finish, he added that if I wanted to he could type it out for me, that always made a better impression. What option did I have? None, except to ask him shamefaced to write the whole report for me.

"I'd be delighted," he replied, but in a way that implied my acceptance of his offer was no longer important. For a while he merely rode along staring at me, his bright, hooded eyes glinting like coins in his sallow face. "The only thing missing is the proof," he eventually said. Bewildered, I asked him what proof he meant. He turned towards me in his saddle, looking exasperatedly at me as one might at a child who is slow on the uptake, then prodded his horse faster, leaving me in his wake. When finally I managed to catch up to him, in what for me was a back-breaking trot, he carried on as if he had never stopped: "The proof of blood, of course. The marines are never going to believe the story about your heroic defence at the head of your troops if you turn up completely unharmed, as though you had a charmed life. Put yourself in the Yankees' shoes for a moment, try to think as they will: the leader of the patrol, not a scratch on him, all the others, dead and buried."

Him saying that really did catch me with my pants down, as they say. I felt myself go weak, and let my feet slide out of the mare's stirrups, so she at once slackened her pace, and he pulled out ahead of me again, with his unconcerned face, a cigarette dangling grotesquely from the corner of his mouth, and the kerchief under a patch of red at the back of his neck. I hung back for a while, not knowing whether to feel angry or grateful, but soon decided to catch up to him once more and raise the subject again. Although he must have sensed I had returned alongside, he didn't turn to look at me, or say a word. We came to a bend in the track covered in thick undergrowth, and he slowed his horse and signalled to the rest of the column to wait behind us. Then he undid the holster of his duty revolver and handed it to me. I slid out of my saddle, and he took the reins. I lifted off the cape, then barefoot and in my pyjamas walked towards the thickest bushes I could see, as if I wanted to relieve myself urgently. As I disappeared into the thicket, I could hear his voice: "Don't feel ashamed, Sergeant, this takes balls as well."

I plunged in, pushing aside the wet vegetation, and followed a narrow path that came out in a clearing where stacks of logs lay as though they had been put there then forgotten by someone, under the branches of a tiguilote tree that also spread over the bubbling, muddy waters of a stream. I sat down calmly in the grass, drops of water falling down the back of my neck from the branches which were still soaking wet from the earlier rain, the leaves quivering in a wind that gave the deep silence of the place an air of mystery. I stared at the nickel-plated gun that weighed heavily in my hand. I held it up in front of my face, the sharp smell of oil making me feel sick. I could see the tips of the bullets, poking out of the front of the drum so harmless-looking, and then pressed the barrel to different parts of my body, flinching at its cold touch. After much hesitation, I pointed it at the heel of my left foot, shut my eyes tightly and, without knowing exactly when, pulled the trigger. Terrified, I heard the hammer click, but it did not fire. The bullet, for some reason that only increased my torment, had not moved into the gun chamber.

I sat for a little while longer weighing the gun in my hand, then decided to get it over with, and pushed the barrel right up against the skin. This time I did not close my eyes as I pressed the trigger. The shot rang out, echoing through the leafy clearing as though it were a grotto: and the last thing I saw before everything went dark was a panic-stricken flock of parakeets darting off from the top of the tiguilote.

I came to lying on a canvas stretcher by the side of the track. One of my trouser legs was covered in blood and there was a kerchief, the one he had been wearing under his hat, tied round my foot; his face was pressed close to mine, waiting for me to regain consciousness, masked by smoke from the cigarette that still hung from his lips about to fall at any moment. He was so close that I could feel the heat of the ash on my cheek. Seeing me come round, he triumphantly showed me the palm of his hand, where the tips of his fingers were stained red with my blood, then clasped one of my hands in a friendly way. I responded as best I could, feeling a sticky wet sensation. "All true friendships are sealed with blood," he said. He obviously felt the bond between us was made.

He had already sent a couple of soldiers to gallop on ahead and inform the marine command in Ocotal that the leader of the patrol attacked in San Fernando was arriving wounded from the battle. Once we got there, he personally took charge of getting me on board the Fokker aeroplane which transported me to Managua, making room for me among some US wounded, all of us destined for the military hospital. I heard him chatting in English to the pilot, saw him nonchalantly take a cigarette out of the man's shirt pocket, completely at ease with the Yankees. Flat on my back as I was, I couldn't help but admire him: He really knows what's what, I had to admit to myself. The plane's engines started up, and he smiled at me, as if to say I needn't worry, that everything was taken care of, then he tried to tell me something, but the noise was too loud for me to make anything out, until he leaned over and shouted in my ear: That wound of yours will probably win you a promotion, Sergeant, I eventually made out, and he looked so serious as he said it that I could not feel offended.

They closed the hatch, and through the glass I could see him standing there on the landing strip waving goodbye, all my fortunes depending on his skill at deceiving the Yankees. As the plane bumped along the gravel runway, in torture from the stabbing pain from my wounded foot—who knows, I might even have shot through a bone, my mind turned to the gold sovereigns my father had sent me off to the war to win, and how I would no longer be of any help to him. He was bedridden, lacking the heart to get up since poverty had come upon him, his passion for dice leading him deeper and deeper into debt. He had called me into his bedroom and said to me: It's up to you now—you're young and with a good head on your shoulders, it's up to you to save El Corozo, the last piece of land we have left. Go and visit your godfather in Masatepe and ask him to recommend you to the American Marines, so that you can join their forces. And I couldn't forget how happy he had been when I came back with the good news that I had seen my godfather President Moncada at *Venecia*, his villa by the lake at Masaya, and that he had given me a letter for Colonel Cummings USMC. In fact, he was so overjoyed I think it gave him a relapse; he couldn't sleep all that night, turning over in his mind how El Corozo would be saved, and all the time casting longing glances at the box where he kept his tumbler and dice.

I can't deny I was very upset by the huge lies in the report they gave me to sign in the hospital at Managua. I even doubted whether or not I should sign it at all before asking him if he couldn't tone it down a bit, at the very least the hand-to-hand struggle at the end; but he was out in the hills and there was no way of getting in touch with him, and there was no time for delays, so I put my signature to the neatly typed original and to the two copies—one for the President of the Republic, which brought me a telegram of congratulations from my godfather, and the other which was for the person signing. But I tore that one up.

CHAPTER 5

"How on earth can waltzes like that become old-fashioned?" Indio protested, standing up. "That's why they're called classical, because they never die."

"I also had an offer of marriage from a foreign gentleman who had discovered an oil lake in the Peten jungle. They paid him thousands of quetzales to keep quiet about it, and only he and I know where the lake is."

"We've got better music of that sort in Nicaragua—what about Gaston Perez, 'Lopears', the man who wrote the bolero *Sinceridad*: that's really famous. 'Just that once I talked with you'," Turco sang, completely out of tune.

"When they heard the music the neighbours crowded round and poured into my grandmother's shop. She tried to shut the door, and took a broom to push them out, shouting: 'These thieves are stealing all my cake!' But she couldn't get rid of them. The racket didn't die down until my grandfather fell asleep dead drunk in his bed and the musicians filed out into the courtyard, expecting my grandmother to pay them."

"How can you think that Lopears is on the same level as a genius like Jose de la Cruz Mena? Do you really think that *Sinceridad* is better than *Amores de Abraham*? Never in this world!''

''Turco, sweetheart, listen to me when I'm talking to you. I've always treated men harshly. However much oil they own, if you say yes, you're trapped for the rest of your life.''

''Locked in her kitchen, my grandmother shouted that she hadn't sent for them, it was their own fault for trusting a drunkard. And she knew too that all musicians were layabouts, and that they had been drinking just as much as he had in the bedroom: if their noses were red when they came out, it wasn't from blowing their instruments but from all the drink.''

The colonel laughed out loud, his naked belly shaking, and looked round to see if Indio was joining in the laughter; but he was staring at the floor, wagging his finger at Turco to contradict him.

''Though you don't like to admit it, that time *Los Panchos* came to Managua—this is true, isn't it, Jilguero? What were their very first words when they got off the plane? 'We want to meet the man who wrote *Sinceridad*.' Did they mention Mena at all? They did not.''

''That same lover begged me: 'Fatima, let me take you home to my country, where I own lots of mansions and land.' But I refused. The only thing he left to remind me of him was a blonde baby girl, who is so golden haired nobody can believe she is from here.''

''They couldn't get a centavo out of my grandmother, so then, furious, they stood outside the kitchen door and launched into a bullfight tune: 'The whore who was your mother, walking the streets all dressed in red'. A great cheer came from all the other houses, gardens and streets in the neighbourhood. My grandmother started to threaten them: 'I'll call the National Guard to you, you impudent scoundrels!' ''

''What have *Los Panchos* got to do with *Amores de Abraham*? That waltz won the music competition at the Leon cultural festival, it's not common rubbish. On the night of the competition, the audience packing the Municipal Theatre stood up at the end and, tears in their eyes, called for the winner to come up onto the stage. They had no idea who he was—the leper, the pariah . . .''

"And another time, Turco, an American who owned Metro-Goldwyn-Meyer saw me dancing and wanted to sign me up as the star rumba dancer for a cabaret in Mexico. He said I was wasted in Guatemala. He was going to get me into films too, playing opposite Ninon Sevilla."

"When my grandfather woke up later that night, complaining about his splitting headache, at first she was still annoyed, but then gradually she calmed down—you know what women are like, Colonel; she took pity on him and took him flannels to rub alcohol on his forehead. In a plaintive voice, he told her not to stay up for him, just to leave the bottle of alcohol at his side so that he could do it himself."

"But, Indio, *Sinceridad* is famous the world over, in other countries that bolero is like the Nicaraguan national anthem. Tell him, Jilguero, you know about music. You tell him, Colonel, you're a man of taste."

"Don't bring the national anthem into this," the colonel chided Turco, his attention distracted from Jilguero's story for a moment. "Our anthem is sacred—you should know that, you were an army officer once."

"What if you had seen my name in lights outside all the cinemas, Turco? 'Today—Fatal Fatima, Singing, Laughing, Dancing, Crying for You'." She traced out the lettering on the neon sign with her stubby fingers in front of Turco's face.

"My grandmother was falling asleep again when she heard footsteps, then banging noises—and who do you think was up, clattering about in the darkness, Colonel? My grandfather, looking for his gramophone. He was drunk again; he had finished off all the alcohol she had left, and could not bear to drink without music, so at midnight his bedroom filled with noise again."

"Play *Sinceridad*, Jilguero, so Indio can see what I mean."

"But it's a tragic piece, Turco, it's not for a guitar. The theatre rang with applause, while outside, the poor musical genius was sitting in a doorway crying, his body covered in sores, leaning on his stick and unable to enter the brightly lit doorway, or to reveal to everyone that it was he who had won the competition, and receive the homage that was his due. A genius of composition, but a wreck of a human being. That's the way of the world."

Jilguero picked up the guitar, but went on talking to the colonel.

"Yes, Colonel, that was my grandfather, Don Chico Garcia. El Corozo's a fine place, isn't it? Carlos and I used to spend our holidays there, but after my grandfather's death, we lost it all. What can you do, you were the one who struck lucky: in life you're up one minute and down the next. He himself used to say that often enough. Your health, Colonel."

Still laughing the colonel gave no sign that he had heard, busy as he was smothering his face in the Schoolgirl's hair.

"Play *Sinceridad* so that Indio can hear it"; Turco shook the guitar.

"You won't convince me like that. You have no taste!"

"Jilguero, do you remember what I once told you?" the shy voice of the Rosemaid came as though from far away: "that I used to be a bullfighter?"

"A bullfighter?" the colonel roared with laughter, his eyes filling with tears.

"It's true, she has been one," Jilguero said, looking over at her affectionately.

"I'm from San Vicente Pacaya; my father was Leocadio Feuntes, known as the Quetzal of the Bullring; with my brother Nehemias, El Charrito, and myself there were three of us. I was the Rosemaid."

"Well, Jilguero? What about *Sinceridad*?"

"A bar room song," Indio insists, without opening his eyes.

"I agree with Indio to some extent," the colonel said, speaking thickly, slurring his words. "Bars were the ruin of our bolero writers. In Nicaragua we spoil everything with our love of drink—just look at our baseball players for example."

"We toured the whole of Guatemala with our bullfighting trio. One day in the ring at San Antonio Palopo they showered us with flowers."

"That's true of our poets too. Dario was a great one for the bottle."

"No, I won't allow you to say that," Indio protested, flinging himself upright.

"That poet Dario you are talking about was really vulgar, all he wrote were disgusting poems—I've heard them. Isn't that true, darling?" the Schoolgirl said, settling on the colonel's lap once more.

"Why do you think we lost the 1942 World Championship in Cuba?—because of drink. I know because I was on the selection committee. We had to go and fish the players out of the bars before each match. The pitchers could hardly stand up when they went out to warm up."

"Our last bullfight was in Chimaltenango. We never appeared again because one night soon after when we were in San Vicente stripping ears of corn on our verandah, a group of masked men came up and started shooting at us with shotguns. My father doubled up and fell into the corn, and they killed my mother too."

"So now you're comparing the Divine Swan with baseball players! Whatever next!"

"In 1949, when the ninth World Series was scheduled for Managua, *el hombre* was very worried that our team would get so drunk again that they couldn't stand, and would betray the honour of our country, so he told me to lock them all up for a couple of weeks before the games began. We sent out patrols to round them up from the shoemakers', building sites, and warehouses where they worked. We shut them up in the Campo de Marte and only let them out under guard for their training sessions. We gave the guards strict orders that nobody was to go near them, in case they slipped them a bottle of something on the sly."

"But didn't Nicaragua lose practically every game in that series? Even El Salvador beat us. Perhaps they needed the liquor after all?" Turco said, as he filled the colonel's glass to the brim.

"In the French court, Ruben Dario mixed with kings and emperors," Indio slumped over, his head on the table. "Duchesses and the noblest ladies passed through his hands. He was a rough Pegasus all right!"

"Do you remember this poem of Dario's, Indio?" the Schoolgirl asked:

That man you saw one day
and called him shitface, if not worse
Now you have to kiss his arse
—and that's the end of my sad verse."

"Nehemiah and I ran into the house. The men shot out the lamp, and set about completing their butchery by the light of their torches. I managed to hide under the bed, but Nehemiah tried to get away through the window, and that was where he was hit by the shots: his little body fell into the mud of the courtyard. Why did all that happen, Jilguero? Because the Sunday before in the ring at Salcaja my father had refused to dedicate a bull in honour of General Ubico's birthday. From the stands, the military governor marked him out for execution."

"It was the manager's fault we lost—he was a Cuban we'd hired for his reputation, but he was a complete disaster. In one of the final games, *el hombre* could not bear his mistakes any longer, and went down from the presidential box, put on his baseball cap, and took over managing the squad himself. We had to drag the Cuban from the field—he refused to leave."

"*El hombre* wasn't much better though. We lost ten-to-nothing that day. I was there, I had to follow him down to the field because I was his adjutant. I can still remember how they booed him."

"Yes, let's hear Indio recite," the Schoolgirl clapped her hands feebly.

"My princess is sad. What can the matter be?"

I leaned over to you, Turco, for you to have a good look at Indio and take his drink from him, otherwise when the time came he'd be no good to us at all.

"When day dawned I was on my own with their bodies, all alone in the world, so at fourteen I set out from home; first of all I lived in San Jose Pinula, then I drifted here and there, and I ended up in Mixco with Lasinventura. That must have been fifteen years ago, Jilguero. If only you had known me in those days—I was so strong and cheerful . . ."

"All these women can do is give us their hard-luck stories," the colonel muttered, silencing the Rosemaid abruptly. "No, the thing was, Nicaragua was already losing badly, the game was lost anyway. What was important was *el hombre*'s sincere gesture. You who knew him well, Turco, who was at his side, you can't deny his sincerity, surely?"

" . . and so sincere," Turco started singing, in a high falsetto.

"What's all this about great baseball players? There's nobody greater than Ruben Dario."

I was still trying to point out to you without them noticing that Indio was too far gone to be of any use to us. You said we wouldn't bother him, he'd done his bit by getting us that far, he couldn't help us much from now on. It was up to the two of us.

The men responsible for making the coffee are already at work in the palm leaf shack that serves as the camp kitchen. It is still dark, but others are also stirring, and as they draw near the fire, they discover that those around it have not been to sleep at all, but have stayed listening through the night.

"It's a different kind of greatness, Indio, but it is all part of our national heritage. Take Chino Melendez for example. The New York Giants struck out nine times against him; not a single player got to second base, let alone anywhere near a home run. 'Chino, let them hit one at least, we're all falling asleep here,' the outfielders shouted to him. But he went on and on, unhittable, pitching his thunderbolts, one after the other dismissing the famous big leaguers. They all walked off with their heads hung in shame. A historic match: Nicaragua 1, New York Giants 0."

"When was that game, Colonel? Nicaragua has never played in the major leagues that I know of."

"Hark! Here comes the courtly suite!" Indio recited, climbing onto a chair.

"The match was held in Havana one evening. Chino Melendez got rid of Lou Gehrig, Babe Ruth—you were very young at the time. The crowd were silent as the grave in the Velado stadium, all that could be heard was the thump of the ball hitting the catcher's mitt. The Giants offered him a contract to go with them, but he said no. 'My country is my country,' he told them."

"Hear the bright bugles call."

"Chino Melendez was a real big leaguer. Stanley Cayasso, the Iron Horse, was another big leaguer; so were Edward Green, the Black Gazelle, Jose Cachirulo Mendoza, Timothy Mena, all uncrowned kings."

"The sword sparkles in the distance..."

"And who helped them escape from their miserable homes? Who made them the stars of the sport of kings? *El hombre*—he was the one who put them on their thrones."

"Come off it, Colonel. There you go praising *el hombre* again," Turco laughed.

"Why not?" the colonel asked, trying to fondle the Schoolgirl's breasts. "*El hombre* has been a true father to all of us; to me, to Indio, even to you. I know how much he cared for you. You can't deny he cared for you."

"Bastards!" wailed Fatal Fatima, and threw her drink over Turco.

"The procession of the paladins!" Indio spread his arms as if he were trying to fly, and fell off his chair.

He and his truant friends from school wander along the shore of the lake at mid-day. There is a white mist hanging in the air; vultures perch on the bare branches of calabash trees growing out of the mud, fly off then land again, their bald heads flattening in the direction of the stench of rotten flesh—a disembowelled carthorse, stiff, poisoned dogs whose matted fur crowns the summit of the heaps of refuse which the grimy waters of the lake lick against then slide away, staining the coarse sand a dark wet colour, oily tongues of feeble waves that barely succeed in ruffling the surface of the lake; heaps of decomposing rubbish, frames of bottomless chairs, handcart wheels, odd planks of wood, pieces of cloth, smashed boxes, and further on, pools of burnt waste that leave congealed scars on the earth; garbage piled to the sky, whose ashes the wind carries and mingles with those from still more distant bonfires; the heaps of refuse stretch on out to the west as far as the eye can see, all along the greasy shoreline—scorched beaches, burnt black mud, gleaming pieces of charcoal; and in the midst of the smoke, lines of shacks built alongside the discharge pipes that empty the city's sewage into the waters of the lake—huts made of cardboard packing cases, cans, refuse gleaned from the dumps; perched on the edge of channels where the filthy sludge oozes along, all the city's excreta flowing slowly out into the lake; whole neighbourhoods that, enveloped in the fumes from the smouldering rubbish, themselves appear to be on fire.

As they leave the shore and walk up towards the Parque Central, one of his friends stops them and points to the steps of the cathedral; they all look expectantly at this promise of a new source of fun. A group of women dressed in black is standing on the steps; they are in a tight knot, and do not appear to notice the glare of sunlight reflecting off the square, as if they were waiting patiently for their photograph to be taken. The boys start to run across to get a closer look when the women at the front unfold a large banner whose lettering is still damp:

STOP THE FRAUD!
RESPECT DR. DESIDERIO ROSALES'
ELECTION VICTORY!

They seem to be waiting for something to happen, as if their dignified passivity were in itself a challenge, and were filling the square with secret vibrations that could let loose at any moment. Soon afterwards, as the cathedral's tall doors are hastily closed and the passersby begin to run towards the park as fast as their legs can carry them, for just an instant their calm immobility is perturbed, and they turn to look at each other anxiously—but at once they regain their composure, while the public employees in the National Palace opposite crowd to their windows, curious to see what is going to happen.

Taleno hears the thud of rifle butts as they hit the pavement, the clink of water canteens against bayonets, and as he lifts his canvas schoolbag up to shield his eyes, he can make out the silhouettes of soldiers on the other side of the square clambering down with deliberate slowness from the same trucks that were used to transport the crowds here that Sunday his father had brought him.

The soldiers take up positions to seal off all access to the square, and one of his friends standing behind him on the pavement plucks at his shirt and tells him to make a run for it, there is going to be trouble; they disappear back towards the lakeshore. He does not move. He stands there, his schoolbag shielding his eyes, his socks fallen down over his ankles, and his muddy shoes fixed to the pavement as if the cement had melted in the heat. Hardly have the women begun to sing the national anthem in timid schoolgirl voices when a tumult of shouts, jeers and yells bursts into their song. Groups of men armed with iron bars, and women carrying sticks, appear at the corners of the square behind the wall of soldiers. Demanding they be let through, they hurl themselves at the troops, who laughingly let them pass.

He watches them rush to the cathedral steps brandishing their weapons, their whips flying, and their shouts recall the echoes of those he had heard that Sunday with his father. The women are knocked to the floor, dragged along by their hair, thrown down the steps, and amongst the groans and cries for help he can make out gleeful shouts of support for *el hombre*. All of a sudden a hand tugs at his hair, he is shaken violently and pushed so that he falls full length onto the floor, and his writing pads and text books lined in brown paper spill out of his satchel. Panting, furious, his father is peering at him from behind the thick lenses, unable to control the froth of spittle at the corners of his mouth, his chin trembling with rage. He drags him to his feet. "Pick up your things at once and get home," he orders him.

He gets a last glimpse of the women in black through his father's legs as he gropes on all fours to collect his trampled books. Defeated, they are scattering in all directions—some take refuge in nearby houses in the Colonia Lugo, whose doors open momentarily to let them in; others push past the soldiers, who have not moved from their positions, and clamber into the garden of the Managua Club, or, still being chased, run along the paths of the Parque Central; others remain on the cathedral steps, resting their bloodied heads against its columns.

The two of them soon also pass through the ranks of soldiers, his father with a firm grip on his ear, shouting at him, not daring to look over towards the jeep parked a block away in the Calle Candelaria, from where Catalino Lopez is directing operations through his field-glasses.

He takes Taleno to the room of the portraits, and leaves him kneeling on a handful of corn that he has scattered on the floor from a bowl used by La Milagrosa to feed the chickens; the sharp grains stick painfully into his flesh. Locked in, he hears people who knock on the front door, the assailants from the square come for their payment. "Tomorrow, tomorrow in the market," is all his father says each time he goes to open it. It is already dark, after the muffled sounds of his father eating dinner alone at his dining table, when he hears him enter the room without switching on the light. He can get up now, and let this be the last time he upsets his father so. Is that a promise?

He stands up, numb and uncertain, all feeling gone from his knees, where the grains of corn have left deep marks. Even after they have gone to bed he still hears his father going on about it, keeping La Milagrosa awake with his worried whining—could he be so unlucky that Catalino Lopez had seen everything that had happened through his binoculars? "A son of Chon Taleno mixed up with the opposition," some jealous tongue from the market might tell him. "He wasn't with them, he was just curious to see what was going on—didn't you say that yourself?" But he will not listen to La Milagrosa's sleepy voice of reason: "The point is, he was there, even before we arrived to break up the women's demonstration. What in heaven's name was he doing there?'' he said, his anger surging back.

By this time, work has already started on the mansion that his father, by now a wealthy man, is having built in Managua near the Bartolome de las Casas park. Its towers preen themselves high above the squalid wood and straw houses that are its neighbours on a high stretch of ground opposite the railway line to Sabana Grande, and it is the only one not to tremble with every train that goes past. The work is being done by a builder named Campuzano, to a design that his father has remembered ever since the day that a black Colombian river pilot drew it for him on the dusty floor of an inn they were to sleep in, telling him that such a mansion really and truly existed in his country, in a place called Bahia Solano, on the top of a cliff overlooking the sea, where it was used as a harbourmaster's office or a customs house. So Taleno's father is having it built exactly the same: a navy blue facade flanked by two pyramidal turrets concealing the roof tiles, fake green columns barely standing out from the walls flecked with black to imitate Carrara marble; a gravel border all round the house; Moorish windows, and above the front door a rose-shaped skylight to let in the electric wires from the pylon out on the pavement.

They haul benches and chairs, kitchen utensils, cardboard boxes full of clothes and shoes, the saints' statues, the dismantled four-poster, and the collection of portraits, to empty rooms that still smell of whitewash. Taleno's father proudly shows them around, leading the way with La Milagrosa trotting after him, moved to tears: ''So you've got a home at last, Chon'', weighed down now with the cares of age, her bushy hair still reaching to her waist, but dried up now like a bramble, all her earthly ambitions relinquished. Alma Nubia, dressed in her convent school uniform, is lagging behind, so he calls them all together to watch as he pompously operates the chain of the porcelain lavatory. Had any of them ever seen a water closet before? He cocks his head to listen to the flush of water, beaming at them triumphantly. They go on a tour of the bedrooms, and he strokes the freshly painted walls, prodding them to test their strength. He looks up at the rafters and the red tiles, peering through his thick lenses to make sure that it really is the ceiling and not the sky over his head.

In the first nights after their move to the new house, Taleno can hear him smashing bottles with a hammer to set pieces of glass in the courtyard wall to stop thieves climbing in, since they live so close to so many poor neighbourhoods.

Taleno only rarely sees his father after that, because he has become a cadet at the military academy, as his father had wished. He makes only occasional weekend visits to the new house when he has a pass. Then on the day of his graduation his father arrives long before time at the zinc-roofed shed in the Campo de Marte where on other occasions courts martial are held; there are stacks of metal chairs against the walls, and milky white streams of creosote trickle across the rough cement floor that has just been washed by the prisoners. The three of them are silent, all alone: La Milagrosa in a taffeta dress, with a black patent leather handbag that she handles with exaggerated care as though it did not belong to her, dangling from one arm; Alma Nubia with her boyish haircut and already budding breasts, daring to talk only to her mother in a whisper, as if she were in her school chapel; and his father, who took his hat off reverently as he came in, wearing a new nylon shirt through which his undershirt, its sleeves rolled up above the elbows, is clearly visible, as is his goldbraid chain.

The prisoners who swept the place clean re-appear; guarded by soldiers they start unfolding the chairs and put them out in rows, then set up a long trestle-table and lay a cloth on it. A conscript places a basket of gladioli in the middle and a cluster of flags behind it, hangs a loudspeaker from the end wall; and it is only when the sun is shining high over the yard and the heat under the tin roof is so unbearable that Taleno's father can feel his nylon shirt sticking to his skin like a piece of sucked orange, giving him an irresistible urge to scratch under the armpits, that the families of the other cadets start to arrive. They scrape their chairs as they settle, and gradually the shed fills with the sound of whispers and voices, scattered conversations, coughs, children crying; then all at once a silence falls and the cadets file in two abreast in their white dress uniforms, with Taleno to the fore, stiffly erect, the leather peak of his military cap pulled down over his eyes, his ears sticking out because his hair has been cropped so short. They are sitting in the front row; Alma Nubia stands up nervously, waiting for him to turn towards them so that she can greet him as he passes by, but her father pinches her sharply on the arm. At that moment there is a noise outside, the guests struggle to their feet, and out in the yard the military band, too numerous to fit inside the shed itself, begins solemnly and raggedly to play the national anthem. Startled as if he had seen a ghost, Taleno's father suddenly finds himself staring straight at *el hombre*'s face, motionless under the lights of a film camera, above the heads of the audience and the white borders of the cadets' peaked caps, *el hombre* in the centre of the platform, flanked by high-ranking officers standing to attention, their caps under their arms, and at one end Catalino Lopez, caught out by the anthem before he could reach his place.

The music stops and everybody sits down, except for Taleno's father, who remains standing, his mouth wide open, staring at *el hombre*, who is complacently chewing on his golden cigarette holder, and who, when he notices him, smiles from afar with roguish insistence as though he were an old friend for whom gestures such as this made words unnecessary—but all Taleno's father can do is to swallow and gape, until Alma Nubia tugs at his shirt sleeve: "Papa, *el hombre* is smiling at you"; only then does he manage to force himself to smile in reply, while he lets himself slowly subside into his seat, still in a daze.

Their son has mounted the platform and is shuffling a sheaf of papers—the first item on the programme is the swearing of allegiance by the 1945-1950 class of cadets, known as the "First of February" cadets in honour of *el hombre*'s birth date, as a reporter from Radio Managua informs his listeners in a whisper. The same man lifts the microphone level with Taleno's mouth, his father's chest puffs with pride, and the noise of the microphone stand being screwed tight again rumbles out over the loudspeakers and merges with his son's voice as it booms out through the room, its shrill tones echoing off the walls, to disappear altogether in an unintelligible squawk as he raises it to pronounce *el hombre*'s name, turning the shiny black peak of his cap towards the guest of honour; and when at length he falls silent, his panting is also magnified by the loudspeaker, before it gives way to applause. Then follows the distribution of diplomas, the handing out of commemorative rings, and the announcement of the prizes for the cadets— all of which go to Taleno. Every time he is called up to receive a medal, his father leaps from his seat as if he had been spurred, and will not sit down again until he has seen Taleno return to his place with the new medal pinned to his chest, staring all the while at *el hombre*'s beaming smile: "like father, like son," he must surely be thinking.

Once the ceremony is over, Taleno's father takes La Milagrosa and Alma Nubia by the arm and pushes them towards the platform, against the crush of people who are holding aloft dirty, crumpled bits of paper, or envelopes with letters asking for *el hombre*'s help before he disappears—because the leader vanishes with the same mysterious speed as he appears, but Taleno's father is not to be shaken off, and elbows his way through, quickly making his request: "Please, would you do me the honour of being photographed with my cadet here?"

There's nothing he'd like better, is the reply, and the bodyguards clear a way for them out into the yard, *el hombre* with his arms around Taleno and his father's shoulders. As they pose beside a dwarf palm, a fat, asthmatic photographer takes their photograph, his fancy shirt flapping as he pops flashbulb after flashbulb around them, leaving a trail of used bulbs on the sand. Catalino Lopez, splendid under the weight of all his badges of rank, joins the group for one picture; he jokes with Taleno's father, and slaps him on the back, then discreetly makes La Milagrosa come over too, though she protests that she is embarrassed at having her photograph taken. And the enlargement of this photo, with all of them standing grouped around *el hombre*, comes to take pride of place in his father's collection in their new house, taking over from one cut out of the *Las Americas* magazine:

CHAMPIONS OF CONTINENTAL DEMOCRACY

which shows *el hombre* together with Franklin Delano Roosevelt, both presidents wearing top hats and sipping soft drinks through straws as they ride in an open limousine.

When the group splits up, Taleno's father asks for permission to say something. He removes his hat with a flourish, as though he were ushering in one of La Milagrosa's clients in time gone by. "I entrust my cadet to your care," is all he says; then, as though what he has said would bear no denial, he thrusts Taleno towards *el hombre*, who receives him with open arms, embraces him, steps back to look him over, then embraces him again. Serious, *el hombre* confirms that he will take care of the youth, that he will take him up there to make a man of him, and that following his example the cadet will be sure to succeed. As he pronounces the words "up there", he jerks his head in the direction of the hill they can see from the barracks yard, with its two crenellated towers the colour of dirt.

Pastorita catches up with the others near the circus that has been set up on the lakeshore. They had stopped to wait when they heard him shouting at them, above the din from the band playing the last tunes before its members go into the tent for the start of the afternoon performance. When he found the door to *El Copacabana* chained up, he thought that this was where he would find them, watching the people going inside the bigtop. A few fathers hurry by, carrying their children on their shoulders or dragging them along, because the excited voice over the loudspeaker, straining to make itself heard above the noise of the band, is urging the public to take their seats. Raul mutters: it's supposed to be a performance for the womenfolk, but there isn't a single woman here.

Pastorita had been to return the accordion to the musician Traña; thankfully he had got it back in one piece. He searches in his pocket for a folded piece of paper that he hands to them: before I forget, have a look at this, though Raul will say I'm the one handing them out:

TO WHOM IT MAY CONCERN
The undersigned Jose (Chon) Taleno
by trade a wholesale merchant
residing in the city of Managua D.N.
WISHES IT MADE PUBLIC KNOWLEDGE
that he is not to be held responsible
for the actions of SANTIAGO TALENO
(former National Guard officer).
Anyone offering him food or money should
be warned that he is wasting them both;
anyone helping or sheltering him should
know they are doing me no favour, and
can expect no reward from me; he is an outlaw,
and as such the undersigned will offer him
no protection.

He's been giving them out in all the markets and main shopping streets of Managua, and in government offices, like adverts for the cinema. I was having a drink down near the Tropical pharmacy on my way back from Traña's place when he came in, handing this to all and sundry.

This fellow was in prison with me, Raul says, tapping the photograph on the piece of paper; he spent the whole time arguing with the guards, demanding that they find his son, a National Guard captain, in the presidential palace, and tell him of the way he was being treated. He also wanted to see the colonel, because his wife was in custody and so was his daughter, the one Pastorita gives mandolin lessons to at the convent school—that's right isn't it, Pastorita? She's one of the girls he's been preparing for a gala evening performance. Pastorita agrees abruptly, and pockets the paper.

The thing is, that man is down, and nobody is going to help him up. His son is involved in the rebellion, so he's been knocked off his perch as the king of San Miguel market that he held thanks to the colonel, Chepito says, coming back with some packets of peanuts. He could never have dreamt that the National Guard would come one night, cart him off and throw him in jail, or that with his house unguarded people would break in under cover of darkness and steal everything, dragging the cane chairs, carpets, saints' statues, buckets, clothes, and blankets out into the street. He wrote to complain about it to the colonel, but he refuses to reply or to see him. "What, have you been back to see the colonel already, Chepito?" Raul looks at him in amazement. "Well, yes, I went to get my pay," Chepito replies, spitting out peanut shells.

Chepito knows Taleno's father's story pretty well, because when he first got taken up by the colonel more than ten years previously Chepito was already doing odd jobs in the barracks; he'll tell them all about it some other time. "No, come on, tell us now," Raul insists, clutching his arm: Pastorita would love to hear his father-in-law's life story. Embarrassed, Pastorita mumbles what father-in-law? as though he hasn't understood what Raul meant.

Taleno's father's friendship with the colonel all started one day when he was brought in for practising medicine illegally: he had given an old woman over in San Judas an injection, and she fell to the floor unconscious, before he could even pull the needle out of her arm. When nothing worked to bring the woman round, they called the police, who hauled him off to the Hormiguero jail. By the time they reached the prison gate there was a crowd of curious onlookers following them. They decided to keep him in jail as long as the woman remained in a coma; three days went by without her regaining consciousness; her relatives laid siege to the prison, threatening to kill him on the spot if he were released.

Then the colonel took a hand in the affair. He had all the woman's relatives taken into custody so that Taleno's father could get home safely, and warned them that if anything happened to him he would hold them personally responsible. The colonel got on well with him, probably because he was such a smooth talker—at any rate, he put him in charge of the political intrigues in the market, responsible for the porters and stallholders who went out to break up demonstrations; all their clubs and whips and so on were in his keeping. He rose to the top like froth, though before that he had failed at everything he had turned his hand to; he himself told the colonel all he had got up to in his life: he had even been a trader in monkeys.

It seems that once, in San Rafael del Norte, he had convinced the fishermen to leave their nets and become monkey catchers, because he had heard that a cargo boat, the *Vespa*, was travelling down the Mosquito Coast buying monkeys wholesale in order to ship them up to New Orleans, where the gringos cut their testicles off in laboratories. Raul butts in that it's true, they use monkey balls for preparing injections that make those that can't manage it virile again.

He had calculated that at two testicles per monkey they could make a fortune, and the quayside was soon full of cages just waiting for the ship to arrive; then he went on to tell the fishermen how he was going to invest what he made from the first sales. That's what amused the colonel so much, because he planned to set up a scientific monkey breeding farm, to fence off a part of the jungle in order to make a kind of monkey ranch where he could castrate them on the spot with special appliances so that he would only have to export their balls to the United States. I was sweeping out the colonel's office at the time, that's how I heard him describe his brilliant scheme, talking enthusiastically across the desk like he was still sitting among the fishermen.

The news spread all along the coast, and people appeared in droves in San Rafael del Norte with cages full of monkeys—so many that soon there was no more room on the quayside, and every night the air was filled with their chattering. Then one day while they were all sitting talking, waiting for the boat to turn up, his elder son Trinidad suddenly asked the hunters what would happen if all the monkeys were in fact females; his father told him off for being so impertinent, but thinking about it decided to go and check the cages anyway. Sure enough, it turned out that most of them were females.

There was nothing else to do but to let them go, so they kicked open all the cages. They refused to be disheartened though, and set off into the jungle once more to gather more specimens, this time making sure they checked between the legs before they caged them. At that point, still leaning on my broom, I plucked up courage to ask what had happened to the *Vespa* in the end; the colonel wasn't pleased that I had interrupted like that, but he did want to know the answer as well—and so too did Pastorita and Raul: did the boat eventually arrive? It did arrive from Tela, loaded to the gunwhales with monkeys that they had already bought at Puerto Barrios in Belize. They did not need any more balls, so the ship continued on its way without even stopping; all they ever saw was a distant glimpse of its smoke.

They can hear the muffled sound of music from within the circus tent, and some ripples of applause, but can see only a few shadows pressed against the canvas on the benches inside. Firuliche's not going to eat tonight, Pastorita says as they move on, leaving the circus behind them. They say he forced the nuns to accept his daughter in the convent school, using the colonel's influence; then he remembers he shouldn't have mentioned the girl, because Raul is bound to start teasing him again, so he looks at the ground to avoid meeting his gaze.

No, Chepito says, the colonel could not do anything for him. "Only *el hombre* can help you," he had told Taleno's father, and fixed him an appointment to see him. After waiting for several days, *el hombre* at last agreed to see him, and he was able to pour out his complaint that the mother superior had not even deigned to receive him in private but in the convent reception room in front of a crowd of parents who pretended they were paying no attention but looked down their noses at him, and she had mortally offended him by refusing to accept his daughter. Her name is Alma Nubia isn't it, Pastorita? He had wanted to take the nun down a peg or two after the insult and, pulling out a wad of new banknotes, he began to fan himself with them as a challenge to her. Was it a question of money? But the foreign nun's reasons were very different: the school would not have children born out of wedlock at any price. Was that right? Only then, after he had finished explaining the whole thing, did he sit down opposite *el hombre*. *El hombre* thumped the desk indignantly, so violently that he sent all the papers on it flying: of course it wasn't right. He called in his private secretary and dictated a letter: dear reverend mother so and so, yours with all respect and so on, then signed it himself and gave it to him personally, saying goodbye at the door with a friendly embrace: who did those nuns think they were, and if the letter didn't do the trick, he was to come back and tell him, they had better heed it. By the time he left the presidential palace night had fallen, but he went there and then to find the colonel and tell him all that had happened, how he had spent so much time talking all alone with *el hombre*, while outside elegant ministers, their briefcases crammed with official documents, were forced to wait, some parliamentarians as well, and estate managers, commissions come to ask for liquor for their village celebrations, for money for local roads or for the repair of a church wall, even a children's baseball team which had come to request bats and gloves from him; several of the boys had fallen asleep on a sofa, to the dismay of the priest in charge. Anyway, he did manage to get his daughter into the school, she'll soon be finishing.

What I was going to say, Pastorita chimes in as he takes the piece of paper out of his pocket again, is that I didn't know that Captain Taleno had escaped, I thought he was still a prisoner. By now they have reached the gangway to the club, and Chepito goes on ahead to undo the chain: he flew out of a window in the presidential palace, down the cliff by the lake. They spent a whole day searching for his body, they couldn't believe anyone could survive such a fall. A priest hid him—do you know the one I mean? He runs the lovers' hotel up on Ticomo Hill. He's been put under house arrest, but he couldn't care less so long as they don't close his business down.

Both Taleno and Jilguero must be well away by now, Raul says, leaning over the guardrail and staring down at the calm grey lake, which is no longer reflecting the sun's rays. That's strange, he says eventually, the middle of April and the sky is overcast.

They have woken to another morning of mist, curled up together against the cold of the damp dawn, and from the open ground on the mountainside that has been their camp since the previous afternoon, all they can make out are the shadows of the moss-covered rocks that border the ravine in front of them, and lower down on the left, a blur of mamey bushes with a hut behind them where Turco has just gone in search of food. Jilguero looks for the almost empty box of matches, and is about to try to start a fire with the wet twigs that Raul has stripped of their bark, when they spot Turco running up across the clear ground. He is dragging another man along roughly, and waves at them with the rifle in his other hand. Jumping up, they grab their own weapons when they hear shots coming from down the slope. Turco stops in his tracks, hesitates, then lets his captive go and dives into the undergrowth, catching up with them after they have followed his example and are climbing up through the trees, which gradually thin out; once again the horseman digs his spurs into the horse's flanks, while somewhere behind him lies his three-cornered hat, trampled by the hooves of his pursuers' horses; his green tunic is in tatters by now, but still he shakes his fist aloft as he did before, immobile on the bevelled glass front of the black cabinet, like a confessional with its carved plumes and garlands of roses, during the days when his sick father re-opened the doors of his pharmacy.

With his grandfather's campaign long since forgotten, the only reminders were the muddied electoral leaflets blown into the gutters of the street, empty now of demonstrators or cries of down with the dictatorship! the side-street wind as always sweeping dust, seeds, bits of vegetation into the shops and the deserted ironmongers, with their bales of cloth and cotton prints, rolls of barbed wire, tin pails, and shop-soiled stock laid out on the pavements, the rubbish yellowing and rotting in the deep ruts left by the oxcart wheels or clogging up the drains of the corner laundries, where mosquitos started to swarm. After the rainy season, clumps of beans sprouted in the gutters, dropped there from sacks being hauled to market: the rain so hard that it dug away the earth and exposed the foundations of the high pavements; weeds pushed furiously against the door frames, and raised their bushy tips among the roof tiles; the walls too were falling into decay—in the silence of the night they would hear pieces crumbling off that littered the pavements each morning; the only people in the street were women selling vegetables from door to door in their sing-song, supplicating voices, or people who had ridden into town and would rein to a halt outside the pharmacy to ask for a remedy without dismounting.

In that period of his illness, when the faint call reached him in his room at the back of the building, his father would drag himself to his feet with the aid of a chair, lean heavily on the preparation bench, then appear between the glass cabinets, his face a mass of purple blotches from his jaw down to his collar. He would stagger forward clutching his baggy, beltless trousers across the dirt of the floor flattened hard by his bare feet, to hand over the medicine or tell the customer that there wasn't any, because by now there was little left in the pots and drawers where he kept his enemas, lengths of rubber tubing, bottles of juniper oil, dried sprigs of borage, ammonia, and marine sponges.

After the customer had gone his way, he would return to the darkness of the dispensary, where the air was thick with the smell of iodine and burnt magnesium, on the wall the unframed, cobweb-covered portrait of Melvin Jones that he had kept with him ever since the time soon after his marriage that, following a prolonged exchange of letters with the main office in Chicago, he had set up a branch of the Lions Club in Masaya. Alone once more, he would return to his passionate pursuit of drinking cheap rum, which he himself went out to buy at the liquor store. Muttering an inaudible "Here's to you", he would down the contents of the thick tumbler in one rapid movement, then slam the empty glass down on the table with a despairing gesture, drawing the back of his hand across his smarting mouth. Then he would sit in silence for a while staring at the bottle, within whose dim transparency the remaining liquid gradually resettled. His elbows spread wide on the table, his eyes gleaming blearily behind the metal-framed bifocals, he would nod, listening attentively but cordially to the sounds of a conversation that came to him from a group of guests who were, like him, at death's door; drinking as he imagined real men did, facing up to the abominable idea of death, or the stabbing pains in his jaw, with a wry smile, grasping the glass in his fist as he imagined they must do in bars he had never entered, either in his days as a surly student in Leon, or since then, married to his carnival queen. His only experience of the social world were the Lions Club charity dances that he organised in spite of endless wrangling with the other members of the committee, dances which always seemed to be held on rainy nights, lit by strings of grimy lamps, in the rooms of the town hall. Even then, he stayed at the door to take the money from the non-members, the sound of sad waltzes seeping out to him as he counted the takings, the mole on his left cheek still bleeding from a cut he had given himself while shaving, the lapels of his striped suit doused in lavender water, the same he sold by the ounce to the barbershops.

Sometimes, their mother would push Carlos or him to go to try and remove the bottle from their father stealthily, but neither of them dared go near him; they could only stare at him from a safe distance, as though he had ceased to be real, immersed in his fate as in the depths of a pond, his bald head caught in the bright rays of sunlight that filtered down through a gap in the roof tiles. Some months later, one stormy November, it was the hand of the father superior of the primary school in Diriamba where their mother had sent them, desperate to get them away from the sight of their father's eery last days, that shook them awake in their beds, side-by-side in the dormitory, a place invaded at night by the croaking of frogs and the endless dripping of water into buckets in the corners of the room. His cassock only half-buttoned, his face still puffy with sleep, the priest seized them by the scruff of their necks as though they were to be punished, then forced them to kneel down to pray on the freezing floor, not telling them until they had completed their prayer of the telephone call from Masaya in the middle of the night to inform them of their father's death.

A customer, curious when nobody answered his call in the deserted pharmacy, had slipped cautiously into the dispensary and discovered him sitting in his usual position at the preparation bench, head cocked listening as though the conversation of the guests had not yet finished, his crumpled clothes reeking of cheap alcohol, as did his whole body for hours after his death, his bare feet seeming outsized after months without the restraint of shoes planted firmly on the dirt floor.

Seated opposite each other in the hazy dawn light on the dark cane benches of the first class carriage, he and his brother passed through the stations of the south, on their way back to Masaya to attend their father's funeral. They wore the navy-blue school uniforms they had fumbled to put on in the school cloakroom, their shoes hastily polished over layers of mud. The zeppelin-shaped coffin was already out in the street by the time they arrived, so they fell in behind it, surrounded by solicitous distant relatives from other towns who tried their best to offer them a considerate, useless protection.

For the rest of that school year they stayed at home to help their mother look after the less and less busy pharmacy, opening the doors in the mornings and conveying the occasional client's requests to her in the bedroom, since she knew by heart where everything was on the shelves. One day in November following the funeral, with the rain pouring down outside and the two of them thumbing through a comic on the top of the counter, a horse and carriage with its licence number gaudily painted on the rear of the cab got stuck in the mud outside their window. The coachman stood up on his seat to whip the pair of horses to pull the carriage out of the churned up mud while his two passengers, frightened by the dangerous angle the carriage was leaning at, were trying apprehensively to get out, though they were not keen to step down into so much water. Finally, the driver succeeded in his manoeuver, and pulled the horses sideways up onto the pavement outside the pharmacy so that the two men could get out protected by the house's wide eaves, so close to the front door that even though they were still in the carriage they seemed to be right inside the house.

The two men came in, shaking the water from their hats. Jostling their briefcases under their arms, they asked to see his mother, and he went to fetch her, calling her name as he walked from room to room. He finally found her sitting in the dark dining room at the far end of the narrow flooded yard; even before he pushed open the door, he could hear her sobs above the hissing of the rain, before he caught sight of her thin body dressed in mourning, her head between her hands on the table where the cold remains of their lunch lay next to the breakfast coffee cups with their dark iodine-coloured dregs, dried spirals of orange peel, the round biscuit barrel with hardened yellow sugar on its rim. He paused with his hand on the damp door knob to look at the dining room's wooden walls, scored with decorations of bunches of flowers, the dining room where for years his father had chewed the gristle of the chunks of fatty meat from his steaming soup with caustic enjoyment, while he launched his vituperative attacks, sometimes even in rhyme, on victims chosen at random according to his mood; behind his chair at the head of the table the wine-coloured sideboard in which their mother kept what remained of the china services they had received as belated wedding presents, their first communion candles, the Christmas decorations. Over the sideboard hung a lithograph of a group of languid, smiling odalisks who lifted their veils as they danced beneath the evening sky of a far-off land, and in the distance, beyond Moorish arcades, blue hills; hills that, whenever he heard his mother crying, as so often before, he wanted to know what country they might be part of.

Carlos was still poring over the comic, ignoring the men who were talking in bored undertones, and when he raised his eyes he noticed Jilguero coming back from the depths of the house; grim-faced, his clenched fists barely visible under the cuffs of his starched shirt, the same one he had worn for the funeral, he crept up behind them and began to shout at them to get out of the house at once. It took them a moment to realise where exactly the shouting was coming from, then they turned, puzzled, to face him, bending forwards to try to understand the gabbling flow of words he was pouring out in his childish voice, but he was already upon them, pushing violently at their legs, leaving the mark of his open palms on their wet white trousers, trying his puny best to get them out of the house. They brushed him aside, and seemed to be trying to push their way further into the house, calling out in alarm to their mother, but now Carlos emerged from behind the counter and joined in the struggle. Thieves! Thieves! he was shouting, though as yet he had no idea why, even if his voice conveyed the same angry, tearful despair at his younger brother's. When the older of the two men, finding himself hemmed in, put his briefcase down on a cabinet and made as if to take off his belt to thrash them, the boys began to kick out at him furiously, and little by little the two men were forced to retreat to the street door, finding it impossible to protect their knees against the sharp kicks from the boys' school boots. They hesitated on the doorstep for a moment, attempting to push their way back into the house, because the rain outside was coming down even more heavily and stinging their faces, but the brothers blocked their path, one of them brandishing the wooden plank used to bar the door, the other a chair, and so the two men found themselves obliged to climb down from the pavement into the flooded street, the brims of their hats bent double with the force of the downpour. They lifted their trouser legs like petticoats and splashed through the mud in search of the carriage, which had moved on to find shelter from the storm.

Alone in the shop again, they came across the briefcase that one of the men had left on a cabinet in his flight. Without a word to each other, they undid the straps and pulled out the sheaves of papers stitched together with thread, then took them to the door.

From under the eaves, at the precise spot where the torrent of rain was at its heaviest, they ripped apart the bundles of papers with their official stamps and the cramped writing of the courts, violet lines which as the rain hit them exploded into pale blue corollas, then wrinkled into dark brown spidery remains, as if the rain had burned them. They threw the papers out into the street, where the gushing stream of water quickly carried them away. Last of all they hurled the briefcase after them. It sailed through the air, splashed into the water, whirled round a few times, then disappeared. Satisfied, they shut the door behind them, then ran to tell their mother she could stop crying, that now nobody would be able to take El Corozo in Catarina from her, the farm she had inherited from her father, all they had left apart from the ramshackle shelves of the dispensary.

The two men returned soon afterwards, but this time Catalino Lopez was with them. The soldiers beat and beat on the door with their rifle butts, and when Jilguero's mother finally opened it, they burst in, weapons at the ready. The commanding officer, who remained sitting in the front of his jeep, nodded his head in greeting when he saw her appear. They were dragged out into the street flanked by guards, and forced to walk over to the jeep with their hands in the air. The officer caught hold of their wrists and began to twist them fiercely, paying no attention to their mother who, held back at the door, was shouting for her neighbours to come to her aid. He wanted to know where the briefcase with the legal documents was.

Suddenly in the confusion of shouts and orders the officer started back, holding up his bitten hand. Jilguero ran off, slipping past the lunging soldiers who tried to stop him, and sprinted down the street through the easing rain, shaking his fist at them defiantly.

When he reached the church at the bottom of the street, he slowed down, climbed its steps, and went in through the half-open main door. In the lonely interior lit only by spermwax candles slowly burning down in front of the shrouded saints' statues, he glimpsed the bottom of a spiral staircase on his left. He began to climb it stealthily, his hand groping up the iron handrail, until he reached a platform of creaking boards where, crawling among music stands, he finally found refuge behind a harmonium. From there he heard the soldiers as they stumbled over the benches down below, and their questions to the sacristan; then later the priest, his voice booming as he came down from the high altar to order them out of the church. When at last night fell and the doors of the church were shut and everything was silent, the pale blue curtains no longer flapping against the worm-eaten columns of the nave, the horseman clasped his three-cornered hat to his chest and, exhausted by the chase, fell asleep on the floor of the choir full of bats, which flew blindly against the bare cane slats of the churchroof.

PART TWO

How many have fallen there!
They stumble all night over bones of the dead,
And feel they know not what but care,
And wish to lead others, when they should be led.

William Blake, "The Voice of the Ancient Bard"

CHAPTER 6

They have just passed the junction to La Paz Centre when the boy starts banging on the roof of the cabin once more to tell them that the coffin has broken free from its ropes again. The driver's face wrinkles with disgust as he brakes sharply to the side of the road in a cloud of chalky dust. They climb down, their shoes sinking into the gravel; Bolivar walks in silence behind the short stocky driver, who sways bowlegged in his walk, cursing the ropes they sold him in Guatemala for not being good enough to tie up a dog with. They scramble up onto the back of the truck, where they have to repeat the chore of securing the coffin, tying the ropes as best they can through the side rails, but less tightly now that there are only a few kilometres of their journey left. Then they throw the tarpaulin back over it, weighting it with stones so that the wind will not lift the canvas.

The clouds of white dust that mark the passage of their truck die down as they speed into the distance along the highway cut through a plain of calabashes and sparta-grass. They are the only travellers in this April night, faintly lit by the pale reddish light of a summer moon that shines on fields with bare stalks and dusty clumps of vegetation on the parched earth of the already harvested cotton fields. Further off to the west, salt pans also gleam white, as does a river where only the occasional glint of water shows among the boulders, to disappear completely beneath the scaffolding of a bridge under construction.

A few yards further on they begin a swaying, curiously balanced descent down a detour overgrown with branches that sweep against their windshield, writhing and scraping against the sides of the truck as it pushes its way through. Finally it breaks free and they cross the river, hardly raising a wave, in the shadow of the bridge that was swept away in the October floods. They can make out the remains of its metal girders in the moonlight behind the timber props. With a hissing growl of the engine, they complete the detour and pull out once more onto the last stretch of the highway. Its asphalt leads straight out in front of them for some distance before curving gently down through an avenue of mango trees, their shiny leaves quivering in secret agitation.

The steady hum of the tyres running freely over the asphalt brings him a great release of tension, as though now all he had to do was relax after the suffocating miles of his journey to Guatemala and back, on the way there with the empty truck, carrying the dead body on the return, since the moment before dawn five days earlier when they had loaded up the coffin in the small yard at the back of the Roosevelt Hospital mortuary.

Since then there has been nothing but delays, and forms to fill in all along the way. It was no simple matter to cross frontiers with a corpse, to drive right across El Salvador, climbing hills and having to make endless detours, and then on to Honduras, where the road was so little used that grass grew between the cracks, and rainclouds hung over the pine-covered hillsides though it never actually rained, then once again they were driving with the sun's glare reflecting up at them off the road surface, the truck sides rattling, and thuds as stones thrown up by the wheels struck the bottom of the cabin. Their shoulders burnt against the sweaty leather of the seat, and the dust gradually built up on his eyebrows and shoes; and in the most desolate part of the route, the last time close to Trinidad, in

Nicaragua by this time, they had to stop and tie the coffin in place after the ropes had come loose and it slid over slowly until it was bumping against one of the sides of the truck. It was then that the driver's son, sitting up on the back with the coffin, would beat with his fists on the cabin roof, or poke his head in at one of the windows, balanced like a tightrope walker, his hair streaming in the wind, waving at them frantically to stop.

Now that the journey is finally almost over, he leans his head back against the worn rest, and gradually dozes off from the insistent pressure of his tiredness, his grit-filled eyes pricking from lack of sleep, a dull, throbbing pain in his side. The truck rolls smoothly along, leaving the cotton fields behind them, and beyond a line of trees a tractor pulled up outside a lean-to, which is full of barrels and piles of wood. Half hidden by the branches along the roadsides are hoardings lit by fluorescent strips that advertise fertilisers; the night air that sweeps through the driving compartment brings him the warm salty smell of the sea, mixed with the stench of cattle devoured by vultures in the distant heat, but also that of ripe fruit, of insecticide left hanging in the air by the crop dusters.

For two days they kept him waiting at the Espino Negro border post, refusing to let him through until they received the go-ahead from Nicaragua. The immigration official, sitting with his feet up on a desk empty of papers, and for decoration only a glass-framed, fly-speckled portrait of *el hombre* standing between his two seated sons, tossed him back the pass issued by the Nicaraguan Consul in Guatemala with a gesture of offhand arrogance. "All that matters here are the orders *el hombre*'s son gives."

Bolivar put the pass away, and politely, as if he really needed help, asked the official what he should do. "That's for you to decide. If you want, you can go to Managua to sort it out, or you can send a telegram from here. All I know is that until I get my instructions from above, your father can't go through." With that he stood up, because from one of the wooden huts on the other side of the road they were shouting for him to come and get his breakfast. Which of the two sons should he address the telegram to? The official turned towards him and squeezed an imaginary trigger: "To the one who has this. To the master of the empty barrels."

So he went over to the shack which served as the telegraph office at the border post, and wrote out telegram number 22:

> EARNEST REQUEST MY SAKE AND FAMILY
> PERMISSION ENTER COUNTRY BODY FATHER
> EX-GUARD OFFICER ALBERTO LARIOS STOP
> THANKS ADVANCE STOP

Shooing hens off the transmission desk, the telegraph operator took the form and began to read it without showing the slightest interest, counting the number of words with a pencil. When he read the name though, he looked up at Bolivar in astonishment, stammering the rest of the message out loud. Even before he had finished he carried the cable over to the doorway and stared at the truck.

"So he's back at last," he said, shaking his head as he returned behind the counter. He spread the telegram out under a glass insulator and sat down again in his swivel chair, sprawling with his arms across its back. "I was stationed in the Campo de Marte as an auxiliary telegraph operator—that's how I got to know your father. I was there when he made his way to the top, I saw him enjoy his years of glory as *el hombre*'s righthand man, I saw him in disgrace." The wind sweeping in from the yard lifted the telegram under the insulator. "I used to send his verses by telegraph to a girlfriend of his, Aurorita Aguilar, in Leon—I reckon she must be your mother." The old man stood up reluctantly, for a moment looked as though he was about to smile, but then changed his mind and instead took him solemnly by the arm. "Don't pin your hopes too high. They won't let a dead man like him through."

Now, as he lets his head loll back on the seat rest, he remembers what he had decided at that moment. He would wait twenty-four hours and not a moment longer; if there was no reply by that time, he would take the body back to San Marcos de Colon, the nearest town to the border on the Honduran side, and would bury his father there. In two or three years maybe things would have changed, and they could exhume what was left of him, if that was what she wanted. It made no difference anyway.

If that was what she, his mother, wanted. Yet he knew that she would not accept things so easily, would not accept the fact that he had returned with an empty truck, to tell her that he had left the body in a foreign country, because that would have been tantamount to insulting her, showing that her husband had never, either in life or in death, been able to get beyond the barrier.

Very early one Monday morning nearly two weeks previously the cotton gin operator had waked him in his bunk in the open shed where he slept, separated from the bales of cotton by a screen stuffed with newspapers. His mother was outside asking for him. Still only half awake after spending the whole night working in the weighing room, he put his trousers on and went out, barefoot and shirtless, into the yard. She was standing there, wrapped in a black shawl and a black mourning dress, which had bits of cotton fluff from the machine caught in it. The noise drowned out what she was trying to tell him, but it seemed that she was not trying particularly hard to make herself heard, nor did he step down from the paved floor of the shed so as to avoid treading in the gravel with his bare feet. Then for a moment the machine stopped, and together with the other sounds that reappeared on the morning air —whistles, shouted orders, a stream of water hitting the bottom of a bucket—he could make out what she was saying to him: "The news is that he has died in Guatemala."

Though her face showed grief, it also contained a kind of hidden satisfaction, as if there was bound to be some pride as well as sadness in the news she was bringing. He squinted to protect his eyes from the cotton fluff that was blowing thickly all around them, and it was perhaps only then that he finally woke up, for when he opened them fully once more, she was still standing there, looking at him. "And he always wanted to come back to Nicaragua, alive or dead."

He put his hand into one of his trouser pockets to scratch the mosquito bites on his leg through a hole, and it was only after he had managed to ease the pain, only after feeling the burns left by his fingernails on the skin, that he replied unenthusiastically that there was no way the government would allow the funeral, there were all kinds of reasons against it. She pursed her lips sternly as she caught one of the ends of her shawl and tossed it back over her shoulder. "This is his country and this is where he will be buried, we'll see whether they will allow it or not," she said, raising her voice and lifting her head defiantly, perhaps even considering shouting, because she glanced around the yard to see if anybody was listening, but changed her mind when she realised nobody was paying her the slightest attention.

He had continued to raise objections in an unemotional monotone, though by now he knew it would be impossible to convince her. Where would they get the money from? It cost a fortune to bring a dead body all that way; but his mother, as though she had been expecting that line of argument, triumphantly dipped her hand into a paper bag she was carrying and held him out a bundle of notes. "Here you are. This was for the flour, but I've arranged to get it on credit this month. So now, get a move on and find out how you're going to get there"; the banknotes smelling of yeast spread out in her hand, ingrained with white from always being in the dough.

He left the telegraph office, hearing how behind him the old man had begun to tap out the message on his Morse key. The sound echoed after him through the silence of the shabby buildings until he had almost reached the spot where they had left the truck, in the shade of some guanacastes, on the far side of the barrier. There was no news from Managua for the rest of that day, so they got ready for sleep without hope of receiving permission to enter the country. The driver and his son slept up on the back of the truck alongside the tarpaulin covering the coffin, while he stretched out along the cabin seat, his legs dangling out on one side, and with both doors wide open. When day dawned and they went off to look for something for breakfast at one of the stalls, the driver took him to one side surreptitiously, despite the fact that they were the only people awake at that hour, and told him sadly that there was a distinct smell of decomposition coming from the coffin.

Bolivar waited until it was eight o'clock, then went to find the official to give him this latest bit of news, that the body could not stand any further delays. It was Sunday however, and the office was closed—all the passports and truck manifests were being taken to the official in bed by a soldier, who agreed to take his message with the others. "If it stinks, lime should do the trick," he heard shouted from inside the room, before the official turned his radio up again.

They managed to get a sack of lime in San Marcos de Colon, and were in time to sprinkle the body with it before sunrise, though they were forced to perform the gruesome task in front of the other travellers. It soon became obvious that the beginnings of the stench had been calmed, and so little by little Sunday passed. In the afternoon, the Honduran border officials crossed over to play cards with their Nicaraguan colleagues in the closed office; all that could be heard was the occasional shout when somebody won his bet. When the lights in the hut came on for a second evening, he can recall that he told himself: as soon as it gets light tomorrow I am definitely taking him back to San Marcos de Colon, he won't last another day.

Shortly afterwards though, the official appeared in the doorway, interrupting his deal of the cards, and waved a piece of paper at Bolivar to come over; he was holding a bottle of beer in his other hand which, as Bolivar came near, he finished off and threw out onto the road. "I've received permission for your father to come through. But on one condition: on no account must his funeral be used to stir up trouble"; he tapped the telegram: "and above all, no speeches." So then they both went inside and the official took out of his typewriter the form on which he listed all the people entering Nicaragua and began to type the sheet of paper Bolivar had to sign promising that the funeral would be held in silence, just as a joyful shout went up from the nearby card players.

He can imagine her standing at the door of the bakery waiting for his truck to arrive, the bakery which in defiance she had called La Opositora ever since the day her husband had fled into exile, as he sits watching hordes of insects flying into the beam of the headlights, to be crushed against the windshield, staining it with a thick yellowy liquid that drips down the glass.

The fluorescent light in the ceiling must have been out of use for a long time because nothing happens when Taleno flicks the switch on, but the light of the moon is streaming in through a skylight high up on the wall, so by its faint reddish glow on the floor tiles he stands with his back pressed against the door, trying to work out what is in front of him. Closest to his feet he can make out some tailors' dummies fallen on the floor, the bald heads glinting with the same red gleam. As he edges into the room, he stumbles against a pine chest full of platinum wigs and Roman helmets; he can just make out in a glass cabinet a jumble of embroidered frock-coats and plumed hats. Imitation shields lie propped against the walls, and bundles of wooden spears stand in the corners; the whole room is a confused heap of objects that give off an insipid smell of glued cardboard and motheaten silk. When at last he has managed to grope his way through to the only seat, a rickety throne covered in crimson velvet which creaks every time he shifts around to make himself comfortable, he cannot help trying to remember where he has seen all this before: the throne, the fancy dress costumes; but all that comes to his mind are vague nocturnal images of his childhood in Managua—his father, as always, dragging him along.

He spends the night awake on the throne, and falls asleep only after daybreak, to be awakened by the rattle of tanks setting off downhill, trucks starting up, people running, shouted commands. He crawls over to the door and presses his ear against it, but the noises have already died away, and all he can hear are the footsteps of the guard outside the room. Some time later, around mid-day, he hears Mustangs roar over the lake flying south, but that is all. There are no sounds of battle, not a single shot as his wristwatch shows two in the afternoon, and he is filled with an overwhelming sense of loneliness because he loses all hope and realises not only has he been captured but that the whole attempt has failed.

It is dark once more in the room when he hears the key turn in the lock. He is taken down a path bordered by laurels towards the presidential garages hidden behind the branches. They make him stoop to pass through a narrow door cut in the lifting front of the garage; once inside, it is some while before he picks out the colonel between the bulky shadows of two black armour-plated Cadillacs.

Sitting on a three-legged stool in the light of a bulb hanging close by his head, he is waiting for him with a sleepy, bored expression on his face. His heavy body is thrust forward, his arms dangling between his legs and his hands almost touching the floor as he slowly spins a cap round in his fingers. As though Taleno's arrival were a tiresome disturbance, he merely glances at him out of the corner of his eye, and the dull look on his face gives Taleno the impression more of disappointment than of hatred, as he points his chin towards him and orders them to strip him.

He can hear the wind gusting over the corrugated iron roof as a hand reaching out from the darkness beyond the circle of light rips off the golden buttons of his dress uniform. They had captured him at the end of a credential presentation in the palace state rooms, surrounding him and disarming him all of a sudden, while *el hombre*, almost as if he were fleeing him, had walked off down the corridor with echoing steps and disappeared behind a slamming door. Someone is still struggling to pull his coat off from behind, so he lets his arms go limp; he kicks his legs to step out of his trousers, while they tie his arms behind his back, so fiercely that the cord bites into the skin of his wrists. Now that he is completely naked, his uniform and all its trappings on the floor at his feet, they push him forward to face the colonel again and he, under the hot light from the bulb, moistens his lips and asks him, with the monotonous voice of somebody having to repeat himself for the thousandth time, to confess, to confess everything that he had to do with the plot.

Taleno, finding it hard to breathe in the heat of the night in the closed space of the garage, says nothing; soaked in sweat that flows down the middle of his back, drenching the inside of his thighs, and running stickily down his forearms pinioned to his sides by the thongs at his wrists, he gives no answer. After a while, the colonel turns to face him fully and looks at him pityingly, then they push him through another door, this one leading into an enclosed garden with a well used for watering plants in the centre, beneath laurel trees. A guard who pushed him through the door whistles, and one of the dark figures standing by the well detaches himself from the group and comes quickly over to him, the gravel of the path crunching beneath his feet. Taleno notices the triangular gleam of his cap badge, and the flash of his teeth beneath the clipped moustache; he hears a familiar laugh and can imagine the man's grinning face: "What are you doing naked at this time of night?" the lieutenant chuckles as he comes over.

He takes him by the arm almost playfully, and goes on laughing as he leads him to the wall, where three others are waiting, soldiers stripped to the waist and with their trouser legs rolled up. The officer lifts one foot on to the edge of the well and carefully folds up his twill khaki trouser leg to fasten the lace of his shiny shoe, the moonlight which is glimmering through the foliage catching the bald spot on his shaven head when he bends down, and when he stands upright again, dancing on his face, from which all trace of amusement has now vanished. He takes his foot from the well-rim, shakes out his trouser leg with great care, then walks slowly round behind Taleno, who can feel the distasteful sensation of his toothpaste-scented breath on the back of his neck, where the sweat has already turned chill. He too urges him to confess. "Tell me everything, or I'm going to have to wring it out of you."

Naked, defenceless in this dry, hostile April night, Taleno looks down at the shapes of his bare feet on the wet tiles and suddenly his mind fills with the tranquil homely scent of freshly cut jasmine flowers one afternoon in a courtyard somewhere, a moment's enchantment that is broken when a hand seizes his hair to force his head down. They lift him and carry him bodily over to the well then, holding on to his feet, they plunge him headfirst into the black waters, his fall shattering the bright constellation of stars reflected on its surface. His body thrashes as he tries to push back and up out of the warm, chlorinated water that first streams across his face, then swirls cold around him in choking veils as he writhes to free himself, his bursting lungs beating against his aching, tormented ribs, desperately trying to push with his legs so that he can get his head back up out of the water—but each time he bangs against an iron grille dropped level with the surface, and he is forced down again into the depths, his eardrums splitting from a deafening drilling noise.

Just as he is about to succumb, the whole of his insides seeming to lose their weight and float free within him, the swirling waters of the well brighten, and to the sound of out-of-tune trumpets blaring out on dark street corners a cohort of Roman soldiers lined up four abreast marches past: docile and embarrassed looking, the country militia who have been taken from their barracks and forced to parade like this drag their sandalled feet through the foul-smelling streets round the markets of Managua, the sweat dripping in white streaks from their made-up faces. They trudge along weighed down with their tufted panaches, while behind their standards and spears other groups of conscripts follow, divided according to their costumes: bewigged courtiers, musketeers with their plumed hats, pages in embroidered livery, heralds and flag-bearers, all escorting a carriage that makes its way to the Metropolitan Cathedral in the midst of smoke from the torches carried in the calloused hands of the newest recruits, got up in the red livery of footmen. Inside the cathedral, beneath the cupola of the high altar glittering with lamps, the old archbishop in his decrepit robes totters over to the throne bearing a crown in his raised hands and places it on the brow of a young girl, the same one who appears on the one cordoba note, her head adorned with an Indian princess's feather. The bells peal out, a cannon salutes in the distance, and Taleno's father kneels among the congregation in the side aisle, and forces him down too.

He comes round in a pool of water on the rough cement surround of the well, twists his head to one side and vomits a mixture of water and bitter bile. The colonel's boots squeak as he walks over from the garage, and he catches sight of the wide bottoms of his stiff khaki trousers as he sits down next to him on his stool. He prods his ribs with the tip of his boot. "Can we have our little talk now, Captain?"

He is almost lifeless as they haul him up by the armpits, but he overcomes his nausea and manages to stand unaided in front of the colonel, who is now searching for something in one of his shirt pockets, his chin tucked down onto his chest in such a way that his jowls fold out more than ever. Eventually he pulls out what must be a photograph, because there is a glint of light from it when the other man goes over diligently to take it from him and push it under Taleno's nose. He lights it from above with a pocket flashlight, and smiles at him in all innocence, as though nothing had happened, although his uniform is streaked with dark patches of water. The colonel presses his weary eyeballs with his thumbs. Does he recognise this person? The flashlight reveals the youthful but mature face of Carlos Rosales, with his bushy eyebrows joining across the top of his nose, his prominent cheek bones, putting on a relaxed smile as he sits in the typical hasty but casual pose of a passport photograph, his hair quickly smoothed down with his fingers, his shirt open at the neck over the lapels of a fashionable jacket. Taleno shakes his head, and as he does so, water from his hair splashes onto the photograph, which the man dries before snapping off his light. Dispirited, the colonel sits for a moment in silence, beating his fist into the palm of his hand. "Give the captain another dip for me, let's see if that refreshes his memory," he says as he heads back to the garage, an attendant trotting after him with the stool.

It is then, or during one of the endless number of times that this scene is repeated in the course of the night, that the other man, squatting down behind him to tighten the ropes, reproaches him sarcastically for keeping them up. How long are they all going to have to stay there getting wet like this? At length he is satisfied the knots are tight again, and hands over the ends of the ropes to the soldiers, so that they can haul him up out of the water at the very last moment before he drowns. Suddenly he grasps Taleno by the hair once more, and as his head is being forced down over the side of the well, he sees him smile as he holds up the grille that will slam behind him after his fall. Then again the fight is on to force his way back up to the surface of the water, but as always he is pushed back down and down; he passes out, and comes to yet again on the dripping tiles beside the well, water pouring from his stiff, numb body. Each time, the colonel is sitting there, and prods him in the ribs with his foot; each time he struggles to stand on his own after they jerk him to his feet, the photograph is lit up in front of his streaming eyes, the same hand wrenches at his hair; then it is back to the well, the drowning, less and less in his senses each time he regains consciousness in the pool of water, unable by now to tell when the starry sky is stretched out across the dark night above him, or when he is shattering its reflection as he hits the water; clusters of constellations shine in the south, stars glittering in the heavens descend to meet his stinging eyes as he falls to the ground, and fade into the distance and disappear in a violent lurch when once again they heave him up and pitch him headlong into the well, where the same starry sky twinkles brightly.

In the end, as he lies there on the cement with a scalding mucus dripping from his nose, dimly aware of a dull roaring in his ears as more scalding water trickles out, cocks begin to crow an unlikely dawn, and the colonel stumps back to the garage: "Take him away and bring him back to me tomorrow."

Just as Larios had predicted, my war wound earned me a promotion and I became an officer. I did not return to the Segovias though, because the Yankees left me stationed at the Campo de Marte in Managua to do administrative work. When, still hobbling on my crutches, I turned up one Monday morning to start work, he was already there, on the other side of the desk to me—Colonel Cummings USMC had got him transferred from the battle front to act as his personal secretary. He got the job thanks to his smattering of English and his ability to type, both things he had learnt at a business school in Leon, where he came from.

Like me, he had been promoted; he always kept ahead of me in the military hierarchy. At headquarters I was his assistant, although he at once made it clear he wanted us to be friends, something I was equally keen on, because of the debt of blood I owed him. From that moment on we were inseparable, calling each other "brother", greeting one another with open arms and much back-slapping.

All I had to do as his assistant was to file documents relating to the war in date order: the cost of aeroplane fuel, accounts for provisions, a list of the number of mules lost in action, because all the pack mules were specially imported into Nicaragua from Kentucky. Apart from checking my work, he used to take Colonel Cummings USMC his private correspondence, remind him of his engagements, or send flowers to Liberal or Conservative politicians' wives on their birthdays. I found the work difficult because I was not used to an office routine, and while I spent the whole day poring over stacks of papers trying to sort them out, he would be chatting away to the Yankee officers; he could make them laugh at anything, or get them to listen to him open-mouthed, as if he had hypnotised them. Whenever he had nothing else to do, he went off to the latrines to read poetry, and the only sign of his presence there was the smoke from the Lucky Strikes he had scrounged from the Yankees seeping through the cracks in the door.

He went so far as to cram the drawers of his desk with typewritten verses: poetry by Ruben Dario, who was his god, others by Vargas Vila that were officially banned. He typed out comic verses on the typewriter poking fun at the other Nicaraguan officers, acrostics and riddles that they fought to get copies of, parodies of *Los Motivos del Lobo* with crude double meanings. He also knew how to use the typewriter to make drawings of peacocks or flower vases, and once he stayed up for nights on end to complete a portrait in type of Colonel Cummings USMC, which in fact turned out quite a good likeness.

He would carry books ostentatiously under his arm, just so that we would go up and ask him what he was reading: Julius Caesar's campaigns, a life of Napoleon Bonaparte, the biography of Simon Bolivar. "Read them, they're useful, the thoughts of these great men have a lot to teach us," he was always telling me, but they were such heavy tomes, with such tiny writing, that my eyes would start to run and I would doze off before I could get into them. He declared his belief in a lot of silly things, or at least pretended to in order to show off: he corresponded with the Order of the Rosicrucians in San Jose, California, and got lots of pamphlets from them about the re-incarnation of the soul: he would go on and on to me about nonsense like spiritual fluids and our previous existences. He made me a freemason. He introduced all the officer corps from *el hombre* down (after *el hombre* appeared on the scene) to freemasonry; somewhere somebody must have all the photos of us taking part in our initiation ceremony in the Great Temple of the Managua lodge, wearing our hoods and aprons, *el hombre* saying a theosophical prayer; from then on we all had to give a secret quiver when we shook hands with each other, to transmit the vibrations from the aether.

Who else but someone with so much impudence would have had the idea of organising a grand gala ball for the daughters of the Yankee occupying officers? They lived shut up in their villas in Las Piedrecitas, and only came down into Managua with a military escort. All we could do was to admire them from afar, listen to them laughing as they strolled along the lakeshore or visited the markets to buy their typical tourist souvenirs—palm hats, hemp hammocks and suchlike, always guarded by marines who kept any curious onlookers at a distance and closed off the streets where they passed by laughing; nobody was allowed to talk to them.

They were also very careful about what they ate: all their food was brought frozen from the United States in warships, and they put tablets in their drinking water to make sure that none of them would catch worms in Managua.

Larios thought the poor girls must be very bored with their sheltered existence, and sent a memo to the United States command proposing the dance. A short while before, some drunken marines and prostitutes had broken into the Managua cemetery, urinating on the graves and smashing crosses; this must have helped the dance idea get fast approval in the hope it would calm down the locals, who were indignant about the desecration. He set up an organising committee from among his friends, and appointed himself chairman. He made Lieutenant Orochena secretary because he was involved with several social clubs and had experience in hiring musicians and barmen; the others on the committee were merely for show—even I was on it, though I knew less than nothing about that kind of function. But who knows, I thought, perhaps this will provide me the opportunity to discover that crock of gold my father was always talking about.

Now Larios spent all his time in the office writing the addresses for invitations, or consulting with Lieutenant Orochena to see how preparations were coming along; they had already hired rooms at the International Club. He breezed in and out of the barracks, and cycled from one end of Managua to the other, sweaty and preoccupied, visiting newspaper offices and the foreign embassies to make sure that the ball was the great social event that the headlines of *La Noticia* kept telling us it would be. Then at the last minute a serious hitch cropped up: none of us knew how to dance.

It was disgraceful; we didn't know a single step. The Yankee girls, so well versed in that sort of thing, would be bound to laugh at us when we led them off clumsily, stiff as boards, or perhaps even trod on their feet. The worst of it was that because of our lack of social graces they would be sure to know, on top of everything else, that we were not proper academy-trained officers; or so he argued, feeling sorry for himself above all. Where on earth did they find such a rabble to dress up in uniform? everyone was going to ask.

So the order of the day became for us to learn to dance as quickly as possible. The question was: how? It was impossible to get women into the Campo de Marte; decent women would refuse to enter army barracks, and anyway, where could we find them? It was impossible to bring in prostitutes; the general staff of the occupying forces were adamant that there should be no women in the camps, everything had to be done outside. But Lieutenant Orochena, the only skilled dancer among us, saved the situation; in the Victory Club they would get the craftsmen to make up the couples so that the club members could learn how to dance; they had a reputation for being magnificent natural dancers. That was how we got the idea of dancing with conscripts.

All we had to do was to choose a squad of the most agile and least repulsive soldiers, order them to line up, and then each one of us pick out his partner, so that Lieutenant Orochena could teach us the correct steps. All they would need to do would be to let themselves be led gently in time to the music; even they could not be so stupid as not to be able to follow the rhythm. So that was what we did. One night after dinner we brought a gramophone into the officers' mess, and the duty officer went round the huts calling out all the men we had chosen. They were marched in in two's, and the door was bolted. When they heard the bolts being drawn and saw us all standing there, they began to look round apprehensively, but Larios at once stood them to attention then made them an eloquent speech to explain that the honour of the army was involved, no less. They did as they were instructed and lined up against the wall without asking any questions. Someone put a record on the gramophone, not too loud so that the Yankee commanders would not hear—how on earth would we explain it if they found all our officers dancing with conscripts? Then off we set into a foxtrot: in the first lessons we concentrated on the foxtrot, it being the most difficult dance and the most fashionable. We stopped the gramophone and put the same record on again and again until we had all learned the steps that Lieutenant Orochena beat out for us, clapping his hands.

At first we found it hard to overcome our repugnance at the sweat and the smell of our conscript partners, and though we took hold of their hands we kept as far away from them as possible, our uniforms barely touching; we would not look them in the face, and they passively followed their instructions, turning and swaying as they were told to. The only problem they had was with their heavy army boots, so it was decided they should dance barefoot; in spite of the stink from their feet, this did help them to slide across the floor more easily. Only once did we have a discipline problem, when one of them refused to sit like a girl so that we could practise asking for the pleasure of a dance: he backed away furiously saying that he was no pervert to be doing that sort of thing with another man, so there was nothing else for it but to have him punished.

That was how we all learned to dance the foxtrot and other up-to-date steps. On the night of the ball, Larios was beside himself with the desire to impress; he had spent the whole day shut in his rooms, a cap jammed on his head trying to subdue the unruly bristles of his hair, which even a pound of Vaseline could not keep in place. As chairman of the organising committee, it fell to him to lead the first dance with the daughter of Colonel Cummings USMC herself, and he did look truly impeccable when he entered the International Club—all of us in fact looked magnificent, the creases in our uniforms freshly pressed, our belts polished, and giving off a manly scent. The ballroom was a blaze of light and a babble of voices; and there were the high-ranking Marine officers, dressed up to the nines, with their astonishingly tall wives by their sides; my godfather, the President, was there in evening dress with all his ministers and the ambassadors of the diplomatic corps. Larios nudged me and was already chuckling at his triumph.

At the sound of a trumpet call from the orchestra, a circle was formed and, looking every inch a soldier, he strode over to ask Colonel Cummings' daughter, waiting for him on her father's arm, for the honour of the first dance. Everyone was looking on as he led her to the centre of the brightly lit dance floor; the orchestra launched into a foxtrot, and then disaster struck. He began the dance the wrong way round, putting his left arm around is partner and leading off to the right, and insisted on continuing like that because that was how we had been dancing the whole time during our lessons with the soldiers, without suspecting our great mistake. The rest of us, lined up ready to follow his lead and invite the other Yankee girls to dance could see that a lot of the guests had begun to look puzzled, but we did not have time to find out just why they were now stifling their laughter: courteously, making a slight bow as Lieutenant Orochena had taught us, we asked them if they would dance, and then started off—but all of us made exactly the same mistake. Though the confused girls tried surreptitiously to get us to change our position, we all persisted in holding them the wrong way round, and made the struggle obvious to all the watching guests.

When the music stopped and we finally realised what had happened, we headed en masse for the rest rooms. There, we gazed at each other in dismay as if we had all just been sentenced to death. Even Orochena, our expert, had held his partner the wrong way. His despair was plain from his talcumed face, bathed in a mixture of sweat and melted brilliantine. Some of us, me included, were all for getting out there and then, but Larios stopped us, told us we should go back to our places at the high table as though nothing had happened, that it would be much worse to desert. A soldier never runs away. Orochena tried to cheer us up: "Come on, you lot—what do those Yankee women know about dancing anyway?"

So we did go back, and managed to dance correctly for the rest of the evening, but our hearts were no longer in it, and Larios, despite his polite manner and sociability, was crestfallen whenever he led a partner out onto the dance floor. He realised it was too late to fulfil the promise he had shouted out so eagerly while he had been getting dressed up: "Tonight everybody will see me dance like a spinning top."

Raul follows the provost marshal up onto the platform and hastily removes his prisoner's cap for the members of the court martial when ordered to do so by the guard. They are sitting behind the table chatting, yawning, passing round a thermos of coffee, having a soft drink from a cardboard cup, or eating sandwiches that they unwrap carefully so as not to get any food on their uniforms. A bright light blinds him as he obeys the order to be seated, and he can hear the whirring of a camera filming his trial. He gropes for the metal chair, screwing up his eyes against the glare, and this picture of his guileless face will later appear in Leo Anibal Rubens' National Newsreel in cinemas all over the country: fat, or perhaps his prison clothes are too big for him, his hair cropped. Even after the film lights have been turned off he finds it hard to see, and it is the voice of the military prosecutor that brings him out of the dazzling shadows, calling on him from what seems like a long way off at the other side of the platform in this zinc-roofed hut in the Campo de Marte, to give his name, age, civil status, profession or trade, and legal place of abode—or cannot the defendant hear, or is he deaf?

Yes, sir, he can hear: his name is Raul Guevara Potosme, and at this, puzzled, the prosecutor leafs through the sheaf of papers on his desk: Guevara? In the records his name appears simply as Raul Potosme. So he explains that since his parents were not married, this confusion of surnames has already occurred several times during the different stages of the trial; he is thirty-two years old. Civil status? He turns round shyly to the official defence lawyer sitting behind him, who leans forward, fanning himself with his newspaper, and whispers: are you married or single? He nods that now he understands and answers "single", and by trade a musical artist. The prosecutor interrupts him and turns to the military judges, showing them he is about to make a joke for their benefit: if he is a musician by trade, could the defendant please tell the court what he thought he was playing at in this band of delinquents? (laughter). The defendant himself laughs, and this is the image of him that appears later in the newspaper, the photograph that Chepito looks at repeatedly in the kitchen of the military canteen, peering at it close up first of all, then at arm's length, muttering to himself: Raul never looks a day older; and it is the same photograph that Pastorita cuts out with a razor blade, taking care not to lop off a part of his ear, then smears with starch and sticks on his barber shop wall next to the photo of Jilguero, which has been stuck up there on a thick coating of starch for days, fading and yellowing, the same one of him graduating from high school. He stands back to get a better view of them both together and thinks: lucky Jilguero, now he'll never grow old.

As for his address, he doesn't really have one. For approximately the past three years, he has been travelling between Honduras and Guatemala, and as far as he can make out, his current place of abode is La Aviacion jail in Managua, D. N. (more laughter). The prosecutor's starched suit crackles as he clasps his hands behind his back and orders him to proceed: he should tell the court all that he knows about or relating to the charges outlined in the indictment, of which he has been fully informed. Raul wipes the sweat from his upper lip with a finger, gazes at the judges behind the table—potbellied officers, balding or grey, one or two with sallow complexion and thick-lensed glasses; all of them wearing fitted khaki uniforms, black ties with tiny knots, the copper badges of rank gleaming dully on their lapels, their military caps on the table in front of them; one of them is laughing at something, another leans behind a third man's back to whisper or pass a cigarette to a colleague. A reporter from Radio Nacional comes up and, breathing fresh mint all over him, tells him to hold the microphone close because they are going to record the trial, pointing out at his feet the spools of the tape recorder winding slowly round with a quiet hum.

"At last we've got the thirty-five cordobas we need to make the recording," Pastorita had said when he finished counting out all the coins among the pieces of clay from the smashed money bank. Off *Los Caballeros* went with their guitars slung over their shoulders to the Estudio Tropical in Colonia Lugo opposite the Plaza de la Republica to record their 78 rpm record, which they were handed shiny and brand new in a brown manila sleeve with a hole cut so that they could read the machine-stamped label: SIDE ONE: Yolanda, *Flor de Todos* (slow foxtrot), words and music by Raul Guevara; SIDE TWO: *El Solar de Monimbo* (traditional song), words and music by Camilo Zapata. Did Chepito still have the record, he wondered? For a long while he had kept it behind the bar in *El Copacabana*; they had never been able to borrow a record player so that they could listen to it, and Lazaro had died without hearing it. It took them more than half a day to record it, and the old-timer who was working the sound equipment behind the glass panel had signalled to them not to get too close to the microphone. "If you do, all people will hear is your breathing," he had come in to warn them: "Don't stand so close as if you were going to take a bite out of it."

Is this all right for you? the radio reporter asks, and the girl stenographers sitting in the first row below the platform, their knees pressed tightly together, hair still damp from their showers, sit poised with the sharpened points of their pencils between their lips or close to hand on the desks in front of them. It is only when he starts to record that they come out of their daze: he speaks slowly and clearly, in the knowledge that his words are being taped. In approximately the month of June 1956—he cannot remember which day exactly—he left Nicaragua by road for Honduras, and during his stay there he met up with Nicaraguan exiles living in Tegucigalpa. If he had had the chance to talk to Pastorita and Chepito, both of them really pleased to see him back after such a long time, Chepito passing him a cold beer to celebrate his return, complaining that he wanted to know what had happened to the guitar, the first thing he would tell them would be that he had met Jilguero living in a slum in Comayaguela, so poor that he only had one shirt to his name, which he had to wash and put straight back on, having to stay in his room while it was drying, unable to go out and sell lottery tickets as he usually did. He lived in such a shanty town that he did not even have a proper address, it would be like asking where someone lived in Miralagos, for example, Raul would say.

Pastorita would be bound to want to know how Jilguero had

reacted when he saw the guitar—because he had sent word to Chepito from Honduras for them to find a way to send him Lazaro's guitar, to help him earn a living—at which Raul had jumped up happily and said he would go and deliver it to him personally. So off he set for Honduras with the guitar wrapped in a pillowcase Chepito had given him, though he had to sleep without one; and when Raul discovered him, Jilguero was cooking bananas in a pot for his lunch. Raul stood in the doorway, smiling in anticipation at the surprise he was going to give him, isn't that so, Raul? That's right, I was standing in the doorway: "Hello there," I said, with the guitar in my hand. Chepito cut in anxiously: what exactly did Jilguero say when he turned round and saw you? Well, he had said: "What's this, what are you doing here?" Raul had held out the instrument to him and waited until Jilguero, silent with astonishment, had removed the guitar from the pillowcase and taken it over to the door to examine it in the daylight. Then he said: "I thought it was better to bring it myself, then nothing would happen to it on the way."

The military prosecutor takes a sip of water but does not swallow it, as if he simply wished to rinse his mouth. The defendant should leave out any evidence which has already appeared in the preliminary hearings carried out by the military committee of enquiry prior to this court martial, and confine himself to telling the court of the events which took place after his return to the national territory as a member of a subversive group that had taken up arms against the constitutional government of the republic. Raul can sense his lawyer craning forward in his seat from behind to whisper something to him, and he nods in agreement, glancing down at the tape recorder on the floor. What happened then? Pastorita would press him. Then they had hugged each other and started to reminisce; Jilguero wanted to know how both of them were: he asked after you, Chepito, whether it was true that it was his fault they had tortured you; and you, Pastorita, he wanted to know whether they had ever given you your accordion back; it was all old news, but he was very out of touch up there on his own. That night I slept in his place: "You'll have to sleep on the floor, just for tonight," he warned me—I was only too pleased. "I'll sleep just like the peacock whose tree fell over but kept on snoring." And next morning, we didn't bother with breakfast, but left at once; Jilguero was striding along: "Now I've got the guitar, you'll see how I get work"; I struggled to keep up with him, trotting along until we reached the Marechal boarding house. Guess who we were going to see there—none other than Captain Taleno, Pastorita.

By then Taleno had already got a lot of good contacts in Tegucigalpa; he was a top life insurance salesman, his photograph appeared every month in *El Cronista* as the salesman of the month, he was even in the Spanish edition of *Life*—that's why they banned that issue in Nicaragua. We found him already having breakfast in the diningroom, dressed in a suit and tie, with his briefcase by his side, all set to start his morning round. Anybody who did not know his past would have known at once that he had been a soldier by the way he stood up to greet us, jumping up smartly to attention just like when he had been *el hombre*'s bodyguard, following his every footstep, right at his shoulder, serving him a drink or giving him a light.

There and then he wrote the recommendation he had promised Jilguero for when the guitar arrived—a letter for a Mr. Florian, a huge fat red-faced Yankee who wore clown's shoes; he ran several businesses in Tegucigalpa, including a bar and a travel agency that flew tourists out to the ruins at Copan, and the Tio Sam bar, on a hill near the Picacho, with a view at night of the lights on all the other hills of the capital. No sense in trying to hide it from them, he might as well tell them rightaway that the bar was in fact a whorehouse; that was where Mr. Florian took them on as musicians; Jilguero was to play Lazaro's guitar, and he himself would be on the grand piano. Have you ever seen one of those pianos, Pastorita? He had never played the piano in his life before, let alone a grand piano, he had confessed to Jilguero nervously—but do you know what he said, Chepito? "The last thing we want is to play something we don't know, but for now we have to make do with whatever we can"; and that in the darkness most of the customers were too drunk or caught up in their dancing to notice, and that everything would sound fine to them. So their musical duo was born, and they called it the *Caballeros del Ritmo*, so that it would have *caballeros* somewhere in it.

The first tune they learned to play, because the Yankee was always singing it in English, was "Managua, Nicaragua, where I fell in love". If ever he met them in the street during the day—something that often happened, for he kept on turning up unexpectedly, with the heavy tread of his clown's shoes as though he were about to cave the ground in—he would shout "Hey, Nicas—Managua, Nicaragua . . . " and begin to dance and clap without giving a damn about where he was. Raul would go on to tell them how that stupid little song had been their duo's greatest success, because when they later went on to play in the bar of the Lincoln Hotel, the place was full of Yankees every night who wanted to hear "Managua, Nicaragua . . . " and nothing else. If Chepito happened to interrupt him to ask why they did not go on playing in the Tio Sam bar, he would have to explain that Mr. Florian had been arrested on fraud charges and that the police had carted everything away: beds, chamber pots, even the grand piano.

You want to hear what took place from the moment we were attacked by the Honduran Army in El Chaparral? The prosecutor waves at him impatiently with the legal briefs in his right hand, and begs the defendant to begin his statement without further delay. Raul cups the microphone as though trying to hatch it with the warmth of his hands, and declares that while they were camping on the night of 24 June 1959 in a place known as El Chaparral in Honduras, approximately eight kilometres from the border, the two columns of about thirty men each who at dawn on the following morning were intending to invade Nicaragua, were taken by surprise by units of the Honduran Army who had surrounded them. They were forced into a gun battle in which they were in a very unfavourable position, so that by daylight both of the columns had been virtually wiped out, with many dead and wounded, and that the survivors had been called upon to surrender.

And if Pastorita had wanted to know what had been the best

time for them in Honduras, he would have replied at once that it was while the *Caballeros del Ritmo* were playing at the Lincoln Hotel. They were earning well, and got their dinner and even highballs free; Captain Taleno had stood surety on a pair of red dinner jackets with fancy lapels, so they looked like real artistcs. But it was just their luck: in 1957 the threat of war arose between Honduras and Nicaragua after the attack on Mokoron, and he got it into his head that he wanted to return to fight for his country, he did not want to live in enemy territory. At first, Jilguero just laughed at him, and so did Captain Taleno: they both told him it would be better to keep quiet, that he shouldn't say anything about the war in public, or he might get into trouble—at the very least they would put him in jail. It was nothing more than a war of words, much better to leave it all to the radios; but he could see how stirred up everybody was in Honduras, all the fundraising that was going on, the way people were giving blood; he could see the squads of volunteers training in the parks, in General Carias stadium, even the old men were begging for weapons to go and fight against Nicaragua; how was he supposed to feel? And it so happened that, one evening, when Captain Taleno was in the bar as well, the manager called them over and told them there was a government ban on performing the boogie "Managua, Nicaragua . . . " Jilguero merely shrugged and accepted: "It can't be helped, we won't play it then"; but he, Raul, perhaps because he'd had more than his fair share of drinks, became obstinate: "Well, I'm going to play it whether they like it or not, goddammit!" Jilguero was angry too by this time and told him he could do whatever he liked, he was a grown man.

Captain Taleno had tried politely to stop him when he had stood up, but he wouldn't listen. He made straight for the piano and began to play "Managua, Nicaragua . . . " until his fingers were raw—he couldn't remember how many times it had been. Standing in the doorway between the bar and the hotel lobby, the manager merely shook his head sadly. When they finished their performance that night they were arrested by detectives waiting for them outside in the street, and Captain Taleno was taken in too for good measure.

The three of them were kept on their own for a whole month in a basement of the central jail, then they were taken to the frontier and expelled to Guatemala. At that point Raul would explain shamefacedly that it was then they had lost Lazaro's guitar. When Jilguero had tried to claim it from the official in charge of their expulsion, he had replied that it had been kept in Tegucigalpa as part of the evidence, and when he had tried to explain that "Managua, Nicaragua . . ." had been played only on the piano, all they had got were hefty shoves across the border. So off they set down the road, the two musicians still wearing their filthy red dinner jackets, Captain Taleno with his insurance salesman's tie stuffed in the pocket of his torn shirt. That was how they looked when, with the sun already high in the sky, they arrived at Esquipulas, in Guatemala.

Whoever would have thought you'd get to know Guatemala as well, Chepito would comment, changing his bottle of beer for a full one.

CHAPTER 7

They are pulling into Leon, and high up in the darkness to the left of the road the red lights of a radio mast blink on and off; opposite an unlit garage they meet a tractor slowly hauling a big wire-caged trailer out to be filled with raw cotton in the fields at dawn, specks of cotton caught in the trailer bars like white birds that the force of the wind appears to be stripping of their feathers. After they have passed the dairy gate and reached the Guadalupe cemetery, the driver reduces speed almost to nothing, and turns right to enter the town down the deserted main avenue.

When Bolivar hears him giving thanks that they have arrived without incident, he pretends to be coming round from his sleep, and leans over to look out of the window, gazing, as though it were ages since he had seen them, at the old houses with their corner posts, the high, worn pavements, all the front doors still closed in the light from the halos of the mercury streetlamps. Then he slumps back in his seat again, this time with his eyes open, and again he can visualise his mother standing in the yard of the cotton depot, the flecks of white flying thicker and thicker around her: "Take this too, to dress him in; a lot of people will want to look into his coffin when you bring it, and there is no reason why a man like him should make anybody feel sorry for him.'' She took something white out of the same bag she had brought the money in, but even before she did so he knew that it was a new shirt, because he had heard the cellophane of the packet rustle.

Days later in the mortuary, as he was struggling to lift the naked, old, yellowing body from the slab to fit its arms into the sleeves, it gradually came to him, without the slightest sense of shock, that for the first time in his life he was holding this stranger who had been his father, this exile of whom he had heard only through his mother's constant praise, this clandestine shadow that had ordained from afar that he be baptised with the name Bolivar, and for whom for so many years she had got up before dawn to knead dough in order secretly to send him money to buy rifles, for close to twenty years siphoning funds from the bakery for ammunitions and arms bought in the black markets of Honduras and Costa Rica for those invasions of his which were always on the point of being launched across the frontiers. And if La Opositora was sometimes closed, forcing the clients to go and buy their bread furtively at the back door, it was because rumours were about that he was already fighting somewhere in Nicaragua.

As he buttoned up the shirt with its lines of grime around the creases, as he knotted the old khaki tie, a leftover from his father's army days, he was also thinking without great astonishment of how only the afternoon before he had discovered that the mysterious twists and turns in the maze of his father's exile led finally to a wretched shack from whose ceiling hung a bunch of forgotten children's piñatas. This had been his last refuge, and after his pauper's death in the public ward of the hospital, this was where he had left another wife and other children, baptised just as he was with the names of dead heroes.

It was only after a long search that he found the piñata workshop. As soon as he had got to Guatemala City he had gone to the morgue to claim the body, but had been told that they could hand it over to him only with the permission of the relative who had signed the hospital admission forms. They showed him the name written shakily at the bottom of the piece of paper: Carmela Dardon Molina. And he had only forty-eight hours to obtain her permission; otherwise, the body would be handed over to the students for their experiments.

They had forgotten though to note down the woman's address, or perhaps had not even bothered to ask her, and he hadn't the faintest idea where his father might have spent his last days—not only did he never write his address on any of the letters he sent them, they presumed that for security reasons he never stayed in the same place for long. He could remember only that once when his mother had been talking in the shop with one of the secret envoys who turned up from time to time to collect her money, they had talked of the Pension Chapaneca in the first district of the city, where he had apparently stayed for some time under an assumed name.

That was where he had tried first of all, in the hope that if he gave them a description, somebody might remember his father's features and help him find out where he had moved on to. But there was a new owner at the boarding house, and none of the lodgers or guests could suggest anything. None of them knew any Nicaraguan exiles, apart from an old municipal inspector who remembered two young men who shared the same room and played the guitar, seeming to spend the whole day laughing over the least little thing: but one day, round about April 1959 it must have been, they had vanished. He was given the addresses of other boarding houses that exiles often stayed in, and he visited them one by one in the truck, until late that afternoon he arrived at the Pension Chabelita, near the American Club. The landlady there clearly remembered a very well-mannered gentleman who, a long time before, perhaps before 1959 even, used to come to visit one of her lodgers, a young insurance salesman who was also very pleasant and courteous. One day when the visitor arrived a little tipsy, he had presented her with his business card for children's birthday parties. She still had it, pinned up with a jumble of other cards collected over the years, next to the rack of keys: so that at last Bolivar could copy down the address.

It was nightfall by the time he reached the unsurfaced road in the twentieth district, in the shadow of a sawmill, where he found the address was that of a lean-to built onto the smoke-stained wall of a higher adobe building, a pig butcher's. The front of the place was painted a bright blue, that in places had already thinned almost to invisibility; between the transom and the roof overhang was a sign, the letters painted in two colours far too big for the size of the wall:

BIM BAM BOOM
Top class piñatas

with beneath it a childish picture of a little girl about to smash open a piñata.

A plump woman came to the butcher's door to sweep leaves and rubbish out into the street. Glancing at the empty truck parked across the road, she told him to knock louder, the children were on their own inside. When finally the door opened, he was struck by the smell of leftover food and damp linen piled forgotten in a corner. A little girl appeared from the shadows, drying her runny nose: her mother wasn't home, but she wouldn't be long. Then she ignored him again and went back to her game of breaking a plate so that she could play with the broken pieces of crockery. He sat on a pine chest to wait, dragging it over to the door to wedge it open, while the driver and his son stayed in the truck.

The piñatas were hanging from the ceiling rafters, swaying gently to and fro, a boisterous collection dangling lifelessly as the dust from cracks in the roof sifted down over them, huge shapes of fruit decorated with torn bits of paper; white rabbits in morning coats; witches with black crepe petticoats; a Pinocchio with a smudged smile—his mouth traced with a pencil, then erased and drawn in again; a Donald Duck. The materials for making the piñatas were in a glass cabinet, one of whose panels had been repaired with newspaper: it contained sheets of cardboard and tissue paper, a big pair of scissors, a pot of starch, and on the floor were clay bowls waiting to be decorated. On the whitewashed wall hung a Nicaraguan flag made from the same crepe paper as that used for the piñatas, with the triangular emblem and its chain of volcanoes in the centre of the white stripe made of silver foil from cigarette packets. So making the piñatas and the blue-and-white flag explained how his father's hands had got stained: when he had put the dead man's shirt on, knowing what work he had done in his last years, he had discovered between his fingers streaks of starch still with traces of the bright reds and purples from the decorations.

He must have slept in that same room under the swinging piñatas: there was a collapsible campbed next to the clay pots, with the sheets still folded inside it. He would have had to move his bed out of the way every morning to make room, while his wife and children (there was a boy too, staring at him from behind the safety of a cord curtain) obviously slept in the other room created by the wardrobe and the curtain.

Dressed in a shirt with no buttons and wearing shoes that were far too big for him, the intrigued boy poked his head through the curtain to get a better look at him, and even ventured a few steps into the room, before hurtling back again into hiding with a clatter of boots. Bolivar tried to think of a way to win him over without getting up from his seat so that he did not scare him off altogether. He beckoned him over and smiled as he showed him the only thing he had to hand, the blue passport in his shirt pocket. The boy edged closer, keeping his back pressed up against the wardrobe, and eventually was standing next to him, though his eyes were wide with fright. He put his hand gently on the boy's head to stroke his hair, and asked him his name. The boy bowed politely just as schoolboys bow to the audience before a recital, and replied that he was Bardo Ruben Dario, at his service. Feeling that she too was included in the question, as though the same hand which had taught her to be polite with strangers were now invisibly pushing her forward, the little girl stood up and, though still absorbed in her game, also gave a rapid curtsy of introduction, holding the hem of her dress out with her fingertips: "Heroina Rafaela Herrera", then sat down once more.

It was only at that moment, it had occurred to him while

dressing the corpse in the mortuary, folding the arms over the chest so that with the help of the driver and his son he could lift him into the coffin—and thinks again now, as the truck's headlights pick out garages, the rising and falling pavement, it was only then that he really believed the two children were his brother and sister. His father had his own saints' calendar, as inspired as it was ill-founded, his lay catechism that was a mixture of mythological heroes, military strategists, and republican champions. He knew a wealth of famous deeds and phrases, unshakably edifying, learnt from his readings of the two-columned Sopena editions or the Gandesa biography series, books that accompanied him in his saddlebags during the campaign against Sandino, though most of them were confiscated when he was taken prisoner, apart from a few still hidden in Leon in a box among the sacks of flour.

Only strap in hand had she been able to get him not to be ashamed of his name, and convince him that to be called Simon Bolivar was a great honour whenever he came home from school with his classmates chanting after him:

> Simon Bolivar
> how silly you are
> born in Caracas
> of a cow and a jackass.

She would end up by dragging him in front of the portrait of Bolivar the Liberator who, astride his horse and haloed with glory on the heights of the Chimborazo, presided over the baker's shop.

In the end though she had excused him the Simon part, insisting only on the Bolivar when, in reply to her enquiry, his father had ruled that the Christian name was unimportant, what really mattered was to try to emulate the glory of the surname. And nobody with the name of Bolivar was to go around making an exhibition of himself fighting in public, and naked on top of everything else; that had been his terse command when years later she had complained to him that their boy was interested only in boxing instead of studying. As a first step she had cut the strings holding the sand-filled punchbag from an orange tree in their yard so that he would be unable to train, until the official prohibition arrived from his father in Guatemala.

He was one of the supporting boxers in the fights held in the arena got up in the burnt-out municipal theater. The ring was erected in what had been the stalls, and the seats for the public were arranged in between the broken columns and the ruined walls; the combats were held by moonlight, advertised on billboards hung from the still intact theatre front that looked out on the dark, cobbled street, where the cheers of the fans echoed. His fighting name had been Kid Bolivar—and that had upset his father most of all, because in her letter of complaint she had included one of the handbills given out in the streets of Leon on one of any number of Saturdays:

MUNICIPAL ARENA
TODAY Ten bloody rounds TODAY
Yambito Blanco vs. Pugnose Porras
Spider Canales vs. Kid Bolivar
STAR BOUT OF THE EVENING
Kid Pambele vs. The Martinican Bull

During one of those fights, his last, just as his second was getting him ready for the third round, he had been surprised to see his mother in the audience. She was using an envelope to waft the cigarette smoke from her triumphantly smiling face. That night he let his opponent knock him about at will: he knew his boxing days were over.

Bardo Ruben Dario, Heroina Rafaela Herrera. At least he had been spared Liberator, Liberator Simon Bolivar. Now the headlights are lighting up the front of a pharmacy, the iron-grilled window of the town's business school, bar tables piled up on a pavement, as they advance slowly down the avenue, the driver sitting solemn at his wheel, as though from the moment they entered the town their progress through the deserted streets had in some way to be stately.

This time they take him not to the room full of costumes but to a cell in the foundations of the presidential palace. He immediately falls asleep on the floor, and wakes up only as the bugle sounds for the evening meal in the barracks, oblivious in his stupor to the fetid, stagnant air and the utter darkness around him, his only real sensation the pulsing burns from the wounds in his wrists. Then, after the curfew bells, he hears the sound of footsteps echoing down the corridor: "It's bath time again, we'll get rid of your stink for you," he hears his tormentor from the night before chuckling hollowly on the other side of the door, before the jailer unlocks it. Dressed in the spattered rags of his uniform, he is led back to the garage, where they strip him, then push him out to the well again.

The torture lasts for perhaps three nights, but the colonel complains that these duckings are getting them nowhere. Mischievously, the man reaches out and grabs him, not by the hair this time, but by the sack of his scrotum, asking the others to hand him a length of rope. "Let's hang him in the well by the balls, then we'll see if he stays silent," he says, putting one end of the rope in his mouth as though about to start tying him—but from his stool the colonel stops him. Wouldn't it be a better idea to put him in the President's zoo? The panther has been feeling very lonely since the death of the lioness, and the cage is empty.

So they force him to walk naked to the small zoo hidden at the bottom of the garden, a solid block of iron cages under the branches of ancient snakewood and guanacaste trees, which shed their leaves into a swimming pool, whose gleaming turquoise water can be seen from high up on the west of the palace. They push him towards an empty, narrow cage, the door of which the man opens as cautiously as possible so that the creaking of its rusty hinges will not disturb the panther in the next cage too soon. One of the guards grips his ankle and makes him stand up on the ledge of the cage's stone floor; others push his head down and force him to crawl inside. He straightens up slowly, his hands in among the shells and dried turds that litter the straw-covered floor, choking in the warm animal smell. On the other side of the bars, the panther begins to stir as it senses his presence, and when they slam the door shut he hears it start to growl, and catches the red flash from its eyes as they shine a flashlight on it. Brought to a sudden rage by the blinding light which they remove from its face only to show the man's naked body, the panther lashes out through the bars, but he crawls to the wall furthest away from the animal, and hauls himself up by the bars until his shoulders are pressed against the cage's roof. Bent double, he crouches with his legs splayed as far apart as possible, alert to every move the panther makes. Time and again it interrupts its sleepless pacing to lunge at him as the beam from the light wounds its eyes; by dawn the next morning he is still crouching, his head drooping as sleep overwhelms him, but jerking awake with a start whenever he feels the claws scratching close to his feet, the bars between him and the animal rattling as it paws in the darkness.

From outside, between the howls of the other animals, comes the colonel's relaxed voice, sitting on his stool next to the cage, repeating the same questions. The other man has a flashlight in one hand and a stick in the other, which he uses to rattle the bars and occasionally to poke the panther in the ribs.

The howls of the other animals have given way to the chirping of birds in the tree branches, and it is bright daylight by the time they leave; the sun is beating down on the calm water of the swimming pool. Some time later the old gardener, who seems familiar to him, comes in. He doles out fruit to the raccoons, pacas and coatis kept in the small wire cages on the far side of the zoo, then walks over with a bucket of raw meat, throwing chunks to the lion cubs and to the puma, but not to the panther. He does not even glance at Taleno as he passes in front of the cage; he picks up a net and scoops the leaves out of the pool, then waters the lawn. As he is about to leave, he bends down to unscrew the hose pipe, and for a few short seconds surreptitiously points the water over in Taleno's direction. Parched with thirst, desperate for sleep, Taleno can barely turn his head, crushed up against the roof of the cage as he is, not daring for a moment to relax his vigilance; all he can do is to let his mouth open slackly to welcome the drops of water onto his split lips, the breath of cool air onto his face.

When they return that night he tells them he is ready to confess. His torturer snaps the flashlight off, sticks it into his trouser waistband, and rushes to open the cage door, shouting to one of the guards to throw the panther some meat to distract its attention. They make him put his tattered uniform on again, then take him to the costume room, where they have set up a tape recorder. The man politely brings the throne over for him to sit on, and hands him the grey, worn microphone. He has scarcely begun to stammer the story of his friendship with Carlos into it before he falls asleep, letting the microphone slip down onto his lap. The lieutenant shakes him roughly by the shoulder and puts the microphone back between his hands, while the colonel presses a button to wind the tape back for him to hear his last words before they faded into the desperate panting of exhausted sleep. "I'm not interested in the dead," he hears the colonel say; "that Rosales you talk about died in a gun battle last Sunday. Didn't I tell you in the cage? What I want are names: the names of the other officers involved with you"; he hears him start the tape recorder going again, and the other man thrusts the microphone into his face. He turns aside, and refuses to say a single word more.

Beside himself with rage, the man suggests they put him back in the zoo, but the colonel shakes his head, drying the back of his neck with a handkerchief. No, not the cage again: they had wasted enough time, none of the others had been shown this much consideration. "This is your last chance. We'll come back in an hour . . . otherwise, get yourself ready," levelling his fingers to make a trigger as he shuts the door behind him. Left alone, overcome by a strange indifference to his fate, Taleno settles back on the throne to let the period of his lying-in drift by emptily, listening to the wind pushing against the round skylight window high up on the wall, through which the reddish beams of an April moon are faintly shining. As his gaze comes to rest on the window, he is suddenly stirred out of his reverie, and remembers one of the many recurring fantasies that had occupied his mind in the cage, in order to avoid falling asleep so close to the lunging claws of the panther: that of escaping.

He sits up on the throne, and tries to judge the height of the wall. Then he drags himself over to the door and presses his ear to it. All he can hear are the sentry's footsteps, so he gropes his way back to the throne, lifts it carefully, then places it sideways on top of the glass cabinet containing the plumed hats, which stands against the wall beneath the skylight. He opens the cabinet door, swiftly pulls all the hats out onto the floor, then uses the shelves as a stepladder to climb up to the throne, which creaks as he puts his weight on it. He stands swaying on tiptoe, and with one hand succeeds in reaching up to the handle of the window. He pulls it towards him, and as the window jerks open, a sprinkling of dust showers his head. Planting his feet as firmly as possible on the arms of the chair, he pauses to wipe the cold sweat from his hands. Then he grips the edge of the window recess and heaves himself up, a stabbing pain shooting through his straining arms, his feet scrabbling to find a grip on the smooth wall. Bit by bit he manages to pull his face up level with the skylight, and as he thrusts his elbows into the hole, he can feel the air blowing freely on his cheeks.

Crouching inside the round hole like a statue in a church niche, he looks incredulously down at the abyss spread beneath him, the steep sides of the ravine funnelling down to the green eye of the lake at the crater bottom, the smooth rear wall of the palace disappearing vertically under his feet, the outcrop of stones and mortar at its base mingling with the vegetation of the highest terrace. On the far side of the crater, an asphalted road climbs up a tree-lined avenue towards Tiscapa, the benches along it tiny in the distance, the yellow blotches of the electric lamps paling in the growing light of morning that creeps over the plains stretching from the southern hills right to the city outskirts, its brightness catching the cones of distant volcanoes beneath an orange dawn.

First he sits astride the window ledge, and as he edges out, it occurs to him without the slightest sense of terror that they may be watching him, pointing their rifles at him from any of the turrets, just waiting for the whole of his body to appear before they rake the wall with machine gun fire, having left him alone on purpose in the room simply to tempt him into flight. He clings for a moment, his face pressed against the cold wall, and remains motionless, expecting the distant rattle of gunfire, but all he hears from the depths beneath him is the rustle of leaves, so he releases his grip.

His fingers scrape the ledge, and then he floats free, spreading his arms wide as his head whirls, plummeting downwards through endless space, not noticing how in his fall he pulls loose tree branches and drags them with him, landing in a heap among them on the ground. He crashes down on his side, and the first sensation he has is the pungent smell of these torn branches; he rolls over and over and finally comes to rest against a smooth boulder on the very edge of the terrace, while above him there is the noise of stones and soil as they cascade after him. Benumbed as if from sleeping too long in one position, he lies flat on his back gazing up at the sky, where a lone pair of hawks wheel.

He sits up, then tries to stand by pushing his grazed hands into the clammy wetness of the rotten leaves, but a pain which shoots from his left shoulder to his fingertips makes him lose his balance and topple headfirst. Eventually he succeeds in getting to his feet, and stumbles off, the leaves squelching beneath his unsteady feet. He is limping, and his torn trouser leg reveals a livid red stripe among the down of hairs. He crosses a small clearing, looking for a way on to the next terrace, his left arm swinging useless by his side. Finally he decides to slide down a bare chute where the palace kitchen waste is thrown, and lies flat on his back on the clayey soil, clutching at flat stones and braking, when the undergrowth thickens further down, on the bare roots of trees that grow leaning over towards the lake, which he occasionally glimpses through the bushes.

He reaches the second terrace and crawls across it, careful to put his weight on his one good hand, then slithers down through another thicket, skirting the vertical drops and stopping more than once as a darting lizard's tail startles him. Soon he has reached water level, so close to the lake that he can see the washerwomen's stones, and he sets off at once to find the start of the footpath that snakes up the crater wall towards the avenue to Tiscapa. He begins to climb, hidden in the bushes next to the path.

He comes out on the esplanade of the avenue much sooner than he could have imagined, scarcely able to believe that the trees, the benches sticky from the drizzle, or the electric streetlamps which at that precise instant flick off for the day can really be so close to him. Still dragging himself along, he turns round before launching himself across the road, and looks back at the rear of the buildings on the far side of the crater. Their windows are still lit, and the skylight he crawled out of is nothing more than a dark hole drilled in the distant wall. Reassured that nobody is following him yet, he hurries as best he can across the avenue, elated as a cripple who can suddenly run. He goes on up past the corrugated roof of a sawmill then, concealed in the undergrowth of empty plots, slips by the sentries at the gate of the Military Hospital, continuing his climb through the outskirts of the city, along dirt roads that soon become country tracks. He clambers over fences, squeezes under barbed wire to get across fields and dairy pastures, staggers down the main avenues of coffee plantations where the barking of guard dogs accompanies him on his way, always aiming south, judging his direction from the sun as the morning grows hotter.

After hours of this tortuous progress, resting only to hide, he reaches Ticomo Hill late in the afternoon; on the hillsides all around him the harvested fields of April are being burnt, the stalks crackling and spitting, and a dense smoke rolls over the slopes. At last he reaches the top, cicadas chorusing on all sides; down below him the city is immersed in the warm twilight breeze, its shadows merging with the outline of the lake, its lines of lights creeping out to the shore, or flashing briefly so that the watching eye expects them to disappear once they have flickered on and off, but which stay shining out steadily, their brightness no more than a dim blur beneath the slate-coloured sky that is slowly dissolving into night.

He goes in at a gate, and the old itinerant priest from his days of wandering from fair to fair comes out surprised to greet him. He staggers, his arm a useless rag, but knows he will not fall now.

Raul testifies that only nine men managed to escape the ambush, but they decided in spite of everything to continue into Nicaragua as they had originally planned, and that it was a certain Santiago Taleno, an ex-National Guard officer, who took command of the survivors, with one Mauricio Rosales, profession unknown, who acted as second-in-command. That on the afternoon of that same day after a forced march without the aid of any field maps they reached the frontier somewhere near Teotecacinate, managing to slip past the frequent patrols by the armies of both countries.

And as they were crossing a rough stretch of ground, he would tell them, skirting the jagged bare rocks of a hillside that sloped sharply down into a deep gully, Taleno, leading them in single file, stopped and pointed to the next range of hills, their tops covered with dark pine woods whose resin smell reached them on the breeze: "We've reached Nicaragua, boys!" As he trudged on, his boots sank into the mud, and it was some time before it dawned on him that this was the mud of Nicaragua—and at once he was surprised that it was not more of a shock, for in the cheap boarding houses where they had been hidden in Tegucigalpa they had always talked of this very moment, when they would actually cross the frontier. They had imagined that the trees, flowers, even the mud itself, would somehow take on a different nature and colour; everything was bound to seem different as soon as they heard: we've reached Nicaragua.

He went on to tell the court that after roughly a week's march they had crossed the mountains in Jalapa, and that from there they continued to advance cautiously so as to avoid discovery by the National Guard patrols combing the area, finally arriving near Quilali in the Segovias; that they camped for three nights on the slopes of Malacate mountain, spending their days reconnoitring the surrounding territory in groups of three. That they abandoned this site as it did not offer them enough protection, and continued in what they calculated was a southeasterly direction, arriving on the banks of the river Coco following a further three days' march. That in a place on the banks of that river which he thinks he remembers was called Piedra Negra, they were attacked by a detachment of National Guardsmen who had been following them, and that despite a lack of ammunition and being physically exhausted from having had nothing to eat in over a week apart from unripe wild fruit, they returned the fire from defensive positions, and managed to break out under cover of darkness. That in the attack they suffered two further casualties, both identified in the military prosecutor's files, namely: Fanor Sagastume, killed in the previously mentioned combat, and Hilario Ardila, wounded, who died later: both of them without any known profession.

Pastorita would still be upset that Lazaro's guitar had been lost for ever: because you know, Raul, those strings were what linked the *Caballeros* to the memory of their old friend; now there was nothing to prevent him falling out of reach. To take his mind off the subject, Chepito would quickly ask Raul where they had headed after arriving at Esquipulas, what on earth they had done, barefoot and without a centavo in their pockets. Well, they had gone on to the capital, Guatemala City, but once more they had been thrown into jail, nearly another month behind bars, Pastorita: there's not much I don't know about jail now. It was thanks to Indio Larios, who hired local lawyers, that they finally got out of prison, but only on condition that they go every morning at eight to sign the book at central police headquarters.

So you had the honour of dealing with the famous Indio Larios in person? Pastorita would marvel. But he wouldn't allow himself to be impressed, he would go on to talk of his friendship with Indio as if it were the most natural and obvious thing in the world: yes, he got us out of jail and helped us find somewhere to live. Jilguero and me stayed in the pension Chapaneca in the first district: Taleno preferred another one some way off. I don't blame him for that, he was afraid we might get him into trouble again.

He goes on to declare to the court that on the afternoon of the gun battle at Piedra Negra, possibly a Friday, in the middle of July it must have been, they reached La Mariposa ranch high up on a mountainside. They spent the night in one of the corrals, thanks to the foreman who gave them shelter and promised not to give them away, and that they were able to have a meal of beans. That the previously mentioned foreman told them the National Guard patrols had passed through the farm earlier that day, and he had realized from their radio messages that they had surrounded that part of the mountain. At dawn the next day, Raul continues, refreshed by the rest and food, they managed to get their bearings and headed out for the heights of Saslaya, still closely pursued by the noise of planes which were dropping leaflets calling on them to surrender, promising that their lives would be spared. That two members of the group decided to accept this offer and positioned themselves in a clearing to wait for one or other of the National Guard patrols: these two persons appear in the military prosecutor's files as: Ignacio Aleman, a law student, and Zacarias Brantome, office worker, both of them tried before a court martial and sentenced to death in a judgment upheld by the appeal tribunal. That at dawn on another day, perhaps a Monday, no sooner had they made camp by a creek on the El Moro estate than they were again attacked by what the defendant believes, judging by the intensity of the gunfire, to have been a sizeable force; and that after a fierce battle they lost two more men, whose names figure in the prosecution files as Cayetano Murcia, salesman, killed in the fighting, and Gerardo Reina, a Honduran national, profession unknown, who also died in the combat.

He goes on to testify that, helped once again by the fall of night, the survivors succeeded in escaping. There were only three of them by this time, and they had only a few rounds of ammunition left. Not only were they exhausted following a two-week, non-stop march, but also they were starving and soaked to the skin by the incessant rain in the mountains. Even so, they pressed on, still sticking to their original plan to find some suitable high ground where they could camp safely and, without engaging any troops, could try to get help or reinforcements. That such a place, in the opinion of their leader, ex-National Guard Santiago Taleno, was Pancasan mountain in the Guabul range in the department of Matagalpa; and that during the following days they continued to make their way towards this mountain, pursued the whole time by the planes and their bombs which fell close behind them, with no other idea of their direction than that given by the inhabitants of the region.

That roughly in mid-August, with heavy rains still pouring down, they camped in various places on the slopes of Mount Quiringua, the three of them having to keep watch the whole time for fear of being taken by surprise or ambushed. That their leg muscles had seized up, and to wear boots was agony for them; that they barely had anything to eat except for the occasional handful of rice, banana, or stale tortilla, being unable to hunt wild animals for fear the shots would give their position away.

He would satisfy Pastorita's keenness to know what the legendary Indio Larios was really like: but you would have been disappointed, Pastorita, he wasn't what he had been, he had no stomach for fighting any more, and though he boasted about his invasion plans, anyone could tell he was just bluffing, when you were talking to him it seemed that he gradually faded into nothing, leaving his chair empty. Pastorita, unable to believe his ears: but on those leaflets last April he was the most wanted man—wasn't he at the top of the list, wanted dead or alive? So then he would have to put on his condescending tone, he would savour his mouthful of beer in silence for a while then shake his head, with the look of someone who has learned to live with his disillusionment, and tell him that Larios never so much as crossed into Nicaragua on that occasion: while the rest of them were getting themselves killed, he was handing out leaflets in the bars of Guatemala City claiming the uprising was on the verge of victory, pretending he had just received the news smuggled out of Managua, when he himself had made it all up. I can tell you that for sure because time and again I heard Taleno, Jilguero and him arguing about it, saying that he had let them down with the supply of weapons and all sorts of other things, over and over they quarrelled. I'm really sorry, Pastorita, he would tell him after swallowing the beer, I didn't want to upset you.

Raul: that their next halt came, as far as he could remember, on the El Olvido estate at the foot of the Guabul range of mountains, and that they moved on, it was possibly a Tuesday, with the rain falling as heavily as ever, walking in single file with their hand on the shoulder of the man in front so they would not stray from each other, and that on several occasions it really seemed they were completely lost. They were delayed so much that it was only by the Thursday of the following week, that is, at the end of August, that they finally reached the foothills of Pancasan, having to cut their way through the jungle with machetes; and that they had to give up their idea of setting up a permanent camp there both due to the torrential rain and to the bombardments which began as soon as the rain eased off. That at the beginning of September, they made for the banks of the Murra River, which had flooded from the continual rain; that they had wanted to cross the river the same day, which he believes was a Monday, but did not dare attempt it because they were afraid of being swept away by the torrent, and so made camp on a ledge above the river until daybreak on the Wednesday, by which time the water level had dropped and they could proceed across, linking hands and making sure that their weapons did not get wet. That on reaching the far bank, and with the morning mists lifting, they lost no time in aiming for the Hielo range in the mountains of Chontales, another spot where their leader, ex-National Guard Santiago Taleno, judged they could make a stand. That according to information they picked up on the way, there were no fewer than five hundred soldiers in the area—and that all the time they could hear bombs exploding nearby and planes flying overhead.

But after that he would go on to explain the miserable way Indio Larios was obliged to live, how poor and miserable his life was, and this would give Pastorita the excuse to say: "You see, that's what poverty does to you—it was need that made the poor fellow dream up all those fantasies, fantasies of invasion or whatever." Poor as a beggar, he would agree, but there's no denying he helped them all he could in the difficult times when they first arrived, seeing to it they had at least the basics they needed, a bed to sleep in, at least one meal a day, and cigarettes, while they were looking for some kind of job. And to provide all that for them, God knows how he contrived to filch the money from his wife out of the piñatas they sold.

Chepito, about to clear away the empty bottles, would plonk them down again and query him, offended: his wife? Larios' wife lives here in Leon; did he really have another one in Guatemala? And as though all through their conversation he had been trying unconsciously to steer them to precisely this point, he would stretch out his legs, slide his hands into his pockets, and tell them nonchalantly: "Of course, a wife much younger than him. And talk about pretty! She ran a piñata workshop, and if you want more proof, she had two children by him. Two children, Chepito."

It seems he met her in the cinema entrance where she sold cigarettes as well as her piñatas; they got to know each other when she let him scrounge some cigarettes—and by the time we arrived in Guatemala City they had been living together for ages. He had taken over making the piñatas, because he was very good at thinking up ideas for animals and dolls to make them from; she concentrated on selling them.

Raul would tell them frankly that he himself had gone out into the streets to sell piñatas; it had been impossible to find any work as musicians in the Guatemalan nightclubs at that time due to the dreadful political situation; they spent all their nights shut indoors because of the curfew. At first Jilguero tried selling lottery tickets, then a Nicaraguan doctor who had lived in Guatemala City for years got him a job as a sanitary inspector. Around then I went off to Puerto Barrios to try to change my luck, and by working hard in the port I managed to save quite a bit, more than I'd ever had in my life, Chepito. But I got hooked on something that had never appealed to me before: I became a poker addict, and that heartless game left me flat broke, so I went back to Guatemala City more dead than alive; that must have been at the start of 1958. In desperation I tried Larios' place, but only his wife Carmelita was there. "If you don't feel ashamed, take some of the piñatas and try to sell them," she told me; so I grabbed as many as I could carry and walked all over town with them, but all I ever got for my trouble was sunstroke, because piñatas are the worst thing in the world to sell. If it's nobody's birthday in the house where you knock, they look at you as though you are mad, with all those clay dolls hanging round your neck. And you can go the whole blessed day without discovering a single child who's having a birthday.

CHAPTER 8

For a second, above the tiled roofs and the lofty fronds of the palm trees, the moon lights up the ashen towers of the cathedral, but then a bank of clouds sweeping westward towards the sea snuffs out the brightness. The truck reaches the corner of a street pitted with potholes and ruts, which has no lighting, so that its blocks merge in the evening; from a distant brothel somewhere comes the sound of a Rockola with the voice of Daniel Santos crooning ''Just a midnight virgin, that's what you are''.

He had been waiting for quite a while, and the boy had completely lost his fear and climbed on his lap, by the time the woman appeared. He could sense when she paused on the threshold, and smell the fresh dye from her mourning dress, although the first thing he noticed as he turned towards her were the pair of old shoes she was wearing, which the shiny newness of her dress made seem even worse by contrast. She was carrying some tomatoes, and looked about her helplessly for somewhere to conceal them from him. Her coarse, lined hands, the nails painted a bright scarlet, looked as though they belonged to a much older woman, because her face, despite its dry scrubbed look, was that of a young woman of about his own age. She finally decided to cross the room under the piñatas and make for the kitchen at the back, walking quickly and with her face averted, to avoid having to look at him. She dropped one of the tomatoes in her haste, but did not stop, so he, feeling perhaps even more ill-at-ease than she did, went to pick it up. He stood there holding it without knowing what attitude to adopt, trying to think of what he should say, to reassure her that he did not want to cause her any trouble, all he wanted was permission to get the body from the mortuary so that he could go back to Nicaragua as soon as possible.

She came back in, but this time scuttled through the cord curtain into the bedroom, the two children scampering after her. He had just made his mind up to knock on the back of the wardrobe to attract her attention, when the little girl emerged: her mother had sent her to ask if he would come in for a minute.

She was sitting on the tattered bedcover, completely composed by now, smoking calmly with her cigarette held up in front of her face, an elbow crossed over the other arm, and the box of matches in her lap. On the bed beside her was a Quaker Oats box tied up with string, and at her feet a cardboad suitcase with tin locks. The two combined to give her the look of someone waiting on a station bench to board a third class carriage. She began to speak, in a harsh smoker's voice, almost as soon as he had pushed through the curtain, her words puffing out like mouthfuls of smoke: "His wish was to be buried in his own country, so I fulfilled my duty by sending someone to tell your mother." She paused in her staccato delivery only to point out the two children, who had crept silently over to cling to her skirt, with a sweep of the cigarette encircling them with its glowing tip. "I had these two children by him; this piñata workshop was mine before he came along." Then, relaxing from her defensive, hunched position, she parted her legs slightly and brought down her arm nonchalantly to throw the remainder of the cigarette into a chamberpot. This was the signal that her responsibilities ended there, she had nothing more to account for.

Night was falling outside by the time he left the room, convinced that he could trust her to go to the mortuary early the next morning and give permission for the body to leave. As he walked towards the door beneath the piñatas which, drained of their colours in the twilight, looked like strange hanging bodies, he had the strange feeling that he was leaving a place in ruins, and this feeling flashes through his mind again in the truck now. In one hand he carried the Quaker Oats box, which was so heavy that the string cut into his fingers, and in the other the case. He opened the case on the tiled mortuary slab, put aside the old dress army uniform, and chose instead the double-breasted striped cashmere suit, with its moth-eaten silk linings. As an afterthought, he tied the khaki tie round his father's neck.

She had followed him and in the doorway had suddenly tapped herself on the forehead, as though she had forgotten the most important piece of news. "Your father's papers are in the cardboard box—I didn't tell you that, did I? He always insisted I should give you the box, he told me so yet again in the hospital. He never lost hope that you yourself would come to take him back after his death. 'He mustn't on any account forget it.'" Just as the driver was starting up the engine for them to pull away, she ran out again to hand him his father's old felt army hat.

In the bedroom she had offered him a cup of coffee, and while he was sipping it seated uncomfortably beside her on the wooden bed, she talked about his father, her hands busy picking at her skirt as though she were unravelling a skein of wool. Listening to her tender, sad words it was easy for him to imagine his father in the hostile silence of boarding houses, the gloomy diningrooms with their cracked windowpanes, the residents looking as though they had just come back from a funeral as they sat down at the tables, or as if they were just about to set out on a night journey to distant, rainy provinces, listlessly stirring the steaming watery broth, sawing through the flakey chunks of meat with a heavy, badly washed knife, idly chewing a toothpick at the end of the meal, waiting for a conversation that would never take place, then finally standing up, taking care not to scrape his chair, shambling off across the ragged-edged, greasy linoleum out into the corridor with its paraffin-waxed tiles, flanked by dried-up palms in clay pots, then unlocking the door to his tiny room at the back of the yard hung with wires and washing. He could imagine his father, with the clatter from the diningroom in the background, sitting on his campbed for a smoke, searching in his worn shirts for shreds of tobacco amongst crumpled receipts, telegrams rubbed through at the folds with their messages of condolence for relatives he had never seen again; then bury his head in his hands, supporting its whole weight as though doing penance, and get into bed, perhaps without bothering to undress, slipping in between the cold, dank sheets, indifferent to the warmth of the shawl folded beneath his pillow and to the voices from the other rooms that filtered through the partitions, conversations and intricate arguments. His father, enveloped in the sickly disinfectant smell from the floors, hearing at the back of the drawers in the wardrobe a rustling sound that was the epitome of loneliness, then after a nap, with night already fallen, washing his underclothes in the cold water of the wash-basin. His father, who had broken out of this sordid routine to seek refuge in this tired old man's alliance, telling himself it would be better to make piñatas than to be trudging the streets in the drizzling rain, the damp coming up through the soles of his shoes, carrying sample volumes of the Children's Encyclopedia around everywhere in a borrowed case, collecting old newspapers to sell by weight, in the middle of the night correcting the proofs of a periodical put out by the Central American Union and read by no-one, giving his Spanish grammar class at an evening commercial school, his trousers spattered with chalk, the money his wife sent him religiously put aside for the purchase of rifles that were invariably intercepted by the border police, or were useless from being buried too long: so in the end, stripped of his rifles, it was in this workshop that he found solace. He was affectionate with his children, and she left some of the tasks to him, cradling Bardo Ruben Dario to sleep in his arms, getting up in the early hours to rock Heroina Rafaela Herrera whenever he heard her cough.

Now that the truck is climbing the narrow road up to the Parque Jerez, between the walls of La Asuncion College and the San Ramon seminary with its high windows, the front of the cathedral comes into view, guarded by its cement lions. Doubtless she has already organised a prayer for the dead man to be said on the steps outside: the following day, when the funeral procession passes by along the Calle Real on its way to the cemetery, she will want a prayer said there in the open air to show more defiance. The crowd will spill over onto the small parking lot and the pavement of the park, the photographers perched on the lions' backs to photograph the throng as it moves off again once the ceremony is over, a cluster of floral wreaths and flags at its head, and in the rear, the unused horse-drawn hearse, empty because the mourners will have insisted on carrying the coffin the whole way on their shoulders, pushing to have the honour, just as the speechmakers will jostle at each street corner for the right to deliver their words of tribute from the moment the coffin leaves the bakery, the last of them having to soliloquize at the gates of the cemetery itself, by the side of the grave, in the light of petrol lamps, for night will have long since fallen. This must have been what his mother was thinking as she peered out of her door to see if the truck was arriving, waiting for all those who in reply to her telegrams would be flocking to the funeral from Managua, from the provinces—committees specially elected to convey their heartfelt grief, all the executive members of the opposition parties; and with all the city's military forces on the alert, as the funeral passes in front of the National Guard regional headquarters, the crowd will start to chant: "Down with the dictatorship!" their hands aloft to give the victory sign.

As it continues down the Calle Real, the truck passes La Rambla on a corner, and he once again pulls out the pledge he signed at the border, but puts it away again without looking at it. Then, as if his mother's proud voice were rising from the end of the street to greet him from the bakery ablaze with lights for the wake, he can hear her reproach him: "If anyone goes to jail for his funeral, it will be me."

We had got over our disappointment at the failure of the ball, though Indio took it much worse and was so downcast he couldn't eat anything for months; the Yankee girls had left Managua with the army of occupation, which had pulled out when they realized it was impossible to win the war in the Segovias. That was when we were brought in to carry out the plan to murder Sandino. It was the Yankees themselves who as they were leaving gave *el hombre* the task of seeing it done, having got him named army commander-in-chief after a few words with my godfather.

We carried out *el hombre*'s orders like the good subordinates we were. Since I had been given another promotion, this time into police headquarters in Managua, it was my job to take him prisoner that February night as he was returning from talks in the presidential palace—he had come in from the Segovias to ask for government guarantees on the peace treaty signed when the Yankees withdrew. Indio, also promoted thanks to *el hombre*, was now in charge of the military secretariat, so it was he who typed out Sandino's secret death warrant, and who made sure that while the ambush was being laid and while he was being taken to the place of execution with his generals, *el hombre* would be sitting in the salon of the Campo de Marte surrounded by his most trusted officers, all of whom had signed the warrant, listening to a poetry recital by a Peruvian woman who was touring Central America at the time.

With Sandino dead, and everything under control in Managua, the troops in the Segovias carried out their orders to fall on the bandits' strongholds along the banks of the Coco River, catching them unprepared in their main camp at Wiwili, where, according to their claims, they had spent the time since laying down their arms prospecting for gold in cooperatives. While these cleaning-up operations were going on, I scarcely moved from the wires in our communications room, waiting for the message that would say: Pedron Altamirano is dead, his body has been identified. The days went by though, and none of the reports mentioned his name: he had given the patrols the slip. I asked *el hombre* for leave and made for the Segovias so that I personally could bring his head back to Managua.

I chose my men from veterans of different campaigns, and obsessed with the idea of killing him, I spent whole weeks up in the mountains, tirelessly searching the areas where we received reports he might be holed up with his followers. We destroyed villages, took people from their homes, interrogated hundreds of prisoners in our efforts to find a clue as to the direction Pedron might have taken in his flight. Whenever word got around that my patrol was on its way the peasants deserted their homes and ran off into the hills for fear of being interrogated, so as a warning we would burn their abandoned crops, any corn fields we spotted, their tobacco and their bean rows; we rode our horses over the sown fields, and butchered all the animals in their corrals and pens.

With so many people either running from us or hostile, it was unlikely they would give us any reliable information about Pedron's whereabouts; we were often taken in, the news we extracted by force was nearly always false or misleading, so that we were marched up and down fruitlessly, sent to the most out-of-the-way places where there wasn't the slightest sign that he had so much as camped, not even twigs from camp fires or ashes. I didn't despair: I knew the hour of our meeting had to come one day, even if I grew old searching for him in the mountains.

I was right. One night when we were camping in Quilali, one of our guards came to tell me that he had found a drunken man slumped outside a bar, who in his ranting was cursing Pedron Altamirano. I trusted my instinct, and had him brought to me. We woke him up from his stupor, and he admitted he knew the place we had been looking everywhere for. He was Altamirano's stepson, eager to get revenge ever since he had been thrown out of their camp for his drunkenness.

We sealed the bargain for fifty pesos and a set of new clothes. At dawn the next day he led us off on what I was sure was the right track; it was a place called Las Congojas, beyond Remango. I wanted more than anything to get the whole affair settled, but on the way I couldn't help but tell myself that Altamirano wasn't going to throw away his life so easily. That's why I offered our informer—who was running alongside my horse and managing to keep up despite having his arms tied with a long piece of rope—another fifty pesos if he agreed to go on ahead, steal up on him, and kill him with his machete. He agreed without a moment's hesitation or even pausing in his panting run: when we reached the camp, he would go on ahead and chop his head off.

We surrounded the camp ready to attack, barely three hundred yards from the huts, which we could glimpse between the pine trees. We untied him, and I ordered him to go on with the machete, warning him not to try to betray us, because if he did he would end up dead like the rest of them. He took the machete and coolly walked off down the track towards the huts, testing the sharpness of the blade on clumps of grass as he went.

We lost sight of him, but they had not spotted us, and nobody disturbed us; they had not blocked the paths to the settlement at all, there were no sentries in the treetops to warn of our approach. Everything was peaceful; war seemed far away. The only sounds were the wind in the tall green grass, and the strident chords of a guitar which the breeze wafted to us. Through the pine branches we could see a group of half-dressed women, pouring water over their heads or untangling their hair with combs, wading in a stream. Near them, some children were washing a mare, and when the guitar fell silent the cool gusts of wind also brought us the sound of their laughter, together with the crying of a baby from a cord hammock slung between two saplings. The last noise I took in as I saw the man bounding back up to us from the stream was the dull thud of an axe chopping wood.

He was in such a hurry to reach us that he kept sliding down, and dropped his hat several times in his confusion before he managed to wave it in the agreed signal. I raised my hand to give the order to open fire, and in the endless moment before I lowered it, I felt I was making them a present of life.

We began the attack, advancing behind a ring of machine guns that never once let up, since we met with little resistance apart from the occasional rifle shot from old flintlock guns, .22s for shooting birds, or antiquated revolvers. We took the whole camp in less than a quarter of an hour, hidden behind a curtain of smoke. I ordered a count of the enemy bodies, as stipulated in the Marines' handbooks, and had the informer brought to me so he could take me to Pedron's body. As gleeful as ever, he told me he had come upon him asleep, worn out from lack of sleep due to a bout of malaria. A single chop to the back of his neck had been enough.

When we entered the hut, his body was lying wrapped in a muddy blanket on a low campbed, with blood still pouring from the neck. In the darkness we could dimly make out the shape of another person kneeling at his feet, which from the quiet sobbing we took to be a woman. She was crying without any hysterics, and did not even look round when we came in. One of my soldiers was about to finish her off, but I stopped him: it made no sense in cold blood like that.

Even when I ordered the head to be completely severed from the body, and had it put in quicklime in a saddlebag she refused to be separated from the dead man. She hesitated only for a moment when she saw them carrying the head away, as she made up her mind whether to see where they were taking it or to stay with the body—but when she had chosen the head, she immediately mounted guard by the side of the saddlebag, which had been tied on my horse.

We threw his body down into the stream, and that was the end of our mission, though we searched the surrounding area for any remaining fugitives, without finding any. The woman was the only survivor. Before we pulled out, we set fire to the huts, and through the thick coils of smoke we could see how hundreds of vultures had already swooped down and were fighting with the wild pigs for the best pieces of flesh, ripping open stomachs, flying up to the trees and draping strings of intestines over the branches then flapping down again for more. But they could not get at Pedron Altamirano's head, that was safe in my saddlebag, proof that peace had returned at last to the Segovias.

For mile after mile I put up with the stench from the head bouncing around in the bag, just as I endured the woman's dog-like moaning as she trotted along behind the horse, never flagging behind, never letting up with her lament, struggling to keep up with us even when out of spite we spurred our horses on faster. We never discovered whether she was his wife, his daughter or even perhaps his sister. We couldn't tell her age from her appearance, and the stepson who had betrayed his father stayed behind in Quilali to drink away his hundred pesos, without my having had the opportunity to ask him. It was not so much that I forgot, more that I was not really concerned to identify the forlorn woman who was following the dead man's head so faithfully, waiting for us whenever we halted, keeping watch all night outside the gates if we locked the head away in any barracks along the way, never eating or sleeping, always the same pattering of her bare feet, caked in white dust from the miles she had run.

She lasted all the way to Managua, and in the yard of the Campo de Marte, where I had the head put on show the morning we arrived, she knelt beside it and set to cleaning the lime and blood from his face with a faded black cloth, somehow realising that this yard, in a town she had never seen before, was our final destination. She tried to push his eyes closed with her fingers, but the lids were stuck open, then to smooth back his hair; in the end though she simply placed a candle on a piece of brick in front of the head. Heaven knows where she got it from. When I brought Larios to look at the head, the candle was already burning.

No sooner had I dismounted and ordered the head taken from the saddlebag and put there for everyone to see, than I went to wake him up in his room, without even stopping to take my spurs off. At first he didn't want to get up, complaining he was suffering from boils under his arms, but in the end he agreed to come, though he was sweating with fever. He didn't even ask me where I was taking him: we stopped under the verandah that looked onto the yard, and I think it was only when he spotted the woman kneeling in the glow from the candle in the grey dawn that he finally shook himself out of his feverish daze. He was hesitating about going any further, but I gripped his arm and pushed him on. "It's Pedron," I told him proudly, "the head of the fearsome Pedron Altamirano": he must go and look for himself. I dragged him across the yard until he was standing right in front of it.

A cloud of green flies were buzzing round the hair, matted with blood and dust. The woman was trying to brush them off with the tip of her shawl. Without letting go of his arm, I urged him to go even closer: Pedron Altamirano would never harm anyone again, he needn't be frightened. "Those were just stories that this old bandit had four lives," I chortled, grasping Larios' hand: "touch him if you like, you'll see he doesn't bite." As disdainfully as ever, he shook my hand off, and held his nose. "Don't you think, brother, you'd do better to get some sleep? You look worn out," he said. "And for goodness' sake, have that thing buried, the stink will be unbearable when the sun gets up." I wasn't having that: it was going to stay there as a warning.

He didn't bother to take his hand from his nostrils, just stared at me, his shining eyes gleaming maliciously as they had done that time so long ago; then turned on his heel without another word. I knew what he was thinking though: "You're right, I remember now, Pedron Altamirano was the one who gave you that wound of yours"; that's what his silent taunt had been.

The defendant states that at about five in the afternoon of what he thinks was a Wednesday in September, their third month on the march, they had reached a mountain in the Hielo range known as Mount La Flor; that they made camp and lay down to sleep shortly before first light. At daybreak their leader, the previously mentioned ex-National Guard officer Santiago Taleno, went in search of food to a hut some four hundred yards away, hidden behind a clump of mamey bushes. That unfortunately he met a National Guard scout in the hut, and was forced to take him captive, starting out back with him to them. That no sooner had they taken in what was happening than they were fired upon from a ridge, with a hail of bullets coming at them from all sides. That they returned the fire as best they could, at the same time pulling back with the aim of climbing higher up the mountain, leaving the scout there unharmed. Due to the strength of the gunfire and the clear weather (the dawn mists had lifted by this time), they decided instead to dig in as soon as they found a suitable position, taking cover among the boulders of a rocky outcrop on the northern slope of the mountain, where they hoped to wait for nightfall without moving an inch so as not to give themselves away. That shortly afterwards they faced a concerted attack of almost an hour, and then, after a pause, another one of similar or even greater length. That it must have been after mid-day when they first heard booming sounds in the distance, shortly after which the whole mountainside began to quake, because the National Guard had begun to fire 60mm mortars at them, some of the shells exploding so close that the muddy earth showered their faces; that each bombardment was followed by a quiet lull, which ended when they heard the scraping of the mortars being repositioned. Finally, after more than two hours of this pounding, a silence heavy with foreboding fell on the mountain.

He goes on to declare that the landscape looked very different, because after so many days of heavy cloud, there was a clear blue sky; that in this brilliant sunshine a squadron of Mustang P-4 aeroplanes suddenly appeared over the mountain peaks, their grey fuselages slowly growing in size, as they headed towards the mountain slope where they were entrenched. That one after another they peeled out of their formation and dived towards them, their machine guns blazing; that after the strafing they climbed in a wide arc until they disappeared from sight, before swooping back again, this time firing broadsides of rockets, which as they exploded set off deep underground rumblings, thunderous, deafening echoes that reverberated into the distance, as though there were answering detonations being set off on the other side of the mountains. That with each bang everything around them turned an incandescent white and stunning blue; they could feel their eyebrows and mouths being singed despite their protected position and them having their faces pressed against the earth, which itself seemed to be giving way under them in an enormous shudder.

That the defendant could see the hour of his death drawing nigh (laughter) and was making ready to meet it (laughter) but that in one of the pauses between the air attacks, their leader, ex-National Guard Santiago Taleno, tried to lift his morale by telling him that both the artillery and the planes were in fact aiming some distance from them, and that it would soon be dark, so the night would rescue them again; but to the defendant it seemed that the day was getting longer and longer, and that night would never arrive (more laughter).

It was late in the afternoon by the time the planes finally withdrew, to make way for a last mortar bombardment; that through the smoke raised by the bombs they could see the army columns clambering up the steep rocks towards them from three sides, but just as these troops had succeeded in getting near their hideout, night began to fall. This meant the patrol had failed in their objective, though the soldiers passed so close to them that they could hear the officers' voices ordering their men to fall back, and the radio operator informing headquarters that the search for the bodies was being called off until the next morning, from which they gathered that the National Guard thought they had all been killed.

In fact none of them suffered a single scratch, and so they were able to move on, after waiting cautiously. They walked past craters blasted in the earth, smashed tree trunks and the charred skeletons of other trees, their blackened shapes looming in the mist which had sprung up from nowhere, the desolate scene lit by a moon which miraculously was new that night. That for a long while they walked accompanied by a chorus of desperate cries from all sides, howls of monkeys wounded by the shooting and bombing; and that since many of them must have been killed during the day's attacks, and a lot more injured, as well as many other animals (more laughter: the president of the court calls for order), there was a terrible stench of burnt meat.

And his words of farewell as he was leaving *El Copacabana* that afternoon, the last he would tell them about Indio Larios, would be how when the time for action came, and the three of them were preparing to return secretly to Honduras to join the invasion forces, Indio had lost all heart for fighting—in fact the last invasion attempt in which he had been at all involved had been the one in 1954. He only ever opened his mouth to pour scorn on their plans, and would laugh like a grey haired boy, making fun of their training methods, criticising their weapons as antiques, telling them high-handedly that their expedition was bound to fail because all the ammunition sold on the black market since the fall of Batista was controlled by the Yankees, and that anyway in Nicaragua they already knew all about the plan, and so on and so forth. This infuriated Taleno, but Jilguero used to do his best to calm him: what use would poor decrepit old Indio be in the mountains anyway? Let him stay where he was, with his obsession for piñatas. For months he had been going on about his idea to change the workshop into a proper entertainment company that would cater for children's parties, hiring out chairs and tables, glasses, tablecloths, supply the sweets and ice creams, as well as the piñatas; and he dreamt of having a film projector with sound so that he could show the children cartoons—but he did not have the necessary capital and I reckon that he never managed to carry out his dream.

That during the following days they continued to head south, knowing that on one side, though invisible, was Lake Nicaragua, and on the other the jungles of the Atlantic coast. They were travelling through plains of tall grass, or tree-covered hills, where the weather was hot compared to that of the heights they had spent the previous three months in; and that since they had failed completely in their original plan, they decided to push on until they came to the San Juan River, and from there cross over into Costa Rica and give themselves up to the authorities. The defendant continues that their physical condition was desperate, especially that of the aforementioned Mauricio Rosales who, due to an ugly wound below his left knee, received in a fall against a tree root, found it very painful to walk; that since the defendant had no idea how far they might still be from the San Juan River, and since he felt utterly exhausted, he decided to accept the offer made on the leaflets the planes had dropped and give himself up, a decision he duly informed his comrades of, though they tried every means to get him to change his mind, telling him that they were determined to continue.

The early evening sky in Managua would be turning to gold as he climbed Dambach hill up from *El Copacabana*, when suddenly he would stop, look round, and wonder whether or not to go back down to the bar, just as the street lights flickered on. After a moment's thought though, he would go on his way; how stupid of him to have forgotten to tell them the most important part: how wide Chepito's eyes would have opened if he had told him how Jilguero and Taleno, with Indio Larios as ringleader, had got their revenge on the colonel in Guatemala: luck had placed him in their hands, like a white dove. He would have made it clear that he himself had not been present to see the fun, because it happened while he was down in Puerto Barrios seeking his fortune—otherwise, he would have been delighted to lend a hand.

Sit down, sit down again, Chepito would invite him, and Pastorita would blink excitedly: we've only heard rumours about what happened. Is it true that, disguised as Guatemalan officers, they pretended to be his aides at the funeral? That instead of taking him to the service they kidnapped him in a car? That alone in the hills, they raped him, then dumped him naked in front of the official deputations at the cathedral doors just as the procession was leaving with the dead man? But his only reply would be to shake his head; it all took place in a rundown brothel in Mixco, Pastorita: they enticed him there with the promise of enjoying some schoolgirls; that was his downfall, his passion for fornication.

It happened in Lasinventura's brothel, which had been famous during General Ubico's presidency because he had reserved himself the right to try out every new arrival who came there wanting to become a Girl Prodigy, as the handmaidens of carnal delights were known. This had made him the brothel's patron saint; his painting was still hanging in the main room. Cement intended for a town hall that never got built was used to give the brothel a face lift; even the statue of a naked woman ordered especially from Italy to adorn the gardens of the presidential palace, which was being constructed at that time, disappeared mysteriously from Customs and a few days later was installed in Lasinventura's courtyard; its heavy pine crate was seen being transported on a gun carriage to Mixco. Ubico provided curtains, chandeliers, ornate mirrors, luxurious armchairs—all of it stolen from the palace furniture.

The day General Ubico fell, Lasinventura's luck ran out. A furious mob attacked her house and smashed the mirrors, her beds and all her fine furniture. Silk screens and handbasins were flung out into the street, while the naked Prodigies fled across the heaps of elegant clothes strewn on the floors, pursued by the crowd, who were trying to burn their most sensitive parts with burning cinders. Lasinventura herself clung to a door frame shouting that they would have to kill her to get her out of there, so in the end they left her among the debris, with the slashed portrait of the general her only company.

After that she was a broken woman, and the brothel's glorious nights were a thing of the past. Only three of her Prodigies stayed on, and because the attackers had destroyed her furniture, all she could buy were cheap metal tables and chairs. It became a third-rate place that couldn't even provide Rockola music, unlike the others that sprang up alongside it in the same street, like vultures congregating around the corpse of a dead animal. From time to time a prostitute would arrive to recover from a bout of sadness or sickness in the undisturbed quiet of the rambling house, so gradually it became a refuge for those whom fate had dealt with unkindly.

But how did you all discover such a strange place? Chepito might ask him. Well, it so happened that one day Taleno went to Mixco in search of clients for his insurance policies, in the difficult days following their expulsion from Honduras to Guatemala, and when by chance he stumbled on the Calle Amargura he was astonished to find such an imposing building among all the cheap bars.

He knocked on the door to try his luck, and Lasinventura herself came to open it, all dolled up in spite of it being so early in the day. Scarcely had it dawned on him what kind of a place he had arrived at, when she politely invited him in; looking round, he could see the piles of old clothes and smashed pieces of furniture everywhere, as though the place had been ransacked only the day before. He realised his mistake soon enough, but thought that since he was there he might as well see if he could sell her some insurance. How much did she reckon her arthritic bones were worth per month? She laughed, and offered them to him for nothing; but then at once felt sorry for him, having to do such a thankless job—it couldn't be easy to knock on strangers' doors, risking insults like that. She could tell from his face that he was thirsty, but as the beer truck had not yet been round that morning, she sent for some water for him.

That was how he met the Schoolgirl, when she came in carrying the mug of water shortly afterwards, and the two others shuffled in in their slippers, their curiosity aroused by such an unexpected visit. Combing their bedraggled hair as best they could, they jostled around him, begging him to tell them news of the outside world. Soon it was they who were pouring out all their troubles to him, speaking frankly and even relishing their misfortunes as if there were something comic or obscene about them. With all their talk, he found the afternoon creeping by, and when night fell he decided to stay and share one of their beds.

Taleno let them all in on his discovery—Jilguero and him first, then Indio Larios later on. Gradually it became a ritual with them to get a bus to Mixco and have a good time on the cheap there thanks to the old woman dressed up as the Queen of the Night and her three attendants. They had credit for as long as they liked, could make as much noise, and talk all they wanted to, without fear of the police arriving to shut them up or cart them off, as they did whenever the arguments between exiles got a bit out of hand in the city centre bars.

But, as he walked down the Calle Calvario towards the east of the city, his impulse to go back and tell them this important news would wane, even if at least Chepito would still be in *El Copacabana* getting the bar ready for that evening. The next day, or some other, he would tell the two of them how they had taken the colonel prisoner: I'm telling it to you exactly the way Taleno and Jilguero described it to me, he would say to them, word for word just as they told us all during one of the last nights of our camp at El Chaparral, before the Honduran Army ambushed us and destroyed us. Then perhaps Pastorita wouldn't be so disappointed with Indio Larios.

The defendant further states that they parted from each other in a sugarcane plantation where they had halted to calm their gnawing hunger pangs by chewing the canes. He had stayed in a nearby stack, getting one of the inhabitants to pass a message to the National Guard patrols to tell them of his surrender, being taken prisoner two days later; that he was taken to San Pedro de Lovago, and from there to Managua, where since then he has been in prison at the disposition of the military tribunal, waiting to face the charges brought in the present case. He knows nothing of what subsequently became of his colleagues, he testifies in reply to a question from the military prosecutor, who also informs the defendant that he has the right at this point to add anything further he may wish to say that is relevant to the trial, before his defence is formally declared closed, but the prisoner declines, everything he has to say has already been taken down.

He has no desire to tell the court that before they moved off on their own, Taleno and Jilguero had tried once more to persuade him to go on with them—hadn't they got through the worst of it—so why not stick out the rest? What if he was killed when the army took him? Jilguero had even managed to raise a smile: "That's Raul for you, stubborn as ever." From the doorway of the ranch he watched as they walked off across first the canefield stubble, then a stretch of flat land full of calabash bushes; even from that distance Taleno, his clothes in shreds and his face filthy, had lifted his hands to his mouth to shout that all they needed to spot was a flight of herons and they would know they had reached the river.

The provost marshal straightens his peaked cap and marches out in front of Raul, who walks meekly between his guards through the empty rows of metal chairs. Behind them only the military prosecutor is left in the court, his head bent over the papers on his desk.

CHAPTER 9

Now that on a stifling April afternoon he is walking in step with the hearse, his hand on the nickel-plated pedestal on which the coffin rests, soaked with sweat and with the button from his shirt collar digging into his neck, his mind returns to the way in which his mother had suddenly burst out crying when they set off. As he laboured under the weight of one side of the coffin, he had seen her stagger back to find a seat, sobbing with frustration and pent-up rage, crying at her helplessness in the face of the great betrayal. Nobody had come to the funeral.

The cathedral bells were tolling in the distance and he was shining his shoes seated at the end of the row of empty chairs set out on the pavement when she came to the bakery door one last time in the hope that she might find, unable now to conceal her anxiety, some sign of people or cars converging on the house. The street was as quiet as ever, the only vehicle in it the hearse drawn up in the shade, the driver in his peaked cap busy polishing the carriage-work. From a billiard parlour they could hear the players' excited shouts and the click of the balls. On the high pavement opposite, an old black man was sitting in his undershirt basking in the sun; a herd of pigs driven by a small boy slipped under a fence into an empty plot of land, while a block away in the Calle Real soft drink trucks went by, and buses full of passengers on their way to Poneloya; a debt collector on his motorcycle accelerated as he passed their street corner. There was no display of troops, not one of the orange Roadworks Department trucks which on the days when there were political demonstrations or student marches would patrol the streets loaded with steel-helmeted soldiers armed with Garand rifles.

He finished polishing his shoes and went to the door of the bakery, which had been stripped of all its shelves and counters for the occasion. He had only to look at his watch pointedly in front of his mother for her to understand that there was nothing more to be done, it was past four o'clock already and the funeral had to start. When he came in a second time from the street with the other pallbearers, chosen from among the few people who had bothered to come, relatives and neighbours who had also been there the night before, he watched as she went over to the coffin to perform one of the rites she had been preparing for days. She unfolded a Nicaraguan flag and draped it over the lid: but now, her gesture seemed lacking in all solemnity, robbed of meaning by the empty chairs out in the sun. It was as if her hands were making a bed or laying a table. Afterwards, she burst out crying.

So there was no need for the awkward conversation he had been planning all the way from the border, to try to convince her to hold the funeral in silence so that he could keep his promise. Almost as soon as the truck had drawn up at the bakery the previous night he had realised that solitude had defeated all his mother's plans. There were only a handful of mourners waiting out in the street. Dazzled by the headlights, they stood up as though suddenly aroused from sleep, and went through with something that was made inevitable by the fact of their presence there at that time of night: they surrounded him in an affectionate silence, and unloaded the coffin with exaggerated care and shouted warnings. He was sure the moment he saw her come to the door with the other women in mourning: though her mouth was still set proudly, she could not hide her dread of this desertion. She was left completely on her own with the dead man before dawn, and later, as the morning sun began to warm the bakery, she alone bent over the coffin to peer at her husband through the glass, like someone staring into an abyss.

By now they are approaching the cathedral. From doorways, curious onlookers stare at the flag-draped coffin and the procession of barely a dozen mourners, who seem to have been thrown together by chance. Some of them even prefer to walk up on the pavements out of the glare of the sun, and mingle with the passersby; the others scurry along as though afraid it might suddenly start to rain despite the stifling heat. In the Casa Prio the regulars are huddled round El Capitan at his table, listening to an Agustin Lara song, which he turns down as the funeral passes by. Near the municipal market, a loudspeaker van drives off announcing the current film at the Orion cinema, a whistled military march accompanying the man's voice: tonight, *The Bridge Over the River Kwai.*

After they left Escuintla on their way to the El Salvador border, he had decided to untie the strings round the Quaker Oats box that he had deposited between his feet on the cabin floor. First of all he came across a mass of papers stuffed in files, with grimy, coffee-stained covers that also had the marks of glasses left on them, and edges burnt by cigarettes. Underneath was a biscuit tin containing photographs, and at the very bottom, a mouldy book bound in red cloth, on which was written in gilt Gothic lettering:

LETTERS TO MY SON BOLIVAR

The first page contained a likeness of the Liberator painstakingly tapped out on a typewriter. Then came the letters themselves, neatly typed and framed in double lines of black ink, all of them numbered and in chronological order, with an index at the end. (Note—the first letters in this volume had to be reconstructed from memory in exile, due to the seizure by the police of the author's archive when he was taken prisoner in Managua, in October 1941.)

He could not remember ever having received any of these letters, dedicated to him with the opening greeting of: My Son! The first were written soon after his birth (later on you will come to understand the lessons I am anxious to impart to you as a guide for your future life, something which is beyond you now due to your tender age); always related to his growing years (today you are ten, Bolivar, and your senses may already perceive the mystical emanations that certain beings and things give off). If they were never sent to him it must have been because they were reserved for posterity (my wish is that through you future generations may come to know that my 1941 rebellion, for which I was condemned to death but miraculously escaped, came about from a desire to preserve the principle of the alternation of power in our country, and to ensure that electoral fairplay be respected); a volume of letters destined to be published one day as a kind of civic catechism for youth (I will now provide you with what I believe should be the honest citizen's ten commandments. First: love your country as you do yourself; always bear in mind that its altar is worthy of the highest sacrifice, no matter how cruel it may seem); interspersed with autobiographical passages (today I am going to devote these pages to writing about some of the useful experiences in my life as an academy-trained soldier, one who graduated at a very tempestuous period for our nation); draft political manifestos for government (despotism, the reasons for which I will not exempt myself from blame, has sapped the strength of our republic, but there is still time for us, men of different opinions and beliefs, to become her saving doctors. Only thus can we ward off the most dangerous evils, making honest the management of public affairs. Proven integrity, above all else); the letters sprinkled with quotations ("Arise, be a man") and lyrical touches in the guise of moral advice ("A drop of mud a diamond may obscure, but if that stone be truly pure . . . ").

The last of them was dated 15 September 1956 (on a day such as today our forefathers wrote in shining letters the central pages of our history when they signed the act of independence . . .) That was where they stopped, the point where he must have sent them to be bound in this first volume; there was no sign of any more in the archive, if in fact he ever wrote any.

In the biscuit tin together with the photographs were cards for masses and funeral services sung in memory of the fallen (Pray to God for the soul of Rigoberto Lopez Perez, R.I.P., who offered his life 21 September 1956. On the first anniversary of his glorious death. Unified Committee of Nicaraguan Exiles (UCNE) La Dolorosa parish, Guatemala).

Then there were the photographs themselves, with messages to Bolivar scribbled on the back:

+ This one is in Dec. 1923 with Chencho Mendieta, on the platform of Leon railway station. We are off to Granada to play baseball against the Salesians ('I was fifteen, and held a star in my hand . . , ' Ruben Dario).

+ Here, somewhere in the Segovias, with Major Pierson USMC, 5th Co. of Marines. Date: 1930, I think.

+ Here I am in exile, a member of the famous Caribbean Legion. On my left is Dr. Patiño, from the Dominican Republic; Dr. Buero, a Cuban doctor, is talking to me, and the third man is Antolin Gonzalez Leon, from Venezuela. (All three of them died in the Luperon beach invasion, Dominican Rep., 1945; the photo was taken earlier that same year.) NB: The Caribbean Legion aimed to fight against all our tyrants; one by one, we were sure, their turn would come.

+ The Malecon in Havana, 1946. We were headed for Cayo Confites, to train for a fresh invasion attempt against Trujillo: the Caribbean Legion again.

+ This is me patrolling the Paseo de los Estudiantes, San Jose de Costa Rica, 1948, after the Caribbean Legion had kicked out Picado's government and installed Figueres. In the end, that victory gave no help to our cause in Nicaragua.

+ Here I am with the youngster Mauricio Rosales, from Masaya, and the ex-National Guard captain Santiago Taleno (both exiles too) swimming one Sunday in the port of San Jose, Guatemala. The other man in the background pointing at the camera is our friend Raul Guevara, an excellent guitarist, a composer with a brilliant future.

+ The same trio taken as they drink a toast in *El Portal* bar, May 1959. They were about to set off on the expedition which in the end cost Mauricio and the ex-captain their lives.

In nearly all the photos his father was wearing his khaki tie over a short-sleeved check shirt. The tie was all he had left from his military wardrobe, apart from a folding cap—but this shipwreck's outfit was enough to lend him an air of soldierly majesty whenever he chaired discussions among the exile groups, sweeping the cap off and beating the sides of his seat with it to emphasize his points, straightening it as though in a mirror as he left the bar. In his hand he was invariably carrying a list of prominent figures who were to become members of the cabinet after the triumph of the armed rebellion. Bolivar found the list itself among the papers, with the names crossed out of those exiles who had sold out their principles in order to return to Nicaragua, promising never to get involved in anything again.

Groups of placid-looking exiles photographed in bad light in a corridor whose shiny tiles reflect the flashbulb, men of all ages perched on a wicker sofa, hats on their knees, those standing behind them trying hard not to lose their resolute, self-absorbed look (August 1944: we are meeting for me to announce Pres. Arevalo's unlimited support for our cause. At that time, it seemed *el hombre*'s days must be numbered . . .)

They had reached El Salvador by the time he got to the last folders. They contained minutes from meetings of exiles' committees, which constantly changed their names and executives: the United Patriotic Front (UPF); Co-ordinating Committee of the Democratic Opposition of Nicaragua (CCDEMON) the Authentic Republican Movement (ARM); Patriotic Revival Action Group (PRAG); each with its grandly headed writing paper, the intertwined initials and artistic designs printed in patriotic blue; invitations to meetings and funerals, reminders that monthly subscriptions should be paid promptly, lists of exiles with their addresses, the telephone numbers of their boarding-houses or of a nearby pharmacy where they could be called in an emergency; commission reports (Finance, Ideology, Solidarity, Press and Culture) and typewritten sheets, carbon copies that contained speeches, proclamations, manifestos, press communiques; and still more papers, torn from duplicated documents with no means of identifying what they were.

Press cuttings held together with rusty paper clips, whole sepia printed pages from Mexican newspapers carrying homages to Sandino at every anniversary of his murder, complete with notes in the margin (Your father soon repented his part in this dark deed—see in this same archive my pamphlet published by the Aurora press of Guatemala "Mea Culpa: the True Story of a Political Crime"). Among the cuttings, carefully folded, an invitation with an oval engraving

PROGRAMME OF THE CELEBRATIONS FOR THE
CORONATION OF
THE QUEEN OF THE NICARAGUAN ARMY,
TO TAKE PLACE ON 14TH NOVEMBER 1941

(NB: I did not undertake this out of servility, but to cover up my plans for rebellion, which unfortunately came to nothing. See copies of the court martial proceedings and *La Noticia* newspaper accounts through Dec. 1941.)

The bottom files contained few documents, consisting mainly of bills for materials to make piñatas with, medical prescriptions for popular dispensaries, bar IOU's redeemed at the last moment. There were no more minutes from secret meetings, or invitations. Only one telegram. He had obviously gone round for days to collect enough money to send it, asking, even begging for contributions: Dr. Castellon (he never turned up at his surgery whenever I went to look for him, or perhaps he would not see me); Tut. Arguello (told me to come back the next day, but he wasn't there); Dionisio Pereyra (gave me what change he had in his pockets; Aristarco 'El Chele' Sandoval (told me he did not agree), a list of the people asked to contribute pinned to the pink copy of the telegram, together with the pawn ticket for his wrist watch, probably the only thing of any value he had left. An old, sick man by this time, he must have sat down to wait, in the hope that a reply would reach him at his address in the 12th district:

> 14 JANUARY 1961 GUATEL (VIA TROPICAL RADIO)
> PRESIDENT ELECT USA
> MR JOHN F KENNEDY
> WASHINGTON DC
> ACCORDANCE PROMISES GIVEN IN REMARKABLE CAMPAIGN SPEECH SAN DIEGO CALIF STOP TAKE TOUGH LINE AGAINST CARIBBEAN DICTATORS STOP WE WISH EARNESTLY TO POINT OUT DRAMATIC CASE NICARAGUA DESPOTIC FAMILY MISRULE 25 YEARS STOP DEMOCRATIC RETURN OUR COUNTRY FIRST CONCRETE PROOF YOUR WORTHY AIMS STOP SINCERELY YOURS STOP

By now they were in Honduras, coming into Jicaro Galan. He held the cable between his fingers for a moment close to the open truck window, the draft blowing it back into his face, then he let the wind snatch it from his grasp. After that he began to get rid of all the papers, tossing out letters, manifestos, newspaper cuttings, which blew back into the cab before swirling off behind the speeding truck, floating in midair as though they were making a last effort to resist, then plummeting defeated, falling limply onto the ground beside the road, littering the streams that flowed through the pines, or being carried still further off by the wind from the bay.

He tore the photos into tiny pieces and threw them after the rest, until all he had left were the bound sheaf of letters and the empty biscuit tin. He tried to tear all the letters out at once, but couldn't, so ripped them out one by one, until all that remained were the red cardboard covers with their gilt lettering.

The funeral is passing the children's park. A swarthy dark-haired man wearing a pressed linen suit stands waiting at the park railings, his hands joined in front of him in an air of silent solemnity. He removes his white panama hat, and one of the two boys flanking him steps forward to take it from him, careful not to get it dirty. The other boy is holding a flag, its stick pressed into his bare stomach. As the coffin draws level with him, the man raises his arm in an imperious gesture, commanding the hearse to come to a halt. He continues in this victorious pose until he has also stilled any muttered conversation among the mourners. Still staring at the hearse, he pulls a wad of papers from his breast pocket, and once he has them in his hand, deigns to put a pair of glasses on. Then he shoots his arm out again in the direction of the coffin, as if to cleave it in two with a thunderbolt. He pauses for breath before launching on his speech, his hand poised erect like a statue.

Bolivar hears the deep rumble as the man makes to start his speech, and orders the carriage driver to move on. The bewildered mourners are caught in two minds, whether to stay to listen to the speaker—who, when he realizes that the procession has unexpectedly begun to move again, raises his voice as if by shouting he can make it halt—or to follow the rapidly disappearing hearse. All of a sudden, almost at a run, they decide on the hearse, and catch up with it just as the driver has reached the final descent to the cemetery, the sun glinting off the black coachwork.

Bolivar, with one hand still on the burning grip of the coffin pedestal, turns for a moment. Back up behind the railing, facing the deserted street along which is passing an uninterested solitary cyclist, the figure of the orator grows smaller and smaller, as he stands there, thumping the empty air with his fist to emphasize his words.

He walked scornfully back to his room to sleep, his elbows stuck out from his side because of the boils. He left me standing in the middle of the yard before I had the chance to say a word, without so much as noticing that I was about to tell him what I thought of him, show him that I had long since seen through his airs, was well aware of his ambitious desire for high command. Ever since my wounding, when he had sealed the bloodbond between us, I had known what he was after. But nobody ever reached high places by organising gala balls, or having his picture taken for *La Noticia* on birthdays, with underneath the printed caption of "an honest soldier" that so pleased him, nor by putting on charity benefit shows, sporting leagues in the barracks, or reading classes for prisoners. And that was his great mistake, the mistake that led to his downfall.

I myself devoted my time to helping *el hombre* amass his pots of gold, because the more he got, the more there was for me. We began with the estates. Every Sunday *el hombre* and I would go out in his car, noting down which of them he liked as we went by, so that I could go back the next day and offer to buy them. Of course, most of the owners didn't want to sell, but that was the whole point: to convince them it would be a good idea. Then when the World War came along, the government expropriated all the Germans who were on a blacklist, and we were able to buy up all their confiscated properties—fine, prosperous coffee plantations, fruit farms, sawmills, dairies; the advantage was that we could fix our own price at the sales for these and all the other properties mortgaged to the banks. I would appear at the auctions with a machine gun in one hand and a bag of money in the other; even if I had gone unarmed, nobody would have dared to raise the price, knowing who sent me.

It was me who thought up the cattle buying scheme as well. First of all we put out a military decree saying that an official permit was required for any movement of cattle in the country. The garrisons in each region sent us reports about any herds that were being sent to market in their area, and we would dispatch an armed patrol to halt them to inspect their permit in a spot a long way from water or pasture. This required a telegram from *el hombre* himself, and while the cattle owner rushed off to apply for it, the herd would have to stay put. Days later, with the beasts dying of thirst and with no sign of the telegram, I would come on the scene in a truck with the weighing machine and an offer to take the animals off their hands. So they had to make do with what I offered—it would have been worse still to leave the carcasses to the vultures.

"Why don't you choose an estate for yourself?" *el hombre* would ask me on our Sunday outings: "choose whichever one you fancy and I'll let you have it." But I was always cautious; I didn't want greed to spoil things. What was his, he could keep; I didn't want to be beholden to him, except when for purely sentimental reasons I wanted to get back El Corozo, my father's old farm in Catarina—then I did ask him to protect me. Apart from that though I always told him "No, thank you very much; but if you agree, I've already thought what my speciality will be, and I hope you'll give me a free hand for that."

I devoted myself to the gambling dens and nightclubs, the dice and roulette parlours, dance halls, big-time betting, foreign whores: there was none of that in Managua in those days, and I cornered the market. Plus the odd brothel or lodginghouse that came into my possession without any effort on my part, as payment for gambling debts, and what I made on granting licences to traders in the market, for butcher shops, animal foodstuff suppliers. So it was me who was on the way up: Indio just had his head in the clouds. That's why when it finally came time to bring him down to earth once and for all I couldn't help but feel sorry for him.

Back in 1941, shortly after *el hombre* had been re-elected for another term, the dance classes in the Campo de Marte suddenly started up again. I got curious when I heard the sound of music coming from the officers' mess, so I asked one of the guards on duty what was going on. Larios had organised the dancing class, but this time there were no conscripts, only officers from all the garrisons in Managua, including the president's personal bodyguard, the police I was in command of, and even some from the provinces. Oh ho, I said to myself, what's all this? A dancing master at his age, and him the father of a family as well?

He had his excuse of course, and a very elaborate one it was too. He had thought up a great social event to crown *el hombre*'s youngest daughter queen of the army, which was to involve three days of festivities in Managua, from morning till night, with concerts in the parks, and on the last evening a triumphal procession through the streets of the city, with a ball as the grand finale. That was the dance that the officers were supposed to be rehearsing for with the gramophone. Maybe it was my mason's sixth sense, but I decided I had better get a spy of mine into the lessons. I chose someone I knew I could trust, and sent him off to dance. He found out that they were all conspirators in an uprising dancing together so they could avoid suspicion while they worked out the plan; that Indio was the leader, and that he would get them to change partners to pass on the ideas—some evenings there were upwards of twenty couples waltzing away. That was their mistake, because among such a crush of dancers, my spy had no difficulty in slipping in unnoticed.

I felt completely dejected, and could not even touch my breakfast the morning I went to tell everything to *el hombre* up on the hill. Horrified at the thought of such treason, at first he would not believe me, his own chief-of-staff, but when I put all the evidence before him, he was forced to change his mind. The men dressed up as royal courtiers on the night of the parade were to be officers loyal to *el hombre*, and the non-commissioned officers and soldiers from their companies were to be the Roman soldiers. When they were all inside the cathedral for the coronation, the others would strike: not a single loyal man left to defend the barracks, all of them in the church with their wooden swords. And what was the reason for all this plotting? They wanted to hand over the presidency to an old, deranged doctor from Masaya who, according to the dancers, had been the rightful winner at the last elections. Talk about a waste of time and effort.

At their next dancing session we waited for them to enter and start up the gramophone, then we moved quickly into position around the hall, and fixed up a machine gun facing the front door. In the middle of a charleston, we switched off all the lights, and ordered them out into the yard at once. "With your partners," I shouted, to add to their dismay; and they should watch their step, or we'd be seeing how they danced the funeral march. For a few seconds all we could hear was whispering in the darkness, but then they began to emerge, with Larios in the lead, accompanied by a police second lieutenant who had been his partner at the moment we had surprised them. Still out of breath from his exertions, his shirt was soaking under the armpits; he tried to step forward to say something to me, but though it broke my heart to do so, I stopped him in his tracks, levelling my gun at him. That brought him up short.

I ordered them tied up with their hands behind their backs, and as the ropes were being wound round them, he still had the nerve to laugh in my face. What are you laughing at? I was going to ask him, making clear how our positions had changed, but he didn't give me the chance. Still kept back by the levelled gun, he cocked his head in the way he always did when he was about to tell me one of his juicy secrets: "If you want to shoot me, brother, you'd better get it over with," I heard him say, for all the world as if he was asking for a puff on my cigarette.

A week later, once the coronation festivities were over, the court martial was held in the same room they had used for their dancing practice. The coronation was every bit as magnificent as he had planned, even though he could only appreciate the cannon salutes and the bells from a distance, alone in his cell. He asked to defend himself, and his wish was granted. He thought his knowledge of the Code of Military Conduct, written in English and left by the Marines, would stand him in good stead, but it was of no use to him at all. Neither was his calling upon his whole pantheon of saints, not even his favourite Marcus Brutus or Simon Bolivar: the court sentenced him to life imprisonment for high treason, while his accomplices were drummed out of the army in disgrace. But I insisted to *el hombre*: "Whatever jail you put him in, he'll escape when you least expect it, he's still got friends inside the National

Guard." Who better than I to know of his bold cunning; there was no way we could keep him sitting quietly in a cell for the rest of his life.

That is why I advised *el hombre* to fake an escape; we would take Larios out into the country late at night and give him the chance to make a break for it, then shoot him down as he ran. I was given the job of organising the details of his last journey, but I got someone else to carry it out. I couldn't bring myself to stain my hands with his blood; I could not betray the fellowship of the masons. Nor many other things. I sat by my window in the Campo de Marte, the only one still lit among the mass of silent huts, waiting indecisively for the telephone to ring with news of how the operation had gone. It was as if I had a premonition of what I was going to hear through the chattering earphone in the electric stillness of the night: he had escaped.

According to the report that the leader of the squad gave me the following day, they had sprayed bullets at him, but none of them had hit despite the clear target he presented in the bright moonlight. They saw him leap over a fence, but could find no further trace of him. A few months later, we learnt from intelligence reports that he had crossed the frontier disguised as a nun, and was now in Guatemala. Oh damn, I thought to myself, now he's going to start causing trouble trying to get back into the country with his armed rebels.

So it turned out. But in spite of his famous invasion attempts year after year, we never saw each other face to face again. The nearest I came was whenever I had to count the dead from his invading forces, but even though I'm not sure I'd recognise the sound of his sly voice these days, I shall never forget his smiling troublemaker's face. I was completely calm the day I arrested him, calm at the end of our lunch that same day in the officer's mess, when without him being aware of it we were saying our last farewell.

We were always in the habit of sitting on a while to chat after we had finished eating, and I am sure he was trying to sound me out in a roundabout way, because he began to read aloud from a book that reeked of disinfectant; passages about free elections, the alternation of power, and other literary ideas of the sort. "Don't you worry, brother, those are just theories," he concluded, snapping the book shut and catching hold of my arm affectionately. Out of pity for him I changed the topic of conversation, poking fun at him for his dancing classes: when he retired he could set up his own dancing academy, like Adan Castillo.

He rose to his feet, picked up the book and tucked it under his arm. "If you gave a hand in teaching the lads the first steps, you'd be surprised what you'd learn too," he said, thinking he was talking to me in riddles. He was right though in that I didn't need to bother with theories, I've never been one for high-flown ideas. "You have to be loyal and grateful, otherwise you'll never see those pots of gold," were my father's last words to me on his deathbed, and I've always followed his advice.

As long as he lived, *el hombre* recognised my loyalty. "If you were my woman, I wouldn't be afraid to leave you shut up in a roomful of men," he told me on the day I was sworn in as the new chief-of-staff. I was completely taken aback, my hand already raised to swear the oath, so I respectfully asked him why.

"Because I know you wouldn't open your legs for anyone, even if they killed you." All the dignitaries and my army colleagues burst out laughing.

Pastorita feels someone touch his shoulder and turns, startled at first, then with a broad smile: Hey, Chepito, what are you doing here? Out on a trip? Chepito laughs back timidly: As you can see, I'm here for the game; and that at first, when he saw him leaving the stand, he had wondered: can that really be Pastorita? It's so long since I've seen him . . . Pastorita, wheeling his brightly coloured bicycle, with its plastic grips on the handlebars and painted rivets in the saddle, says: we've got to celebrte this, how about a few drinks down at *Las Gordas*, Chepito?

There is a large crowd leaving the baseball stadium in Granada after the game Sunday mid-day. They stream across the avenue or disappear down side streets, walk over the pitch itself, jump the metal barrier with its painted advertisements. The two of them are swept along with the others down a dusty road in among the motorcycles, horse-drawn carriages, and taxis, while behind them a loudspeaker van plays a marimba jingle to advertise Rayo talcum powder, and ice cream vendors ring their bells. When Pastorita asks what he's been up to since *El Copacabana* had to close, Chepito comes to a halt and looks at him sadly: You see? The lake got it in the end. After that he became a cook in the military canteen, thanks to a recommendation from his protector the colonel, who's retired now from the National Guard, by the way.

Pastorita takes one hand from the handlebar and rubs his fingers together as though he had a wad of notes in his hand: Your colonel must have a good few of these by now. Chepito nods in agreement: Stinking rich he is all right. You can imagine, he's moved on to better things than nightclubs—he sold all those to some Cubans from Miami. All he cares about now are his pedigree herds, his cotton, and getting still more land. What do you think he told me the last time I went to see him at the villa he's had built in Catarina, where El Corozo used to be? A real luxury villa it is, with a swimming pool and everything. "Listen Chepito," he said: "I never used to dare consider myself a millionaire, but now I can." And he's got the orphan girl there to look after him; she came back from the United States and he decided to move in with her. But his eyesight is getting worse and worse, and she's the one who looks after the business affairs now—his, and the ones she runs on the side, things like buying pay cheques from public employees in advance, or lending money at colossal interest.

That girl was so sweet and gentle—is that how she's turned

out? Pastorita sighs. He saw her once in Managua, pacing up and down outside the door of the National Palace like a wild animal, making sure that none of those who owed her money slipped past her; she's even put on mourning clothes so that she can claim her money. Then he blinks and appears to lose track, before going on to tell Chepito about his barber shop in Jalteva. It must have been about a year earlier that he had decided to move out of Managua; he bought the chair and the equipment from an old barber in Campo Bruce by the name of Luis Carlos Rivas. He knew nothing about the business, but picked it up by looking. The bicycle pedals are immobile, the chain clanks noisily as they turn down a street lined with shady gardens; tall palm trees sway in the distance. The palm trees alone, Chepito thinks, would tell anyone who had never been to Granada before that there was a lake nearby.

A few blocks further down the street Pastorita carefully lifts his bicycle up onto the pavement, and they go into a smokey, adobe house, with a big room divided into two by a screen plastered with faded cinema posters. Pastorita says hello to one of the women sitting peeling corn, and they go on out into the tree-lined courtyard. He leans the bicycle against a tree, locks it, then takes off his clips, and the two of them sit at a frail table that wobbles on the sandy earth. Overjoyed at their unexpected meeting, Pastorita cannot stop beaming, with the Kolynos smile that Lazaro used to say was his trade mark, his teeth gleaming white like a toothpaste ad.

He claps his hands, but the noise can hardly be heard above the hubbub from the other drinkers at the tables discussing the baseball game. If suddenly you could no longer hear their voices but just see their gestures, it would look as if they were practising some religion or other—well, you know baseball is almost a religion, Pastorita tells Chepito, as they look round at the others. By the way, did you see Raul with his head shaven and a face like a foreign priest in the newspaper? He did all right, Chepito replies, trying to make the table level. Whatsmore, he's been to visit him a couple of times in the air force jail: Raul hadn't changed a bit, up to his neck in trouble, but still as cheerful as ever. When I pointed out to him that according to his staement in the newspaper they had crossed nearly the whole of Nicaragua on foot, even he could hardly believe it. "I've always hated walking, Chepito, but you're right; otherwise, how did I get where they found me?" They might let him out soon—Chepito has heard talk among the staff officers in the military canteen. The son of *el hombre* reckons that Raul only played a minor role in the rebellion: they have already accounted for the two ringleaders.

At that they fall silent, looking at each other, neither of them wanting to say any more. A distant breeze from lake Cocibolca rustles the leaves of the trees; they imagine that the drinkers have all of a sudden paused in their noisy chatter to turn their heads to watch Jilguero come in and sit in the empty third chair at their table. When the woman comes over to ask what they want to drink, Pastorita asks for a half bottle of Santa Cecilia with three glasses. The woman counts the two of them with a nod of her head, smoothing her hair through a grip she has opened between her teeth, and asks why they want three glasses? Pastorita, as if she were shaking him awake: Ah, what? Yes, only two then. I bet you didn't know, did you? Chepito queries, chewing on his fingernails: they killed him in San Carlos along with Captain Taleno in mid-September last year. The government has told their relatives that they escaped to Costa Rica, but that's all lies. Do you remember how Carlos died back in April 1954—and we learnt all about it because Raul overheard some soldiers talking when he was in jail? Well, the strange thing is, they go and kill Jilguero in exactly the same way, shooting him after making him dig his own grave, and I come along and find out the details through an eyewitness too.

They have brought a tin container with crushed ice and limes in it, freshly washed glasses, which leave a wet ring on the table, warm soft drinks and the half bottle of Santa Cecilia that Pastorita opens between his knees; they have already poured the white liquid into the eight-sided mugs, raised them carefully, wished each other health, and drunk the first drink when Chepito, lowering his voice, bends over to Pastorita.

"There's a sergeant in the supply corps who knows the details, but he's not allowed to say anything,'' somebody whispered to me one day in the canteen. I made a mental note, and the next time we got our supplies, I went and looked for this sergeant. I chat to him, then the next time he comes I offer him one of the American cigarettes he's brought, and bit by bit I work on him until finally I invite him to come and see me at the canteen. He agrees, I lay on a big spread for him, open him a can of foreign beer, and as though in all innocence, I lead the conversation around to the topic that interests me: ''Was it right that I heard you were stationed in San Carlos, Sergeant?'' Then all I had to do was wait for him to finish his mouthful of food:

The rain was pouring down in San Carlos, and in the darkness all they could hear was the roaring river that swept along branches and water lilies; they had no way of knowing whether the lake was rough, or quiet like a mirror. From the outpost they finally made out the lights of the launch patrolling the river. The sergeant picked up his cape and ordered his only soldier to follow him down to the landing. They plunged through the flooded town, where all the doors were bolted and the windows shuttered against the downpour. Not even the dogs barked at them, and there was no sound from the disgruntled shivering cocks on the horse-rails. They reached the oil drums on the landing, picking their way through the alleys between warehouses and bars, and the sergeant shone his light down into the swirling waters beneath the rotten planks.

The launch's motor stuttered to a halt as it drew in. He caught the rope they threw him to moor it, then helped the officer up the steps. He would never forget the lieutenant's dark glasses at that time of night, dripping with rain. They found some shelter under a shed stacked with oil drums, and when the man removed his hat to shake the water off, he noticed how the hair had receded from his forehead: a young man too, and already going bald. Who do you reckon it was, Pastorita? I guessed from the sergeant's description: the very same Lieutenant Quesada who broke my ribs for me that time. He came back from the Canal Zone after learning all the techniques for hunting down rebels. ''What information do you have?'' he wanted to know.

The sergeant told him the story of how two strangers had arrived in the town, exhausted and dejected, asking to stay the night at Ofelia's. "Who is this Ofelia?" the lieutenant asked him, still with his condescending tone. Ofelia was a woman friend of the sergeant's, a schoolteacher in San Carlos. The two men had said they were lost hunters, and she had agreed out of fear to let them stay. "But as soon as she could, she came to warn me, Lieutenant, that's why I called you on the radio. They asked her to find them a boatman who would take them to Costa Rica by Los Chiles, but instead she came to tell me."

They were talking as if neither of them had really been there, their bulky forms under the capes only barely distinguishable in the darkness, and all the time the rain beating against the sergeant's back, which stuck out beyond the roof. "They're up there stretched out on her floor, they've done nothing but sleep since they arrived, Lieutenant, they didn't even ask for food. One of them is badly wounded in The leg, the blood keeps oozing out." The lieutenant wanted to know, finally, what weapons they had on them. There were no heavy calibre arms in sight. Perhaps revolvers in their rucksacks.

The ten or dozen soldiers in the patrol had all left the boat by now, and were formed up on the jetty waiting for their orders. "Go back up to the fort and wait there for any new development. How many men have you got?" the lieutenant asked him. The whole garrison, from the commanding officer down, had been called to Granada for the state of siege: he had only one man left with him. Nonetheless, they were to return to the outpost. Did they have a machine gun? Loaded and ready. Well, then, he was to stay on guard up in the fort with his one soldier. He didn't dare go after the lieutenant and ask him to look out for Ofelia if there was any shooting, and had wearily started the climb when he heard the officer call him back. "Aren't you the one who knows where the house is? You lead us then, and send the soldier back to the fort on his own." He was happy to obey the change in plan: if he was on the spot he might be able to protect her.

The house was shielded behind a clump of papayas, below the

track up to the military outpost. The rain was already easing off by the time they reached it. The lieutenant posted two men as hidden sentries at the end of the street, sent another two round the back of the house to block any escape that way, and with the rest of his men covered the front of the building. Then he squatted down alongside the front door, and warned them all to stay in their positions. The night was turning to grey dawn as he signalled to the sergeant to knock on the door, but there was no alarmed noise from inside at his rapping. They were dead to the world.

As the door inched open, the lieutenant charged in, knocking the woman aside. He screamed: "I'll shoot anyone who moves." Searchlights lit up the room, making it broad daylight inside. The lieutenant pointed his gun at each of them in turn, shouting out again the order for them not to move, his voice far too loud for the tiny room and the silent, sleeping men. Still without much notion of what was going on, the two of them finally sat up on the floor, rubbing their eyes like a couple of children, and it must have been the simple innocence of this gesture which prevented the lieutenant from shooting them there and then. When he made them stand up with their backs against the wall, they were still barely awake. He prodded their rucksacks with his foot, and a soldier emptied them out: pieces of stale tortilla, a plantain, a tin of Vicks Vaporub, a cigar butt, one flashlight, one hunting knife and two .45 automatics with empty magazines.

"Kneel down" he shouted again, his voice choked with saliva as though he found it hard to catch his breath. He pushed Jilguero to the floor because he had not kneeled properly, bending only one leg—but it was his wound that prevented his doing so. "Stand up," he ordered, and they did so. "Turn round," and they turned to face him, Taleno helping Jilguero. When they were face-to-face, he looked them over with a smile on his lips, his eyes still invisible behind the dark glasses. The room was full of soldiers, but the school teacher, as though nothing at all were happening, was curled up on her bed rubbing paraffin into her feet.

"Sit down" was his next command, "with your hands out in front of you, palms on the floor here", pointing to the spot with his gun barrel. "Your little trip is over," he said, then turning to Taleno: "You got out of the cage when I had you, but now, I'm very sorry, but my orders are to take no prisoners." Taleno looked up at him, his face blurred in a cloud of weariness. "Carry out your orders, then." The lieutenant repeated that he had no other choice, but Taleno's curt, annoyed voice interrupted him: "I've already told you not to worry, carry out your orders and have done with it, Calzones." Either because he couldn't bear such defiance from a condemned man, or because he didn't want his soldiers to hear his nickname, the lieutenant lashed out and hit him in the mouth with his gun. At once Jilguero, lame as he was, threw himself on him, but a soldier hit him in the stomach with his rifle butt, and he collapsed in a heap on the floor. "Tie them up," the lieutenant shouted in a rage, and the others fell on them and bound them with a long rope. "Lead them out," and they walked out into the daylight dragging the prisoners with them, the sky still dark and stormy. As they were filing up to the fort along the narrow path, the sergeant went up to the lieutenant to tell him that the one with the wounded leg wouldn't make it, pointing out Jilguero, who was leaving a trail of blood behind him. "Who asked your advice, smartass?" was the only answer he got, so he said no more.

They reached the fort, and left the prisoners seated out in the yard for a while, bare chested and tied back-to-back, while they sent to town to get the lieutenant some breakfast. His mouth full of French bread, resting the plate on the rail of the verandah that looked out over the river, he asked if there was any clearing nearby in the woods. The sergeant told him there was, a place where they had been felling trees about half a mile from the outpost. It must have been seven o'clock or a little before when they got the prisoners to their feet and walked with them into the forest along a track that spurred off from the side of the fort. They disappeared under the branches of the sodden trees, while in the treetops the birds were still silent because of the heavy layers of cloud.

When they reached the clearing, the lieutenant chose a spot for them to dig in among the stumps of the felled trees. They were untied, and as the sergeant went up to Jilguero to hand him a spade, he could feel him burning with fever as their hands touched. He must have looked so desperately ill that the lieutenant wanted to stop him digging, but he shook his head, tightened his grip on his spade, and dug the hole as quickly as Taleno.

The sergeant finished off two helpings, then wiped his plate clean with a piece of bread. "Can you imagine what they did as the soldiers lined up to shoot them, Chepito? They started to sing the national anthem: they were still singing 'Your two-coloured banner . . .' when they toppled into their graves. Who on earth would dream of singing when their time comes like that? I know I wouldn't even have the voice left to ask for water."

EPILOGUE

—. . . Now we've reached the plain!
—Now we can take heart again!

The Gueguense,
an anonymous 17th-century
Nicaraguan ballet play

CHAPTER 10

Indio struggled to his knees, and was trying to get a grip on the edge of the table to heave himself up to his feet, but found it impossible, so stayed kneeling, his chin sunk on his chest like a penitent. Turco, who had leapt to his feet as the drink splashed him, shook his trousers so that the drops of liquid could trickle down to the floor. He took out a handkerchief and cleaned off the lemon seeds and spiked slivers of ice that still stuck to his shirt.

"I'll defend you, Turco," shouted the Rosemaid, hurtling out of her corner and throwing herself at Fatal Fatima, tearing at her hair. When he saw them locked together rolling under the table, Jilguero, still holding his guitar in one hand, tried to force them apart, but Fatima was already prone on the floor, one arm flung over her face, and the Rosemaid was sitting staring at her. They were both dressed only in bras and panties, their dresses hanging slackly over chairs, the red die of their old, battered shoes seeping into the pools of melted ice.

Oblivious to the commotion, the colonel was stealthily trying to undo the buttons on the Schoolgirl's uniform. Each time he succeeded, he pretended he was going no further, like a youth undressing a shy girlfriend; half asleep, she let him do as he pleased, though whenever his groping fingers tickled her too much, she would giggle as if laughing in her sleep.

By now Indio was snoring loudly, slumped against the table; Turco went over to a corner of the room in the shadows beyond the light from the ceiling bulb, and pushed his chair against the wall. Hardly unsteady at all, he was chewing his fingernails, seemingly no longer interested in the drunken farce. Dawn would soon be on them, the deathwatch hour. The colonel, it seemed, suddenly felt romantic: when he heard Jilguero's guitar music (he had finally decided to play *Sinceridad*) he led the Schoolgirl out to dance. In the midst of the shamble of chairs and clothes, he hugged her to him, swaying her round heavily without moving from one spot. He bumped with his backside into the sleeping Indio, and when he knocked the light bulb with his head, the shadows of the room whirled round dizzily. The Schoolgirl, her uniform crumpled by his lecherous fondling, was dancing pressed tight against him, then he bent over with a bleary smile and whispered in her ear that they should go to her room. She went to pick up her shoes while he, terrified she would not come back, peered blindly after her with his arms stretched out imploringly.

When he succeeded in raising his head, Indio managed to focus on what was going on, and asked thickly where they were off to. The colonel made no reply, but stumbled out, the Schoolgirl trying to steer him through the door from behind, like a cumbersome wardrobe. As he left the room, the colonel waved mischievously, to which Indio responded by beating his fist feebly on the table, before falling fast asleep once again.

Both Turco in the corner and Jilguero hunched over his guitar were silent after the colonel and the Schoolgirl had left the room. It was not a silence of their own making, but it deepened and tightened, a silence of the end of nights of drinking or wakes, the moment when the realization comes that despite the darkness it will soon be day, and it is so quiet you can even hear the furniture creak. When a bright line appears under the door, the arrival of day comes as no surprise.

"We can't count on him at all," Jilguero said, peering at Indio draped over the table.

"The two of us will be enough," Turco replied, pushing himself forward and the chair onto its four legs.

"Let's get him now and have done with it," Jilguero nodded towards the dark corridor where the couple had disappeared.

"No. Let him have that last favour."

"He'll have enough trouble getting his leg over as it is," Jilguero joked, still staring at the door.

"If he doesn't piss himself." They smiled at each other, weary from lack of sleep.

The Rosemaid had dozed off, her head resting against a table leg and one hand on Fatal Fatima's forehead. Turco had begun pacing up and down the room, and Jilguero was about to say something more to him when the colonel unexpectedly reappeared. He was shoeless, the flaps of his shirt hung down over his naked legs, and there were dribbles of vomit on his chin. He staggered into the room, then straightened up as he tried to work out where he was. The Schoolgirl came in behind him, carrying his jacket and trousers.

"He couldn't do it," she whispered to Turco, "and the pig went and puked in the bed."

The colonel appeared to have got his bearings at last, and stood swaying in front of the snoring Indio. There was a smug smile on his puffy face, and he was trying to get Indio to smile back at him.

"The drink must have gone to his head when he lay down," the Schoolgirl commented to Turco, still keeping her eyes on the colonel, who persisted in his efforts to get a smile from Indio. "He even dropped a revolver he had in his pocket without realising it. Shall I fetch it for you, Turco, sweetheart?"

"No, leave it where it is. And listen, when you go to bed, hide it carefully, do you understand? Put it under your clothes in the trunk."

Just at that moment, Indio woke up, opening his eyes without lifting his head; when he saw the colonel pawing at him, he tried to push him off in disgust. The colonel kept waving two fingers in front of Indio's face.

"He claims he did it twice," Jilguero looked mockingly towards the Schoolgirl.

"He's a filthy lair, he couldn't even manage once," she chortled.

Indio stood up, brushing the colonel aside. He looked completely alert again, as though he hadn't drunk a thing the whole night. He tried to light a cigarette, but the matches he picked up from the table were too wet.

"Come on, dearie, let me put your trousers on"; the Schoolgirl took the colonel by the hand, while he was still waving his two fingers in the air for everyone to see. She sat him down, knelt in front of him, and began to try to fit his legs into his trousers.

"All right Indio, brother. A deal's a deal. As soon as I get off the plane, I'll go straight to *el hombre* with your request. You know he can't refuse either you or me anything. He's still got a real soft spot for you, I know." He was talking of *el hombre* as if he had still been alive. For him, he still was alive.

Indio had put his jacket on and, perished with the dawn cold, stuck his hands in his pockets.

" 'So-and-so and so-and-so are to be allowed to enter the country without hindrance.' You have to promise me though not to get mixed up in any armed nonsense. Yes, you have to promise me that, I'm the one responsible for you to *el hombre*," and he went up to Indio, carrying his trousers once more because he had thought somehow that was what the Schoolgirl had been trying to do.

"You were against *el hombre* because you didn't know him deep down: he's a good man at heart. He knows how to forgive people, to care for them." At this he broke into sobs, until he brought up more vomit into his mouth, managing to turn away towards the wall before being sick, spashing Indio's legs as he did so.

When Jilguero left the room, Indio immediately went after him, catching him up in the toilet. He stood beside him silently to relieve himself.

"Jilguero," he heard him say as he was buttoning up his trousers, and he could guess at his faint-heartedness, because a fearful man gives himself away by the tone of his voice.

"Yes, Indio, what's on your mind?"

"Let's leave it at that. He's a poor old man, a blind old fool."

Jilguero did not reply, and stood as though he were still pissing.

"What will it get us?" Indio insisted.

"All those drinks have turned you sentimental on us," he answered, trying to make light of it.

"I'm fine and sober," Indio protested.

"So much the better. Then you can be the first, as you said you wanted to be only yesterday," Jilguero snapped, striding out into the yard.

Indio followed him again, and as he came alongside gripped his arm, his foul breath hitting Jilguero full in the face.

"Jilguero, I'm old enough to be your father. You know all I've been through for the cause."

Jilguero let him retain his grip, but seemed ready to shake him off at any moment.

"Take my word for it, tomorrow you'll look back and remember I was right."

"There's always someone who backs out when the time comes," Jilguero muttered as though talking to himself, shaking himself free.

"Jilguero!" Indio hissed from behind, afraid to raise his voice too loud.

Just as he was about to go back into the room of mirrors, from where the sound of the colonel retching could be clearly heard, Jilguero turned to face Indio.

"So it's those of us who've got it where it counts that are left," he said, gripping his own trousers around his crotch.

"It's not because I'm afraid, dammit! It's not that," Indio said over and over in a choked whisper.

"Indio's backed out; we have to get a move on," Jilguero warned Turco in passing as he walked over to help the Rosemaid and Fatal Fatima up from under the table.

"Pick up your clothes and get out as quick as you can," he told them, handing them their dresses.

"Come on, sweetheart, don't be sick anymore, or this place will be worse than a pigsty," the Schoolgirl encouraged the colonel, taking good care that he didn't splash her. He had nothing left to bring up anyway by this time, and stood there retching helplessly.

Turco caught the Schoolgirl's arm and led her towards the door, while Jilguero and the Rosemaid dragged along Fatal Fatima.

"My handbag with the jewels," she demanded, her eyes tight shut.

"Forget about your silly bag, just get a move on!" Jilguero said, giving her a slap on the backside to hurry her up.

As the three Prodigies reached the door, they collided with Indio coming in. He walked past without so much as glancing at them, and went straight over to the colonel.

"You'd better be getting back to your hotel, Catalino: I'll take you," they heard him say.

"I'm not moving from here. I won't walk out on any of you. Ever."

"Farewell, my little old man," the Schoolgirl blew him a kiss from the doorway, before Jilguero could shut them out. Even when they were in the corridor they heard them stop, whisper something among themselves, and giggle; then their voices died away in the recesses of the house.

Goodness, why have all the women left me? Call them back again," the colonel shouted. Then, as if playing a game of hide and seek, he began to coo out their names in turn. Indio steered him away from the pool of vomit and tried to help him get his trousers on.

"What's this? Are you going to dress me now, Indio, brother?" He shook his head in disbelief, and lifted his feet obediently. Indio was struggling to get the pair of trousers on properly; Jilguero and Turco made no attempt to stop him. He put his belt on, tied his tie after several attempts, wiped the traces of sick from his chin, and last of all did up his shoes. Once the colonel was dressed, he put his jacket round his shoulders and made to lead him over to the door. The colonel pushed him away and slumped into a chair.

"It's morning already, Catalino, time for us to go," Indio cajoled him, trying to get him back onto his feet.

"I've already told you I'm not leaving here, so don't bother me,'' he replied, giving Indio a push that sent him crashing into the table, knocking off the few things that were still left on it.

Jilguero was standing guard at the door, blocking any exit. Turco switched off the light, and as he strode over towards the colonel only the glow of dawn lit the room.

He scoops aside the leaves so he can drink and for a few moments stares down at his face reflected in the calm water of the puddle as in the shiny surface of a guitar. Lying flat on his stomach, he drinks thirstily, and when he pauses to lift his head, he sees Turco smiling at him, pointing at something in the distance. ''The herons,'' he says, helping him up, ''the herons at last!'' Beyond a palm grove they see a flock of white birds flying south, towards the far bank of the river, where their march will be at an end, and when the horseman will at last be able to unsaddle his mount for it to rest, to graze at will on the grassy plain, free from its bit, free from the lashing reins.

He picks up his pack, and Turco helps him to walk the last stretch. They pass wire fences, a track that widens out as it reaches the riverside port, an overgrown baseball field. They walk instead along a gully sloping down to the fertile river meadows, and wait there in hiding until nightfall, when they cautiously approach a wooden hut on the edge of the dip. ''Lost hunters,'' they tell the woman who is washing dishes by candlelight in the open-sided outhouse that is her kitchen. Startled, she looks up at them without taking her hands from the soapy water. ''We set off hunting days ago over on the Oluma plains, and we got lost,'' Turco explains. ''Could you find us a boatman to take us across the river to Los Chiles? My friend hurt himself in a fall and needs a doctor.''

The woman now does take her hands from the water, dries them on her apron, and raises the candle for them to follow her into the house. It has only one room, with a narrow bed in it that is piled high with washing. Turco hands over a damp, wrinkled bank note from his trouser pocket, then they sit laboriously on the floor. "Try to persuade him to take us tonight," he begs her. Still without saying a word, the woman puts on a waterproof cape she has taken down from a nail on the wall, then disappears out into the night. The two of them are unaware that the rain has started to pour down again; they do not hear the door bang as she opens it, nor feel the wet gust of air that sweeps through the room, because they have already fallen asleep slumped against each other on the floor; the rider has fallen asleep in the saddle while his horse, no longer feeling the pull of the reins, takes him on with slow steps, nibbling in the darkness at the grass of the wayside.

The sudden glare of searchlights, the rap of the rifles' safety catches, encircle them only in their sleep, and only in their dreams do they stand up, obeying remote orders, only in dreams is he hit in the mouth, do they force his arms behind his back to tie him up. As during the years of wandering with his father the pedlar, he instinctively curls up his bare feet to protect himself from the sharp gravel on the way up to San Carlos fort, a prisoner, with the lieutenant's machine gun barrel stuck in his ribs. He turns his tired, bruised face to look at the tin roofs of the port, with their streaks of rust showing in among the green vegetation, the streets with their tufts of weeds, the lavatories at the water's edge, the canoes tied up at the landing-stage; and the faint morning smell of ground coffee and frying breakfasts reaches him just as it had one morning long before in that same San Carlos as he sat waiting on a pavement for his father to finish selling his skins and make his purchases of salt, lard, candles and matches.

A tailor with a tape measure hanging round his neck stood in his shop doorway swinging a brazier of live coals that smoked like a censer; the earth floor behind him was littered with pieces of cloth, and a cockerel was strutting over his cutting table. In the store next door an enormous fat woman was shouting instructions from a tiny chair, her face hidden among strings of garlic hanging from the beans and sacks of cereals whose necks were rolled down as they empty; there was a cold, sad-looking loaf of bread in a glass case, and at the door of the shop an old cripple squashed in a wooden child's trolley stared out at some herbs drying on the pavement as he listened to another barefoot old man who was stripping corn cobs into a basket with the blade of a black handleless knife. And a pregnant woman had stopped as she passed by, turning her head under the load of her basket to look at him, sitting there on the kerb; then later on in the company of another, younger woman who might have been her sister, she pointed to him from a distance, smiling, feeling sorry for him.

Taleno's father arrived with the waterproof bag full of provisions, plonked Taleno's palm hat on, and they walked off down to the landing, meeting up with Trinidad on the next corner, clutching the cage full of parrots he had been unable to sell. "I met two women who asked after you, Papa; they send their regards," but their father pretended not to hear, and merely shifted the bag on his shoulder.

It is only when they are taken out of the yard and set off walking up to the woods that they perhaps at last fully wake up, surfacing gently from the depths of sleep, just as he once woke after sleeping against a fallen tree trunk when the Catarina church bell rang, his legs submerged in a sea of tiny yellow flowers that sprouted in the damp grass, down below him among the rocks, Lake Apoyo. It was December in El Corozo, and even before night had fallen, a star had appeared in the clear sky; there was smoke from a wood fire rising above the rocks of the crater rim; a train crossed high up on the slope, the distance softening its clatter, and the stones from Carlos' slingshot rattled among the trees; a stream rushed down its gully as though trying to bury itself underground; and beyond that, only silence. His brother reappeared without having caught any birds, and the two of them set off back to the farm, the rider holding the reins of the horse which loped along obediently after him; their mother was waiting for them on the verandah lit by a kerosene lamp, the old farmhouse, like a dovecote beset by chirruping cicadas, surrounded by the yellow dryness of the midsummer vegetation.

They pass by a gnarled mass of roots that protrude from a decaying terrace at the base of the fort wall; a little further on the track narrows, then they are showered with raindrops from the soaking branches; they must have come down the river with their father the night before from Melchora, or perhaps Sabalo Real. They paddled into San Carlos, the canoe rocking gently on the waters of the lake, the waves lapping at the piles of the broken-down jetty, with bits of branches, banana leaves, floating lilypads bumping against the sides of the boat. His father lifted him to his chest that was rancid with sweat, then stood him carefully on the worn steps. "Wake up, we've arrived," he shouted to them, and Trinidad came out of the shelter he had made among some sacks at the back of the canoe, carrying a cage with great care. They clung on to the wet railing to climb the steps, then scurried along under the wide eaves of the wooden houses, a man-made tunnel in among empty crates, oil drums, and hens' roosting nests. Their father hurried them along: the next day they would see what a nice place San Carlos was.

On their way back to the farmhouse, Carlos and he heard voices in the distance, one person calling to another who did not reply, a meaningless shout whose only aim seemed to be to ward off the silence or dispel it. Then the voices drew nearer—a boy calling to his dog, then whistling, a man laughing, women talking, the metallic ring of a machete hacking at branches to clear a way through, the voices gradually getting louder and more distinct, close to them by now, carefree, about to emerge into the avenue of the plantation where the two of them had halted to wait and see who these strangers were.

They reach the clearing, with the fort out of sight behind them. They are untied and take the spades thrust at them. They start to dig; the edge of his spade slices through the fresh, tender roots of the grass tufts, then he digs deeper, into the dark, sodden earth, and tosses it up over his shoulder, enjoying the sensation as a fine film of soil sprinkles his throbbing face. Where are they sailing to now, after leaving San Carlos, with the sun beating on their faces? Taleno's father grumbles at him for letting the wind blow his palm hat away—he tried to catch it but it was too late, his hand clutched the top of his head uselessly as he watched it soar away, whirl around, then fall into the swift current, which carried it off. How often does he have to tell him not to dangle his hand in the water? his father scolds him further downstream. "We'll see what you have to say for yourself when a shark gets it."

All of a sudden, the voices fade again, the laughter dies away, and nobody emerges from the woods, nobody comes out onto the path; he hears only gunfire. The horseman's raised fist crumples as he slips from the horse's side, it bolts at the sound of shots, and drags him along by the stirrup. The dirty stain of his green jacket appears further and further in the distance in the mud track where his body finally comes to rest, while the horse, riderless, wanders across the fields with its reins dangling free.

All the ice in the tin mug has melted, and the squeezed lemons are floating in the water. Overcome by the heat, the other drinkers have quietened down, and no longer seem to be discussing baseball. Pastorita, his face puffy from the drink, stares at Jilguero's chair and shakes his head sadly, pondering its emptiness. Chepito is savouring his last mouthful, staring blankly in front of him as he swallows: so the colonel's happy at last, his mortal enemies shot in a pit, rotting like animals, god knows where in the jungle; he had sworn to get revenge on them ever since that time in Guatemala: did Pastorita know about that? Pastorita tries unsuccessfully to push a lighted match into the empty bottle held between his knees to get the devil out of it: of course he did, what they had done was famous. Dressed up as loose women, they had accosted him in a dark street and led him on with lewd promises to a luxury brothel where Indio Larios, also dead now, was waiting for them, disguised as the madam of the place. When they had got him stripped and aroused, they gave him a thorough beating up, then pushed him out into the street naked—isn't that how it happened? Chepito shakes his head and, daintily inserting his little finger into his mouth to remove a scrap of food, says: it was much worse than that, but I don't like to talk about such a delicate matter. Pastorita laughs, standing the bottle on the floor without having succeeded in getting the lighted match into it: what on earth can it have been, for you not to want to talk about it? To avoid being tempted, Chepito suddenly stands up: it's getting late, Pastorita, I have to get back to Managua. Pastorita gets up with him, and seizing hold of his arm, almost begs him: don't go yet, please. What have you got to do in Managua? Why don't you come and see my barbershop instead?

So they leave *Las Gordas* bar and wheel the bicycle down dirt roads where washing is spread out to dry on hedges, men stripped to the waist are playing handball in noisy groups, a horse carriage with empty shafts and torn hood leans against a kerb; they pass an adobe church alongside a square overrun with weeds, and walk on and on until they reach Pastorita's barber shop in Jalteva—called Breezes of Xolotlan in honour of the good old days. He undoes the rusty padlock, heaves open the door, and they are in a room of whitewashed blank walls, in its centre a chair with an adjustable headrest, the blue leather of the seat worn and split. The floor is littered with dry dark hairs, which waft to and fro in lifeless bundles as they are stirred by drafts from the yard door which Pastorita has opened. As more light streams into the room, the words scrawled in white on the mirror become visible:

HAIRCUT	1.50
SHAVE	1.50
HAIRCUT & SHAVE	2.50
SHAMPOO	
MASSAGE WITH COLOGNE	
NO PRESSING OF HATS	

Underneath the mirror is a shelf where empty lotion bottles stand next to big rusty pots of Heno del Camp talcum powder, brilliantine, and combs sticky with dust and grease. A guitar with a faded blue-and-white silk ribbon hangs from a nail on the wall, surrounded by calendar pin-ups of nude blondes, their nipples covered with aluminium foil stars. Pasted on the wall are the newspaper photos of Jilguero and Raul. Chepito goes over to look at them, and warns him he can get into serious trouble for having banned photos like that on show. Pastorita brushed out a chair for him to sit on; they can do what they like, we all have to die some time.

Chepito dozes in the chair, his eyes almost closed, realising that the moment has come to satisfy Pastorita's curiosity: because the reason behind the long walk from the bar to the lonely barber shop was for him to talk about Alma Nubia Taleno; but still he lets a few more moments go by before he asks: do you remember the day when you ran off with Alma Nubia Taleno from her convent school? He squints at the pleased smile on the other's handsome face, sees him nod in agreement, then closes his eyes, laying his head back in the barber's chair as though about to have a shave, yes, to tell the truth, so does he.

Chepito kept her in hiding in *El Copacabana* for a whole week. She cried softly to herself all the time, locked in her room. You can't imagine how scared I was to see you arrive with her, Pastorita, how on earth did you manage to get her away from the nuns? Pastorita replies—that guitar over there had a lot to do with it, it was by teaching her to play in the rehearsals for the recital they were putting on that he had won her over. He abducted her just as the gala function in honour of the mother superior was about to start; they crept away from the school along deserted streets. He had already decided where he would take her—to *El Copacabana*. As he walked, he kept his distance, as though to avoid anyone thinking they were together, and took her arm like a respectful father at street corners, looking round every now and then to make sure nobody was following them. You can't imagine how ashamed of myself I felt not having enough money for a taxi, Chepito—I've heard of poor peasants living in the country a long way from Managua who if they win the lottery have to walk for miles along the road or the railway track to collect their prize – that's exactly how I felt.

Once the deed was done, he was more than willing to honour her with marriage, but her father would settle for nothing less than a prince: who was I to be marrying her? A third-rate musician he called me, trying his best to do me down, or to set the National Guard on me, but he'd fallen right out of favour, and no-one would listen to him. Chepito yawns—heaven knows how they found out where we had her hidden—I was scared out of my wits when her mother appeared that morning; as sure of herself as if she had had a map, she went over without making a sound and knocked on the door: "Alma Nubia, I know you're in there, open up." She led her out, helping the girl avoid all the chairs as if she had been blind, and they left without even a goodbye to me. I went out to the gangway, and watched them walking off up the shore, the girl still in her white uniform and clutching her mandolin, her mother walking slowly behind her, the wind whipping clouds of sand around them. At least I could sleep in my bed again, not on the tables.

Pastorita turns to look in the mirror and touches his face, seeming all at once to discover that he is a different man from the one of that far-off April in Managua. He hesitates, then watches his lips start to move in the stained surface of the mirror. I only touched her once, Chepito. Chepito nods that this is true, he only slept with her that first night there, after that he had called every morning and afternoon to find out if she had been crying or if she wanted to eat, but hadn't even gone in to see her. You avoided the nights above all, Pastorita, you never came again at night. Were you frightened of her or something? Scared of getting her pregnant? If that's the case, it was no use, because you had her once and she did get pregnant, just like in the radio serials.

It is some time before Pastorita opens his eyes, and notices that night is falling outside. He has dozed off like this on many other afternoons in his barber's chair, and then too his only thoughts have been of her. Do you know what's become of her? he asks Chepito, standing up. But Chepito is no longer in the room with him—tiptoeing over the mat of hair clippings so as not to wake him, he has left to try to catch the last bus back to Managua. Above the squawking of the hens in the yard, he hears the invisible Chepito reply: he heard once she had married an American and had gone off to live in San Francisco, California. Pastorita complains to his vanishing friend that he had never seen the boy who was his son. Her father had died, but somehow he never got round to visiting her again. Later on, him being a barber now and without a guitar, there would have been no point. So she had got married then —and here am I, a bachelor all my days.

Some fireworks explode, the noise softened by the distance, and through the twilight he can just make out Chepito smiling, the smile of a toothless old man, and hears him shout that they're better off on their own, that way nobody can be asking them what they've been up to. He gazes at the guitar hanging from the wall, indistinct in the dusk, and thinks to himself: *Los Caballeros* are a thing of the past.

"That's the way it goes," Chepito calls back. "At least they left you memories."

Berlin, October 1973-May 1975.

Chronology of Events

1930 While camping with his troops in San Fernando, National Guard Colonel Catalino Lopez is ambushed in a cinema by a column of General Pedron Altamirano's troops, and is routed and humiliated. He makes the acquaintance of Indio Larios, also a National Guard officer, who saves him from disgrace.

1932 Taleno's father arrives at San Juan del Norte with his sons Trinidad and Santiago Taleno (Turco) and settles in the port to start up a trade in monkeys.

Indio Larios, now working in the US Marine headquarters in Managua, together with Catalino, organizes a ball in honour of the US officers' daughters.

1933 Taleno's father takes his sons first prospecting for gold then as wandering pedlars on the Atlantic Coast.

1934 In Siuna Taleno's father buys a wheel of fortune from a dying man, and travels with it from fair to fair.

1935 After the assassination of Sandino, Colonel Catalino Lopez hunts down Pedron Altamirano, helped by his stepson's treachery. He massacres all Altamirano's followers, and brings his head to exhibit in the Campo de Marte in Managua.

1936 Trinidad, Santiago Taleno's brother, is gored and killed by a bull during the fiesta of San Pedro de Lovago. Taleno's father meets La Milagrosa.

1938 Now living with La Milagrosa, Taleno's father moves to Managua to practise faith healing. His daugher, Alma Nubia, is born. He meets Colonel Catalino Lopez and is set up in business by him; he also becomes leader of the Somoza Popular Front in the San Miguel Market, Managua.

1940 Doctor Rosales, Jilguero's grandfather, is nominated opposition candidate to stand against *el hombre* in the presidential elections. The election campaign begins at the same time it is learned that Jilguero's father has cancer.

1941 Doctor Rosales wins the elections, but is robbed of victory by *el hombre*'s electoral fraud. He goes mad.

Turco, a schoolboy, happens to witness a demonstration by women in mourning in the Plaza de la Republica, Managua; they are protesting at the electoral fraud. His father, at the head of his gang, catches him and punishes him.

Indio Larios rebels against *el hombre* and organizes a plot to take place when they crown *el hombre*'s daughter Queen of the Army. Catalino Lopez discovers the plot, and Larios is put in jail. He escapes by miracle, and flees to Guatemala.

1945 Turco enters the military academy.

Jilguero's father dies. He, his brother Carlos and his sister Liliana are left with their mother in Masaya.

1950 Turco Taleno graduates from the military academy and becomes *el hombre*'s adjutant.

1952 Lazaro, one of the *Los Caballeros* trio, is murdered on the lakeshore in Managua.

1953 Jilguero's sister Liliana, and Colonel Catalino Lopez's adopted daughter are the two main rivals for the Miss Nicaragua contest. Fraud again ensures that Catalino Lopez's daughter is the winner.

1954 April rebellion. Jilguero's brother Carlos, after being interrogated by Catalino Lopez, is shot by firing squad in Las Esquinas. Jilguero hides and manages to escape. Turco Taleno, the leader of the revolt inside the National Guard, is captured, tortured by Lieutenant Quesada, and interrogated by Catalino Lopez. A prisoner in a cage in *el hombre*'s private zoo, he succeeds in escaping and goes to Honduras. His father repudiates him.

1955 Pastorita, another member of *Los Caballeros*, abducts Alma Nubia, Turco Taleno's half-sister. He takes her to the nightclub *El Copacabana*, where the barman Chepito looks after her.

1956 Raul, another member of *Los Caballeros*, leaves Nicaragua for Honduras to look for Jilguero and give him Lazaro's guitar. He stays in Honduras with the other exiles, and meets Turco Taleno.

1957 Turco, Jilguero and Raul are expelled from Honduras and settle in Guatemala. There they meet Indio Larios, and discover Lasinventura's brothel in Mixco. Colonel Catalino Lopez comes to Guatemala to attend the funeral of the dictator Castillo Armas; Turco, Jilguero and Indio trick Catalino Lopez into going to Lasinventura's, where after getting him drunk they take their revenge on him.

1958 Taleno, Jilguero and Raul return to Honduras to try to join the guerrillas in Nicaragua. Indio Larios stays behind in Guatemala with his wife, who owns a piñata workshop.

1959 The guerrilla column enters Nicaragua through Honduras, and after repeated clashes with the National Guard and Honduran troops, is gradually broken up, until only Taleno, Jilguero and Raul are left. They try to make for Costa Rica, crossing the whole of Nicaragua; Raul leaves the other two to turn himself in. Taleno and Jilguero are captured in San Carlos by Lieutenant Quesada and shot. Raul is taken prisoner and tried by a military tribunal.

1961 Indio Larios dies in Guatemala, and his son Bolivar brings his body back for burial in Leon.

Colonel Catalino Lopez is living with his adopted daughter, Miss Nicaragua.

Chepito and Pastorita meet one last time in Granada, where Pastorita is a barber.

New and Forthcoming Books
from
READERS INTERNATIONAL

Sipho Sepamla, *A Ride on the Whirlwind*. This novel by one of South Africa's foremost black poets is set in the 1976 Soweto uprisings. "Not simply a tale of police versus rebels," said *World Literature Today*, "but a bold, sincere portrayal of the human predicament with which South Africa is faced." Hardback, 244 pages, summer 1984. Retail price, US$12.50/£7.95 (UK).

Yang Jiang, *A Cadre School Life: Six Chapters*. Translated by Geremie Barmé and Bennett Lee. A lucid, personal meditation on the Cultural Revolution, the ordeal inflicted on 20 million Chinese, among them virtually all of the country's intellectuals. "Yang Jiang is a very distinguished old lady; she is a playwright; she translated Cervantes into Chinese . . . She lived through a disaster whose magnitude paralyzes the imagination . . . She is a subtle artist who knows how to say less to express more. Her *Six Chapters* are written with elegant simplicity." (Simon Leys, *The New Republic*) "An outstanding book, quite unlike anything else from 20th-century China . . . superbly translated." (*The Times Literary Supplement*). Hardback, 91 pages, autumn 1984. Retail price, $9.95/£5.95

Ivan Klíma, *My Merry Mornings*. Translated by George Theiner. The finest and wittiest stories to date by this popular Prague writer, who was officially silenced after the 1968 Soviet invasion of his country. Nevertheless, his works continue to circulate in typed, handbound, clandestine "padlock editions". Highly regarded in Western Europe, Klíma is virtually unknown in the English-speaking world. Hardback, ca.150 pages, early 1985. Retail price, $14.95/£8.95

Antonio Skármeta, *I Dreamt the Snow Was Burning*. Translated by Malcolm Coad. A cynical country boy comes to Santiago to win at football and lose his virginity. The last days before the 1973 Chilean coup turn his world upside down. "With its vigour and fantasy, undoubtedly one of the best pieces of committed literature to emerge from Latin America," said *Le Monde*. Hardback, ca.225 pages, spring 1985. Retail price, $14.95/£8.95

Yahya Yakhluf, *Najran Below Zero*. Translated by Marilyn Booth. A tour de force, banned throughout most of the Arab world, that explores the mind of religious fundamentalism. The book demonstrates the dissenting role of the Palestinian intellectual. During years of civil war, the people of the border region of Najran are buffeted between intimidation and resistance, between Saudi religious repression and an infant Yemeni republic—always with an American presence, hovering and anonymous. Hardback, ca.110 pages, spring 1985. Retail price, $12.50/£7.95

READERS INTERNATIONAL publishes contemporary literature of quality from Latin America and the Caribbean, the Middle East, Asia, Africa and Eastern Europe. Each of the books in this first annual series was initially banned at home: READERS INTERNATIONAL is particularly committed to conserving literature in danger. Each book is current—from the past 10 years. And each is new to readers here. READERS INTERNATIONAL is registered as a not-for-profit, tax-exempt organisation in the United States of America.

If you wish to know more about Readers International's series of contemporary world literature, please write to 9 East 46th Street, New York, NY 10017, USA; or to the Editorial Branch, 8 Strathray Gardens, London NW3 4NY, England. Orders in North America can be placed directly with Readers International, Subscription/Order Department, P.O. Drawer E, Columbia, Louisiana 71418, USA.